PRAISE FOR *SPLENDITUDE*

In the best traditions of Algren, Bellow, and Dybek, Eileen Lynch's *Splenditude* presents a Chicago of the mind and of the street, of quiet interiors brewing with storms, of street lights streaking by. The novel follows Deirdre who yearns for an inward richness and companionship but whose life is circumscribed by convention. With rich detail and a gift for capturing time and place, Lynch's novel draws a line between the intensely local and the universal, between the intensely felt, and those feelings that threaten to burst us from within.

—Raghav Rao, author of *Missy*

A powerful new story from a wonderful writer, Eileen Lynch has created a very human world where characters are as flawed as they are relatable. Giving the reader a fresh perspective through the trials and tribulations of Deirdre Collins, a young woman on the verge of finding herself and losing herself, this book gives us plenty of love, loss, and lots and lots of books, making for a compelling read about reinvention and rebirth. *Splenditude* will dazzle anyone who has ever been to, lived in, escaped from, or wanted to visit Chicago, as the author paints a picture so simultaneously real and surreal that even the most reluctant readers will be engrossed within the first few pages. Strong character work and an even stronger message make Lynch's debut novel a worthy entry on the must-read list.

—Jeff Hill, author of *Dead Socials*

"This compelling novel captures the raw struggles of artistic ambition and the unpredictable paths of human connection. Deirdre Collins is a deeply relatable protagonist whose dream of publishing a book is both her driving force and her greatest heartbreak. Her journey from creative despair to personal renewal is rendered with empathy and nuance, particularly as she finds purpose in working with at-risk teens, channeling her pain into compassion for others. The reappearance of Max Fletcher, once a beacon of hope and now a symbol of betrayal, adds a tense and emotional layer to the narrative. His promise of publishing connections is seductive, but Deirdre's discovery of his plagiarism forces her to confront her ideals and past. The author deftly explores themes of mental health, artistic integrity, and the resilience of the human spirit. Poignant and thought-provoking, this novel reflects on the complexities of creativity, the power of redemption, and the painful beauty of finding one's voice. Fans of character-driven fiction and literary dramas will find much to savor in this heartfelt and emotionally resonant story."

—Mel Jackson, NetGalley

SPLENDITUDE

A NOVEL

EILEEN T. LYNCH

HIGH FREQUENCY PRESS

Copyright ©2025 Eileen T. Lynch.
Cover art: ©2018 Val Fischer, "LaSalle Bridge".
Acrylic on canvas, 24"x36"
Limited edition prints are available at valfischer.com.

Cover and layout design: Shanna McNair.
Author photo credit: Madeline Bedoe.

All rights reserved. No part of this publication may be reproduced, distributed, or transmitted in any form by any means, or stored in a database or retrieval system, without the express prior written permission of the publisher. Published by High Frequency Press. www.highfrequencypress.com.

Postal mail may be sent to:
High Frequency Press, PO Box 472,
Brunswick, ME 04011.

This book is a work of fiction. Names, characters, places and incidents either are the product of the author's imagination or are used fictitiously, and any resemblance to actual persons, living or dead, businesses, companies, events or locales is entirely coincidental.

NO AI TRAINING: Without in any way limiting the author's [and publisher's] exclusive rights under copyright, any use of this publication to "train" generative artificial intelligence (AI) technologies to generate text is expressly prohibited. The author reserves all rights to license uses of this work for generative AI training and development of machine learning language models.

ISBN: 978-1-962931-19-9
LCCN: 2025901414
Printed in the United States of America.

To my parents
To C-G SPED

*We all leave one another. We die, we change—
it's mostly change—we outgrow our best friends;
but even if I do leave you, I will have passed on
to you something of myself; you will be a different
person because of knowing me; it's inescapable . . .*

—Edna O'Brien, *Girl with Green Eyes*

Part One

ONE

Chicago, Illinois
October 1995

THE ORGANIST SOUNDED THE OPENING NOTES OF WAGner's "Bridal Chorus" as Hugh Devlin and I arrived at St. Benedict Catholic Church in Chicago. We had made a wrong turn off Irving Park Road. The church was full; both the bride and the groom's side were equally packed. Hugh steered me toward a pew with just enough space to squeeze next to a large family. A stained-glass window radiant with deep reds and true blues depicted Mary cradling baby Jesus on her lap. Rays of sun illuminated Hugh's curly light hair, receding but still thick. Thin expressive eyebrows gave him a serious look. His skin was white as a cloth dinner napkin, lightly freckled. He often joked that he glowed in the dark.

We had been dating a year except for September when Hugh did not call. He did not explain, and I didn't question his absence. I was too shy to demand answers. Nightly phone calls resumed with an invitation to his friend Thomas Pratt's wedding.

Our elbows touched as Hugh thumbed through a missalette. The smell of a particular paper used to print church bulletins reminded me of Sunday. Of Sunday morning mass.

Hugh and I had met at a Christmas party atop the John Hancock Center on Chicago's Magnificent Mile. Elliott Law Partners, my employer, held their holiday dinner in the Signature Room. Dinner was prime rib with twice-baked potatoes. My coworker Jeanine Devlin smuggled her brother Hugh in after dinner. Red wine served with dinner made me less shy. I talked to Hugh over a melting baked Alaska. He asked me out every weekend for dinner and a show. We spent hours during nightly phone calls, debating whether to see *Dangerous Minds* or *Casino*. Hugh teased me about my highbrow tastes. He claimed suburbanites like me sat behind picture windows drinking wine and laughing at poor people. That his family lived in a working-class Chicago neighborhood made no difference to me. I didn't care if his father drove a truck to work while mine took the train. That he had resumed calling and we were attending a wedding together gladdened my heart.

The bride glided up the aisle, escorted by her father, to her waiting groom. They recited handwritten vows as they exchanged Claddagh rings, a pair of hands cradling a heart topped with a crown—hands for friendship, heart for love, crown for loyalty. They transferred rings from their right to left hands, hearts pointing inward, signifying their hearts were committed in marriage.

Six tow-headed children stair-stepped in height sat next to us. Their father stopped Hugh as we exited to talk union business. Hugh was a carpenter, studying accounting in night school. While they spoke of an upcoming election, I walked outside to savor the last bit of autumn warmth. Golden light like the fingers of God separated red maple and yellow oak leaves from skeletal branches. In Chicago, such an October day was a gift. Winter was staging in Canada, cool breezes foretelling December's hawk wind.

At the reception hall, a long line snaked from an open bar. I stepped around a cadre of old-timers gathered around Hugh's Uncle Aloysius. Following his lead, they upended whiskey shots in their beer mugs. Hugh knew I was shy in a crowd. He handed me a screwdriver. I stopped counting how many after three.

"Twist and Shout" brought the crowd to their feet. An old gent shouted, "Play 'Reilly's Daughter'!" Inhibitions lowered, I pointed at the dance floor. A slight head shake let me know Hugh didn't dance.

Aloysius' weathered face was mapped with tiny red veins, his gait steady. Standing no taller than 5'6," his bald head balanced on shoulders built strong hauling garbage for streets and sanitation. "Hugh Devlin, introduce me to this lovely redhead." Aloysius' deep voice carried, embarrassing me.

Hugh gestured toward me. "Her name is Deirdre Collins."

"Ah, Deirdre of the Sorrows. Most beautiful woman in Ireland. Legend has it she dashed her brains on a rock rather than surrender to King Conor who killed her one true love."

My too-high heels made me wobble. Hugh laughed. "Take it easy, Uncle A. Can't you see you're scaring her?"

Aloysius extended a silver flask. "A sip of my elixir will set you right."

I tipped the flask and swallowed. Lightning traveled my throat to an empty stomach. Crystal prisms from a large chandelier illuminated a golden hinge joining Hugh's glasses to their stems. Dizzy, I grabbed his hand, steadying myself.

Hugh squeezed my shoulder. "Let's get some air," he said.

We didn't reach his car before we started kissing.

"What did I drink?" I asked. "I'm riding a rocket ship to the stars."

His hand circled my waist. "Poteen."

"Never tasted anything like it," I said, curling under Hugh's arm.

"Irish moonshine distilled from potatoes. During the potato famine, peasants made poteen from tree bark."

Tumbling inside his car, we kissed until we couldn't breathe. Hugh turned over the ignition. We had never gone all the way. As both of us lived with our parents, we had no private place. I had thought tonight Hugh might rent a room, or we might sneak into his parents' basement.

He drove me straight home. I wondered if he believed in waiting for marriage. Nikki Adamos, my former college roommate, said I needed confirmation of where we were headed, but I didn't want to scare Hugh. He was a reliable boyfriend, a believer in weekly movie and dinner dates.

He was stable and unemotional. We talked about books and movies, joked about our families. We came from the same stock. He was first generation Irish; I was third. We expressed love, anger, welcome, and irritation through humor. Feelings were muck and mess, better dealt with never. We drowned them like stray cats, shouting lyrics about an Ireland I had never visited, the land of happy war songs and sad love songs. Hugh and I were in our early thirties, too old to be living at home. Our friends were married and having babies. We were late bloomers, blossoming in each other's company.

I never loved him as deeply as I loved Dan Ahern, a boy I'd met in a college poetry seminar at the University of Illinois in Champaign-Urbana. Dan shared my coloring along with my dark and light moods. He encouraged me to talk about everything I thought. On a spring night when the world was coming alive, he took me walking miles from campus, stopping to kiss me in a meadow sprouting bluebells.

Just when I decided I could love him for a very long time, Dan told me he was leaving for a Peace Corps assignment in Ghana. In his letter was a poem circled by bluebells. I thought he had written those words for me until I heard them played over speakers at a college party. Jackson Browne's words, not Dan's. I burned Dan's letter, but kept an envelope adorned with multi-colored stamps to remind me the world was a big place.

Hugh didn't discuss his past nor ask me about mine. I did not tell him about last year's suicide attempt. No need for confession. The past was the past. My birthday gift from Hugh was a black lacquer pen. Light between my fingers, the Montblanc glided gracefully as a figure skater performing figure eights.

We kissed outside my parents' small brick ranch until a neighbor walked his forlorn beagle a second time. Hugh disentangled himself from my arms. "I better go, Deirdre. Working tomorrow. I'll call you."

I stepped out of his car and then returned to give him another kiss. Hugh transferred his Claddagh ring to his left hand, heart pointing outward. Engagement. Wearing a Claddagh ring on the right hand, as he had when he picked me up, signified a relationship. Did he consider us engaged, even though we hadn't discussed future plans? Even drunk, Hugh wouldn't do such a thing lightly. How exciting. A giddy hope flashed inside me: our names might soon join on a wedding invitation.

My parents were asleep. Our kitchen clock displayed 11:00 p.m.

I didn't want to be alone. My thoughts turned dark when I was alone. Since I'd returned earlier than I thought, I called Nikki, thinking we might get coffee. We hadn't seen each other since I'd dropped out of University of Illinois. Even though our friendship hadn't always run true, Nikki and I had shared adventures in Champaign, and farther afield, when we attended a Grateful Dead concert, hitchhiking to St. Louis.

We talked in our shared bedroom at school, Fleetwood Mac's "Rumours" on the stereo. Nikki was wilder, taking drug-fueled risks— speed when she needed to get things done, Quaaludes to relax. I wrote her a thank you note the night I tried speed, scribbling away at a story that made no sense. My brain was tricky enough without adding chemicals. Alcohol was the only way I altered reality.

Nikki said she was too tired to go out that night. I tiptoed to my bedroom. The hall was dark. My parents' bedroom door, closed. There were two other bedrooms, mine and a smaller one my twenty-two-year-old brother Kevin had abandoned when his friends helped him build a room in the basement.

In a full-length mirror, I caught sight of myself in my slinky cerulean dress that hugged my curves. I mentally subtracted five pounds, maybe ten, that would make me a knockout. The deep blue fabric magnified my indigo eyes, a gift from my father's family.

A tiny scar bisected my wrist usually hidden under long sleeves. Sitting on the pink ruffled bedspread Mom had bought, I remembered the day I tried to kill myself. Depression had felled me after high school graduation. My once busy brain slowed until I couldn't put a sentence together. College was impossible. I worked retail for a year. When I enrolled at University of Illinois the next fall, my depression returned even worse.

My family doctor provided a psych referral. Dr. Karlsberg was a tall man who protected his bad back by balancing himself on his desktop with his elbows. I sat mute in his visitor chair, unable to explain how depression had destroyed my mind. My thoughts had slowed until words disappeared. Forming a sentence took so long, I stopped talking. Since I had always been a quiet person, my friends who were busy getting ready to go away to school didn't notice I was getting quieter.

Terror and despair descended when I realized I wasn't getting better. Shame that I had been a top student who couldn't navigate college kept me from seeking help. The night before I landed in the hospital, I swallowed half a bottle of Sominex I'd pocketed at Walgreens, where I worked part-time. Sleeping pills failed to kill me. They didn't even make me sleep.

After my parents left for work, I smoked cigarettes and read Phillip Roth's *When She Was Good*. It depressed me. I cursed myself not having researched efficient ways to commit suicide. Dad had a straight razor packed in his shaving kit. I pulled it out and dragged it across my wrist. A trickle of blood ran down my forearm.

The back door squeaked open. I had forgotten my mother came home for lunch. I entered the kitchen where she was spooning cottage cheese on a plate. She gasped when she saw my outstretched wrists, razor in my left hand.

"Help me finish the job," I said.

Mom walked toward me. "Honey, don't hurt yourself." She took the razor from me.

"Please put me away," I said. "I can't live like this anymore." My limbs felt so heavy, I couldn't move. My ears droned with a constant buzz, my stomach knotted. I wanted to explain but couldn't summon the words.

She grabbed a towel. "You don't mean that, Deirdre. You don't really want to go to the hospital, do you?"

"I'm not myself," I said. "I don't know where I went."

Before I comprehended what I had done, Mom called Karlsberg's office. "Get in the car," she said. Tears ran down her cheeks.

A hospital administrator separated me from my mother while a nurse searched my bag for dangerous objects. Dr. Karlsberg was not on site. I was told to make myself comfortable in the dayroom where patients played games, watched television, and smoked cigarettes. A blue haze hung over the room. Everyone smoked. I lit a cigarette.

After dinner, I was called to the medication cart and given two small Dixie cups filled with pills. Dr. Karlsberg had never prescribed medicine before. "What are all these pills?" I asked the nurse.

She consulted my chart. "Well, you're getting an antidepressant three times a day with Valium, Dalmane at bedtime." Seeing my confusion, she said, "That's a sleeping pill, honey. Swallow like a good girl. Next, please."

Over the next three days, antidepressants made me groggy but not less depressed. Dr. Karlsberg switched me to mood elevators. Escalators, elevators, I was stuck in the basement, going nowhere. My lack of progress made me so anxious I stopped sleeping again.

My grandfather, who hated hospitals, visited me every day. Grandpa Molloy was my mother's dad, a kind and congenial man who had loved me since the day I was born. He and Grandma attended every school event. He secured my first job in town so that I would learn how to work. "How is the hospital treating you?" he asked, slipping me a chocolate bar.

I hung my head. "The pills they're giving me aren't making me better."

Grandpa had a word with the nurse. Dr. Karlsberg saw me for a five-minute appointment to discuss medication dosage. A family conference was held. My mother wanted me to stay in the hospital. "You need to face your problems." Her tone made me think she was angry with me.

"Tom Knuth said the pills Deirdre is taking don't work for everyone," Grandpa said. Mr. Knuth owned the pharmacy in town and was a family friend. Grandpa continued, "Deirdre can live with Grandma and me until she feels better."

Mom gave her consent, although I knew by the set of her jaw that she did not agree.

Dr. Karlsberg discharged me against medical advice with a sheaf of prescriptions. Frustrated by my lack of communication skills, the doctor gestured toward a Ficus on his desk. He cradled a tiny watering can. "Deirdre, you must find something you care about as much as I love my plant."

Grandma made the guest room bed with freshly ironed sheets. Every Sunday morning, we went to church. I sat between my grandparents on a hard pew at St. Paul of the Cross Church as Father Donlan recited Latin mass.

After church, we returned to my grandparent's tidy ranch house, four blocks from my parents' house but a world away. Grandma prepared a traditional Sunday dinner of roast beef, mashed potatoes and cauliflower. We watched baseball all afternoon. Grandma was a Cubs fan. She sat in her newly decorated living room complete with plush carpet and an upholstered couch delivered from Marshall Field's.

Grandpa retreated to his room to cheer his beloved White Sox. He refused the Fannie Mae Candies I brought him in favor of Cracker Jacks. His room was simply furnished with a dresser and a comfortable chair in front of a small tube TV. A cross hung over his single bed. On a white side wall was a picture of his three brothers, two sisters, and a host of cousins at a picnic. I returned to the living room where Grandma sat in her red velvet Queen Anne wing chair. I sank deep into the couch. With the volume turned low, we closed our eyes and napped until Grandpa returned.

"Sox won," he said.

The Cubs beat the Mets, rounding out a long, slow afternoon. My grandparents' house was so much calmer than the buzzing energy at my parents', where everyone wished they were somewhere else.

Monday morning, Mom picked me up for a doctor's appointment. As she pulled into his driveway, I told Grandpa I didn't want to see her. He surprised me by saying, "Put your arms around her. She is the only mother you will ever have."

Water running woke me from my reverie. I opened my bedroom door to see who was up. Dad crossed from bathroom to bedroom. Ever modest, he wore a plaid robe over blue cotton pajamas. "How was the wedding?" he asked.

"Great," I said. "Authentic Irish music. You would have loved it."

"Sleep tight," he said and closed the door behind him.

TWO

THINKING I'D CHEER MYSELF UP, I WENT DOWNSTAIRS to listen to music. My brother Kevin was out with his friends. An old stereo occupied a rec room corner, Jefferson Airplane atilt on the spindle. I lowered the needle. Grace Slick singing "Crown of Creation" blistered the silence.

A thumping noise joined a bass guitar note, underlining Grace Slick's screams. Not until a pause between tracks did I realize someone was knocking on the basement window. An upside-down face, mouth where eyes should be, grimaced at me. Nikki had showed after all. She bounded downstairs, a Gucci purse slung over a T-shirt clad torso and GUESS jeans.

"I thought you were tired," I said.

She sipped from a Starbucks cup. "Got my second wind. Let's take a ride. We can catch up," Nikki said. She grabbed my purse and led me upstairs. Her BMW almost hit the house as she navigated our driveway's slender ribbons.

"Careful," I said.

Her smoky laugh purred deep in her throat. "Don't worry. Leo owns a repair shop."

"You're not seeing Mike anymore?"

"Dude had no ambition. He loved getting high between shifts at Western Electric."

The daughter of a construction worker, Nikki had escaped her working-class roots by trading up boyfriends every time she found a richer one. We had shared co-op housing with eight women when we attended University of Illinois. Living at Simmons House, we paid reduced fees as we cooked our own meals in an antiquated kitchen.

Nikki studied chemistry late at night while I wrote poems my English professor called idiosyncratic. He was more enthusiastic when I ran into him at Murphy's Pub. As my roommates scanned a crowd of international exchange students and rugby players for future husbands, I learned how to drink like a great writer.

Nikki merged onto the Kennedy, city bound. As we passed the Mayfair Pumping Station, billboards offering Winstons and Newports made me crave nicotine. "I forgot my smokes," I said.

"Leo says smoking isn't ladylike. I quit." She handed me a dope pipe shaped like a Viking's head. "Take the edge off," she said.

"No thanks. Makes me tired."

Nikki retrieved her one-hitter from my palm, inhaled a deep toke. A sharp sweet smell took me back to our dim dorm room.

"Why don't you ditch your secretarial job? Finish *Seesaw*," she said.

Seesaw was a fictionalized account of my depression, a way to explain the mood swings that had torpedoed my life. Comforted by the intimacy of being enclosed in a car, strangers living their lives inches away, I debated confiding in Nikki. I was pleased she remembered my work.

Smoke escaped through an open window. A rush of chilly air sobered me from the wedding cocktails. I decided not to mention my hospital detour. Nikki was a doer who despised weakness. I had learned the hard way that mental illness carried such a stigma. It was better hidden, even from family and close friends.

A speeding sedan entered the reversible express lane at Irving Park. Nikki squeezed my hand. "Not everyone has your talent. Let me spring you from your parents' house."

"I can't stay out late," I said, knowing we would be out until dawn if I let her take control.

"Where's my girl who proclaimed the weekend begins on Monday?" A car changing lanes made her slam the brakes. She flung her arm across my body. "Why don't you finish *Seesaw* in New Mexico? Stay with Lizzy until you find your own place."

Our college housemate Lizzy Monroe studied cello. When we met on move in day, she declined our invitation to drink beer at Murphy's. Lizzy claimed practicing four or five hours daily was necessary to secure a job with a top orchestra.

The Ohio Street exit delivered us into the heart of downtown Chicago. My heart beat faster seeing streets, cars, people converging. "Nikki, I don't think I told you I enrolled in Loyola's weekend college. The only way I can afford tuition is living at home a while longer."

"You like Loyola better than U of I?" Nikki asked.

"They have a wonderful English faculty. Small classes, dedicated teachers," I said. "My lit professor said I write as well as their day students." I didn't mention my favorite teachers were former nuns who turned their dedication from Catholicism to literature.

Like a parting of clouds, a parking space opened on Rush Street. Nikki backed into it, cutting off an approaching driver. "You need room around you. The West is a wonderful place to write. Nothing but open sky."

At The Lodge we chatted with orthopedic surgeons attending a convention. Nikki collected business cards. At closing time, we were still thirsty. Nikki's beemer was parked in front of Moe's. "Let's stop."

"Not this dive," I said. A half memory surfaced of finding Moe's after Nikki's birthday celebration in Greektown. Cradling a wine bottle, Petros, a middle-aged Greek with a lithe body and flashing smile, held diners hostage while he danced. Our party of college roommates drank so many glasses of Roditis, we barely tasted our moussaka and dolmades when they finally arrived.

Putting my hand on her forearm, I said, "Listen, Nikki, I've been dating a great guy. Can't leave Chicago right now."

"Just a short one," Nikki said.

Moe's was a 2:00 a.m. joint. Patrons arrived already drunk after regular bars closed. A good night was both bathrooms stocked with toilet paper. Three crumbled cement stairs descended into a dark barroom.

Nikki eyed a sharp-dressed fellow entering the bar. A Chicago Board of Trade badge bounced off the vest of his three-piece suit buttoned tight at 2:00 a.m. Nikki made a space for his barstool. They discussed market fluctuations, a subject that bored me.

When overhead lights blinked closing time, Nikki wrote her phone number on the trader's hand. We climbed stairs, Nikki steadying me as my heel caught an uneven piece of concrete. We paused outside. I'd seen the look in her eye before. If I let her, we would be out until dawn. "Let's call it a night," I said, guessing Hugh wouldn't like my carousing unsupervised in the city.

Nikki fired the ignition. "Get serious about your life, Deirdre. I'll call Lizzy. We'll fly you to Albuquerque."

"After I get my degree," I said, extracting a cigarette from a crumpled pack of Winstons I'd cadged from the trader.

My parents were asleep when I snuck inside. As mad as we got at each other, I loved spending time with them. They had raised me to share their interests. Our house was lined with Mom's history books and Dad's novels. *1000 Years of Irish Poetry* and Ambrose Bierce's *The Devil's Dictionary* shared space with William Styron and Philip Roth. A floor-to-ceiling bookcase lined the hallway. My parents permitted me to read whatever I chose, granting me a freedom denied by their strict Catholic parents. They let me watch movies like *Spartacus*, which had been banned by the

Catholic Legion of Decency. My sheltered Sunday school classmates at St. Paul of the Cross were envious.

I stubbed my toe on an album case as I hung my jacket inside the coat closet. Dad's jazz was in a blue box: Ramsey Lewis and Herbie Hancock because they were from Chicago, Dave Brubeck and Bill Evans because they played piano. Mom's classical albums were in a white box: Beethoven and Bach. My favorites were Debussy and Ravel. "Bolero" marched through our living room loud as an approaching army when Mom cleaned.

All was quiet. In a couple of hours, Mom would pull Joan Baez from an orange box and sing: "'All men are false, says my mother. They'll tell you wicked, lovin' lies'". She sang and vacuumed. Dad escaped the female angst swelling through the house by removing everything from our garage and hosing the cement floor.

Sunday after Mass, Dad took control of the turntable. Dave Brubeck played "Take Five" as we ate an overcooked roast with super smooth mashed potatoes.

My brother Kevin hated folk music, especially The Clancy Brothers, who Mom started playing months before St. Patrick's Day. When Kevin was home, which was less and less since he'd gotten his license, he retreated to his basement bedroom. Whether my brother played Jimi Hendrix or Jethro Tull, an urgent pounding bassline sounded like *get me out, how do I get out, let me out.*

I shut my door quietly. My room contained a single bed with a reading lamp attached to the headboard and a matching dresser. Instead of reading, I watched the sun rise over a catalpa tree. As kids, Mom paid my brother and me a nickel for collecting long seed pods that fell from spindly branches. We pretended they were cigars.

Best to avoid Nikki until she stopped talking about sending me to Albuquerque; I had Hugh, and he was all I needed.

January brought three feet of snow and a dangerous boredom. At work, I rushed through my tasks to type my memoir. The more time I spent on my writing, the more excited I became about publishing and leaving office life behind.

Hugh was working so much I hardly saw him. I didn't mind, convinced he was saving money for our wedding. Although we'd never talked about marriage, the idea Hugh might propose on St. Patrick's Day had captured my imagination. Sleep had become elusive, but I didn't care. Senior seminar required I read Virginia Woolf's body of work.

Even my parents were restless. Small, dark-haired, with bright blue eyes, people mistook them for brother and sister. Evenings, Dad sat on the floor in front of Mom while she ran her fingers through his thick black hair.

They decided to host a dinner party. Mom cooked Julia Child's Boeuf Bourguignon for twenty guests. Dad opened bottle after bottle of red wine. Before the dinner parties started with their new set of friends, Mom and Dad rarely drank. Alcohol was not served at family dinners or holiday celebrations.

Conversations got louder over Bob Dylan and Joan Baez singing "It Ain't Me Babe." After dinner, their friends danced to The Band.

New noises invaded our quiet house. Doors slammed as heavy-footed men traveled the hall to our single bathroom. Dennis and Geraldine Barnes were loudest. I hated Mrs. Barnes' shrieking laugh and Mr. Barnes' smelly cigars. Mom wore a tight purple dress I hadn't seen in her closet. Sometimes we shared outfits.

I fell asleep reading. Sometime after midnight, I woke to the sound of Mom's laugh—and a deep voice. "Kiss me," the deep voice said.

"Get out here, Dennis," Mrs. Barnes yelled from our living room. "I need help opening the wine."

By the time I finished another chapter of Woolf, party guests were leaving.

Dad was cleaning the kitchen, a towel over his shoulder, a glass of red wine at his elbow.

"I left laundry downstairs," I told him. *To the Lighthouse* was tucked under my arm.

Kevin was watching TV in the basement rec room. "When I was coming home, the Barnes almost hit me. Pretty loaded. What are you reading?"

"Virginia Woolf. My professor mentioned Woolf killed herself by stuffing rocks in her pockets to ensure she didn't surface and then walked into the River Ouse."

"A depressing fact only you would know," Kevin said. "Why is that ashtray filled with match ends?"

"An experiment. Woolf says you never do figure out life's meaning. We need to look for daily miracles, illuminations. And matches struck unexpectedly in the dark."

Kevin pursed his lips and looked at me as if I were crazy. "Don't fry us, finding the meaning of life." I resumed my lecture about Woolf. His look silenced me. "I was alarmed they sent you home from the hospital eating so many beans."

"Beans?'

"Pills. They brought you home like a piece of furniture. Now that you're off them, you never sleep. When is the regular Deirdre coming back?"

I laughed. "I've never felt better."

We sat on adjacent couches. Kevin switched channels, searching for a good movie. Finding nothing but commercials and reruns, he turned off the television. I returned upstairs.

St. Patrick's Day fell on a Friday. My favorite holiday. No gifts to buy, just good times with friends. A thrill went through me as I walked east into a biting wind. Plumber's Union employees dressed against the weather piloted a small boat. They pitched orange dye into the Chicago River, turning sludgy gray water shamrock green. People of every ethnicity wore green.

Since my boss was not in the office, I worked all day on my memoir. At 5:00 p.m., I received a summons from HR. Jan Arnold, who had smiled like an old friend the day she hired me, shot me a stern look. "Deirdre, we have a problem. Lately you've been, well, irresponsible. You come in late, leave without warning. Your work is full of mistakes. Please sign a notice of termination."

"Mr. Friedman gave me a good performance review," I said.

"That was six months ago. Something's changed," Jan said as she slid a typed form across her desk. "Mr. Friedman thinks you need help. He said you're not the reliable girl we hired."

Fear traveled through my stomach as I realized college tuition was due. "I promise I'll do better," I said.

Jan shook her head. "Mr. Friedman's wishes are clear. I'll walk you out." An elevator mirror displayed a portrait of the artist as an unemployed woman wearing a crooked smile. A man wearing a "Kiss Me, I'm Irish" button grabbed the door to let in a throng of coworkers dressed in green.

The shock of losing my job made me forget what day it was. Nikki was waiting downstairs. "Did you forget our plans?" she said, handing me a brush from her purse.

I hadn't seen her since we'd gone to Moe's. She rarely invited me to her house, complaining her family lived like immigrants. She was ashamed of their cramped three-story frame on Chicago's northwest side where her widowed mother and gang of brothers shared the ground floor. Her grandparents lived upstairs. Their kitchen smelled of oregano or cinnamon, depending on whether Yiayia was roasting lamb or baking pastries.

Crazy Aunt Cora, who'd never married, lived in her parents' attic. "Never married" might as well have been part of her name because no one ever called her plain Cora. Screams erupting from her crazy cupola were a wild keening, not the joyful noise of boys yelling from the ground floor where they slept stacked in bunk beds, or the Greek chorus sailing from Yiayia and Papoulis' living room window.

When she was feeling good, Cora wore three dresses and a pair of white anklets as she wandered the neighborhood. Everyone knew her. The corner vegetable merchant walked her home when she strayed. My secret fear was ending up like Cora.

Nikki wore an expensive camel hair coat, looking more like a North Shore matron than a child of immigrants. "Happy St. Patrick's Day," she said, hugging me. Her thick dark hair smelled of cigarette smoke. She pushed me inside a bar packed with revelers. No hope of getting a drink. We retreated to a crowded sidewalk.

"There's a bar hidden in the basement of my office building," I said. "Shouldn't be crowded."

An escalator delivered us to the lower level. Fantan's was a wood paneled place with minimal lighting, an establishment where execs huddled with their office wives. Nikki chose a back booth. She ordered a beer; I requested ginger ale. "Finals are next week," I said.

"Lizzy called," Nikki said. "She said her place in Albuquerque is available while she's in Europe. You can finish *Seesaw*."

Loud laughter preceded a group of six spilling into the bar. Hugh's sister Jeanine was one of them. I hadn't seen her since she'd left Elliott Partners on maternity leave. Tables were pushed together, drinks ordered. Hugh Devlin entered last, escorting a girlish brunette.

My stomach sank. When Hugh didn't call, my rational mind cautioned he had lost interest. I hadn't allowed for the possibility I had been replaced. Fueled by reading books like *Jane Eyre*, I had concocted a story that our slow burning passion might burst into flame.

Hugh leaned close to the brunette. I thought about escaping. Too late. Jeanine spotted me and rushed over. She scooched next to me. "Did you meet Hugh's girlfriend?" she asked. Gin from Jeanine's glass spilled, dribbling on my skirt. "They grew up together." She dabbed the tablecloth with a linen napkin. "About time they made it official."

Hugh's party had downed a drink and was heading out.

"I better rejoin my group before they leave without me," Jeanine said.

My stomach sank. Hugh had disappeared. I was sure he had seen me across the bar. Anger followed by deep hurt he hadn't chosen me. I thought we were in love. Had he not told his sister we were dating?

Lights burned in apartments perched over tracks as Nikki and I rode The L to Cumberland. Nikki patted my hand. "See those windows? Behind one of them is someone a hundred times better than that pasty-faced Hugh Devlin."

She pulled a tissue from her purse and blotted my tears. "Deirdre, you told me in Champaign you wanted to publish *Seesaw* more than you've ever wanted anything. I'll help you."

At Fullerton, I dug Hugh's Montblanc pen from my purse and flung it on the tracks. Steel wheels smashed Hugh's expensive roller ball pen to smithereens.

21

THREE

SATURDAY MORNING, FLAKES OF FAST-FALLING SNOW doubled my hour-long drive. Loyola University was perched on the curve of Lake Michigan at Devon and Sheridan. A light dusting of snow had fallen all night, but there was not enough accumulation to make me miss my morning class. My car skidded as I turned right onto Sheridan Road. As temperatures fell, icy pellets pinged my windshield. At Loyola Beach, Lake Michigan rolled gray and ominous. My mind rolled with the waves, unable to find a place to land.

No close parking places were open. I drove six blocks into a residential neighborhood until I found a narrow spot where I could sandwich my car between a Volkswagen and a Ford. I headed toward campus, slipping on icy sidewalks. I ran upstairs to the second floor instead of waiting for an elevator, breathless as I entered English 340—Reading James Joyce. I loved Professor Griffin, who encouraged my creative writing as much as assigned analytical essays.

Miss Griffin stood at a wooden lectern, her sweet face crowned by waves of white curls. She was beloved for how she helped students fathom genius hidden in difficult texts. Chatter abated when she opened *Dubliners* to read from "The Dead." Tragic young love remembered in middle age. She balanced reading glasses on her nose: "Yes," she read, "the newspapers were right: snow was general all over Ireland. It was falling softly upon the Bog of Allen and, further westwards, softly falling into the dark mutinous waves. It was falling too upon every part of the lonely churchyard where Michael Furey lay buried.'"

Gale force winds bent an ash tree outside the window. My thoughts fired so fast I could not distinguish individual words or break them into sentences. I pieced together the minutes Hugh and I had been together last. We saw *Heartburn*, a movie neither of us enjoyed. No drink afterwards. He carefully navigated slick streets. No good night kiss, or even a proper goodbye. He held my head between his hands, grazing my forehead with his lips, his expression ticking from love to pity to alarm like a clock's second hand.

Instead of kissing me, he held me at arm's length. After helping me navigate our icy front walk, he left me on my front stoop. "Get some rest," he said.

I stayed awake at the window, hoping for Hugh's return. I wanted an explanation. My brain assembled an image of Hugh's right hand when he reached across me to open his car door. His Claddagh ring hugged his ring finger on his left hand, heart facing outward. I hadn't realized he was engaged but not to me. The brunette had been his intended all along. What bothered me most was that he had never told me. He'd just stopped calling.

I raised my hand. Usually I considered my words, stacked them neatly and tied them in a bundle before I opened my mouth. Today they tumbled over each other, like boys wrestling after mass. "Better a moment of passion than a lifetime of boredom," I said. Miss Griffin's bowed lips flattened into a tight line. Digging sharp nails into my palms, I continued, "Joyce's relentless snow overpowers every human intention." Red rivulets streaked my palms. I gestured toward the window. "Watch the lake's rock and roil."

My voice was too quiet. No one was listening. I screamed, "Is Lake Michigan not the collective unconscious of Chicago? What might wash up if we paid attention?"

My professor closed *Dubliners*. Her kind smile hovered over me like a halo as she walked me to the registrar. Paperwork was produced and I signed, not reading the content.

I emerged from the building in no hurry to get home. My thoughts were so scattered I searched residential blocks surrounding campus until I spotted my car on Pratt. I pulled onto Sheridan, turned right, and drove west on Broadway. Snow hit the windshield in furious circles. Driving was impossibly slow. Cunneen's was open, so I stopped. Light glinted through stained glass gracing the bar entrance.

Two middle-aged men wearing work clothes played pool. Opening notes to "Thick as a Brick" played on a turntable behind the bar. Regulars loved that Cunneen's bartenders played album sides. I selected a hand-crafted wooden table nestled in an alcove overlooking Devon Avenue as I eyed the payphone, thinking of calling Hugh. Surely he missed me by now.

Before taking my order, a tall shaggy-headed bartender flipped *Thick as a Brick*. He pulled a tap marked Harp to fill another pitcher. Tray balanced on his forearm, strong gnarled hands ending in long bony fingers, the bartender brought me a beer and a pitcher for a table behind me. Two men and a woman discussed their favorite authors.

Snow coated the windowpanes. A stretch limousine I hoped Hugh had hired made its way down Broadway. Perhaps he sat in the back with our wedding guests. Any minute now Hugh would spring out, tell me our breakup was a misunderstanding. We were getting married after all. Tinted windows kept me from seeing inside. When the light changed, the driver accelerated.

The table behind me argued who was the best Chicago writer. A petite blonde leaned against her boyfriend. "You smug North Siders make me sick. Bellow and Algren defined Chicago literature. The West side is the best side."

A bearded man at the table behind raised a glass of clear liquid. "What about Dybek?" he said.

"And James T. Farrell," I said. "Can't forget the South Side."

"Mind if we join you?" the blonde asked. They gathered their drinks and moved to my table. They introduced themselves as graduate students and the bearded man as their cousin. "Sebastian is studying for the priesthood."

"Not sure I would include Farrell as a great Chicago writer," the blonde said.

"Are you even from Chicago?" I asked. "*Studs Lonigan* defined the experience of South Side Irish families." Another pitcher of beer arrived and a round of shots. I continued, "My father knew Farrell. They played pick-up basketball in the Mount Carmel gym. Locals called him 'stinky feet Farrell' because he wore his street shoes instead of changing into clean socks and sneakers."

"Funny," the blonde said. "Farrell's stories read more like case histories than serious fiction."

Pitcher empty, the couple stood. "Snow is letting up. We can walk back to the residence hall. Buses are running, Sebastian."

Their discussion had revealed Sebastian was attending an evening wedding at St. Nicholas Cathedral in the Ukrainian Village.

"I'll drive you," I said. Anything to delay telling my parents Loyola had dropped me.

"Won't I take you out of your way?" Sebastian said.

I waved him toward my car. I wanted to continue our literary discussion. The blonde had talked so much, Sebastian hadn't had a chance. When I got excited about Farrell, he stroked the back of my neck to calm me. His touch didn't feel like I imagined a priest's touch. He brushed my car windows clean with ungloved hands.

The snow had stopped, leaving dirty black ribbons. Clumps caroming from tires of passing traffic hit my car door as I turned on Western Avenue. Sebastian guided me while we talked. "Bellow's Russian Baths are on Division," Sebastian said. "If you park on a side street, you'll be able to make a getaway. A church parking lot after mass is more dangerous than the Roman Colosseum."

I parked and followed Sebastian. Thirteen turquoise domes topped the cathedral. "They represent Christ and his twelve apostles," he said.

Elderly women wearing black wool coats struggled up the steep front stairs. Their heads were covered by babushkas to protect their beauty shop sprayed helmets of hair.

"Would you like to witness the wedding?" Sebastian asked. "All are welcome."

The top button of Sebastian's coat was unbuttoned. He wore a priest collar under his navy wool sweater. At Cunneen's, I thought he had touched me with love. I realized he had touched me as a priest.

"I should go," I said. Sebastian turned toward the church.

Street signs had familiar names frequented by my grandparents who had been West-siders. I turned on streets they had mentioned—Augusta, Damen. Bellow's bathhouse was on Division.

The front door was as heavy and solid as the towel-wearing old men who passed between sauna and tearoom. No women in sight. I leaned forward to remove my snow-caked boots, an expensive pair Mom gave me for Christmas. Boots Nikki had hidden in her closet when I left school.

The front desk clerk eyed me funny. He was a tired-looking fat man, not a character from *Humboldt's Gift*. I had to leave. Back on the street, I didn't remember where I parked my car. Panic built as I walked unfamiliar blocks. I tripped over a high curb and fell, tearing holes in the knees of my pants.

A patrol car stopped. A cop lowered his window and asked if I needed help.

"I can't find my car," I said.

"Get in. What's your license plate number?"

"Don't remember." I told him my problems as he cruised residential blocks.

"Be quiet a minute, will you? Hasn't anyone ever told you everyone has problems? Maybe I had a fight with my wife before I went on duty because she's tired of sitting alone on Saturday night."

The officer's sharp tone shut me up. We drove around the block. My car was on Damen, where I had left it. That I'd forgotten worried me. I never forgot anything. I thanked the officer as I exited the squad car.

My car was covered with sheets of frozen snow. Windshield wipers ground over icy patches. Even with the defrost on full blast, the windshield wipers didn't remove icy patches. Using a combination scraper and brush Dad had placed in the glove compartment, I dusted snow from the glass with bare hands. My gloves were not in my pockets.

After I cleared the driver's side windshield at eye level, I started the engine. So much snow had fallen, I couldn't get out of the space. A young man wearing a Pike's Peak sweatshirt and a big smile rapped on my window. Desperate, I got out of the car.

"Let me help you," the young man said in a confident voice. He asked me what I was doing out on such a nasty night.

"I'm stuck," I said.

"I know. I've been watching you from the window. You're not just stuck. You're lost. I specialize in rescuing lost girls."

Before I could say yes or no, he had taken my car keys.

The man got into the driver's seat and rocked the car back and forth until I feared for the transmission. On the fifth try, the car leaped into the street.

"Hop in," he said. "You can give me a ride to work."

The man smelled of beer but didn't seem drunk.

"I'll drive," I said.

"You're in no shape to drive. Trust me." He squeezed my thigh. I batted his hand away.

"Sorry, darlin'. My name is Wayne David Miller. Where I come from this is a light dusting."

"Colorado?" I asked, looking at his sweatshirt.

He winked at me. He drove through a neighborhood of two-flats and squat bungalows to Lake Shore Drive, taking a wrong turn down a one-way street. My anxiety mounted, watching the gas gauge plummet.

"You shouldn't be out alone," Wayne said. "A man got stabbed last night on Argyle. Do you even pay attention to the news?"

He talked as if we knew each other. I didn't answer, unable to concentrate. I had always been able to find the thread of my thoughts. Lately as soon as I had a thought, another was chafing to take its place. Sparks flew when I closed my eyes. I thought of them as the electrical fires of my brain.

Snow hit the windshield, frosted recently shoveled sidewalks, and disappeared into Lake Michigan. We hit a patch of ice, sending the car into the next lane. Luckily, traffic on the Drive was light.

"Slow down," I said. "Or let me drive."

"Don't worry. The weather is keeping the crazies home."

"Where do you work?" I asked, trying to figure out where we were headed.

"Let's just say I freelance. Meeting someone at the Italian Village. I'll buy you dinner if you pretend you're my girlfriend."

A long, disjointed story followed. Wayne drove with one hand on the steering wheel, the other around my shoulder. I let it rest, hoping to be downtown soon.

"What kind of business are you in?" I asked, trying to distract him.

"An important man sent me. You'd know his name if you watched the news." He talked without taking a breath as we passed Wilson and Montrose. He had grown up in Michigan and went to college in Colorado, where his roommate introduced him to the drug trade. A face-off with another dealer ended in murder. "Lucky for me, I was in Michigan on spring vacation. My roommate did the deed."

The closer to downtown we got, the more opulent the buildings became. High-rise condominiums and turn of the century apartments were as large as a family home. Windows alternating lit and dark like a toothless child's smile. Listening with one ear, I deduced Wayne needed money to right a romance gone wrong. I didn't ask questions, as I didn't want to stop his stream of consciousness delivery. Stuck inside a story, whether James Joyce or a stranger driving my car, I felt safe. Stories were a world I understood.

We passed Belmont, then Fullerton. The gas gauge ticked empty.

Removing his hand from my shoulder, I said, "We're out of gas." As I turned toward Wayne, I noticed a shiny silver bulge in his jacket pocket. *A gun*, I thought. My sheltered suburban background had never brought me face to face with a gun.

"Don't worry, darlin'. Your tank has a reserve. You can drive thirty miles on empty." We were back downtown. Wayne's chatter had ramped my anxiety to complete disorientation. I couldn't tell if we were on Madison or Monroe. He pulled in front of the Italian Village. A valet approached.

"I'll pay for parking," I said.

Wayne put his arm around me as we stood on the shoveled sidewalk. I grabbed the keys from the valet. "Forgot my lipstick," I told Wayne. "You go ahead and find your friend."

Once Wayne was safely inside the restaurant, I gave the valet money and got back in my car. I snaked around Wacker toward the Chicago River. I knew how to get home from there. To celebrate, I parked at Lake and Wacker to search my purse for cigarettes. The dashboard clock showed 1:45 a.m. I should have been tired, but a weird energy was building. "Won't Get Fooled Again" played on WLS. I blasted the song.

Radio playing, I stepped outside to lean against an ironwork bridge. The temperature had dropped since I left Loyola. During daylight hours, I loved the streetcorner symphony of the elevated trains clacking overhead, barge horns lowing, irate taxi drivers honking.

At 2:00 a.m., a strange silence reigned. A homeless man stirred under a cardboard blanket inside a doorway. No pedestrians moved toward commuter stations. Terror at how alone I was buzzed through my body. I sprinted back to the car. It wouldn't start. I tried repeatedly until I realized my car had run out of gas. A pay phone the city had forgotten to remove promised safety. Who was awake at this evil hour? It was too late for 2:00 a.m. taverns and too early for morning coffee.

I dialed home. Dad picked up after two rings. "Hello, Deirdre, is that you?"

Verging on tears I said, "I'm at Wacker and Lake. Ran out of gas."

Dad rattled paper on the other end. "If you hurry, you can catch the last train tonight at 2:30 a.m. We'll worry about retrieving the car later."

My racing heart slowed a beat, hearing Dad's pleasant voice. On the commuter train, I held my purse tight, checking every other minute that my car keys were safely zipped inside.

Dad waited for me, wearing a wool topcoat and an Irish cap. The fact that epilepsy kept him from driving didn't deter him from walking wherever he could.

"No cabs at this hour," he said. "Let's walk."

Our house was a mile away. I hurried to match Dad's quick pace. He held my elbow when I slipped on a patch of ice. Everything was closed—the grocery store, gas stations. The YMCA. We walked in companionable silence all the way home.

FOUR

DAD WENT TO HIS ROOM TO CHANGE. MOM HUDDLED at the kitchen table reading *The Sunday Tribune*. We ate meals there, as our small brick ranch did not have a dining room. Pink petunias climbed a trellis on cheerful yellow wallpaper. African violets brightened our kitchen window. An ashtray that was stored out of sight until after dinner occupied the kitchen table, filled with smashed cigarette butts of varying lengths. Smells of coffee and toast mingled with Silva Thin smoke. I had never seen Mom smoke before breakfast.

"Where were you?" Mom glared at me like a cat holding back a hiss. "Are you drunk? We've had two calls regarding you. Loyola is dropping you this semester. Your job will send items you left in your desk. When were you going to tell us the law firm fired you? You were typing a memoir."

"In my free time," I said.

"What's wrong with you?" Mom said. "Are you pregnant? You're a walking time bomb, and I can't be around when you go off. We were so worried Dad called Hugh Devlin's house around midnight. Woke his father. We were about to call the McBrides."

"Stop calling people." I didn't want to admit I left the car downtown, so I lied. "I stayed at Nikki's."

Mom gathered newspaper sections. "I thought you weren't friends after she stole your college boyfriend." She grabbed ceramic coffee mugs, chipped one as she banged them together, taking them to the sink.

"Old history," I said.

"She's not like you are. She came from nothing. When we moved you out of the dorm, her closet was lined with your clothes and new leather boots. Don't you see she wants what you have?"

No use mentioning Nikki had been promoted twice in a year. Her job sent her to labs worldwide. She was able to buy everything she wanted. All I had was a hangover.

Dad returned. "Deirdre, why don't you sit down?" His tone was calm and kind. "Loyola thinks it would be better you skip this semester. They'll accept you back when you're feeling better."

"I feel fine. James Joyce is only offered every four years. Everyone knows you can't read Joyce without a guide," I said.

Dad finished his coffee, rose to make a fresh pot. "I made arrangements with the registrar. They'll welcome you back when you return."

Mom shredded her flower-decorated paper napkin. "Hugh spoke to your father. He said you called him from a bar called Cunneen's. Weren't making any sense. He thinks you need help."

Dad put his arm around my shoulders. No memory surfaced of calling Hugh. "He told *you* I need help?" Dad tightened his grip on my shoulder. I removed a slim cigarette from Mother's pack and lit it even though I hated Silva Thins' papery aftertaste.

Kevin paused at the back door wearing a ski jacket. "Brad and I are going snowmobiling in Wisconsin."

"When will you be back?" Mom asked, already missing her fair-haired boy.

"Sunday night." My brother was gone before I could say goodbye.

Mom turned toward me. "Why don't you see if Walgreens will give you your old job back?"

"That was my high school job."

"You can't live at home and not work," Mom said. "It's early. Go while everyone's still at church."

I rode my bike in the snow, not wanting to reveal that the family car was downtown.

My old friend Alan Preston was filling prescriptions. When he asked me how I was, I told him my life was a mad whirl. Alan's expression remained serious. Alan, who couldn't tell you the time without making a joke. He invited me into the pharmacy where a coffee maker rested on a small table. I added cream to a mug of coffee and drank half of it.

He held me with his gaze. "You told me about your job, your mother, your boyfriend. When you walked into Walgreens at sixteen, I saw how intelligent you were. Talented. Promise me you'll seek help. There's a new psychiatrist on staff I've heard wonderful things about. You should see him."

"My parents made me see a psychiatrist. All he did was scratch notes on a yellow pad. Reminded me of Goldenrod tablets. Prescribed pills that didn't work. 'Mood elevators,' he called them."

"Listen to me, Deirdre. You've come to a place in your life where your family and friends can't help you. And you can't help yourself." He slid a card across the table. "Make an appointment with Dr. Shea. Tell him I referred you." Alan had never adopted such a serious tone or spoken so intimately.

At home, I gave Mom the card Alan had given to me. She called immediately.

"They'll see you tomorrow morning. Your father and I have work. You'll have to drive yourself."

I retreated to my room. Dad brought me buttered toast sprinkled with sugar. "Grandma Heatherly made this for me when I was a boy."

His kindness touched me. I fell asleep and was awakened by Mom wrenching open the door. "You lost the car downtown? How will I get to work? Dad and Uncle Jim just left to find it. I have a headache. Please check the refrigerator and figure out what you can cook for dinner."

I did not like Dr. Shea at all.

After Dr. Karlsberg diagnosed me as schizophrenic, the idea of seeing any psychiatrist agitated me. I was ready to walk when Dr. Shea called me into his office.

"It's all a mistake," I said. "I'm perfectly fine. Just stayed up for a couple of weeks drinking coffee while I sorted my life."

He interrupted me as I was talking. He wouldn't tell me if he followed Freud or Jung. "I read Freud and Jung in college. I must understand your approach," I said.

"Not important you know, at this time."

"There's nothing wrong with me a good night's sleep won't cure. I'm happy to take a break from school and leave that phony job. I can get another one easily. I type ninety words a minute and have a good vocabulary."

"You're not in a position to know what you want," Dr. Shea said.

"How dare you tell me that? You've only known me twenty minutes."

He peered over the rim of his glasses. "You're right. I don't know your typical behavior. I'll talk with your parents and a close friend who's seen you recently." Dr. Shea handed me scratch paper. "Write down names of two people who know you well. And their phone numbers. I need to get an idea if how you are acting now is part of your normal personality."

I gave Dr. Shea phone numbers. He wrote a prescription for lithium and ordered follow-up lab tests. "Blood draws are performed downstairs." The nurse who took my blood was kind.

Band-aids dotting my arms, I drove home. My parents were preparing dinner. "I had a long talk with Dr. Shea," Mom said. "He wants to keep you out of the hospital. Much easier to resume normal life. He will schedule frequent blood tests until you're stabilized." After she thought I had left the room, Mom told Dad, "Dr. Karlsberg cautioned us not to expect much of Deirdre."

Dad set his coffee cup in the sink. "Karlsberg never established a relationship. Let's see if Shea is a better diagnostician."

"I hope she makes it this time," Mom said. "We can't afford another hospitalization."

Lithium stabilized my mood so quickly, I forgot the disruption Dr. Shea called a manic episode. Within a week, I was able to sleep normally and think coherently. At month's end, I interviewed with an ad agency. They hired me based on my typing score and vocabulary test. I took an early train to see Dr. Shea before work. As I felt like myself again, our appointment went better.

I was embarrassed when I remembered our first meeting, manic and out of control. My memory was faithful as a watchdog, not slipping when I was at my highest or lowest. The first thing I noticed was how handsome he was. Dark intent eyes scanning everything in the room including me, lithe in his movements.

My moods stabilized as my brain stopped chattering. When Dr. Shea retrieved me from the waiting room, I followed him quietly to an office outfitted with a small maple desk flanked by comfortable upholstered armchairs. I took a seat next to a huge jade plant in a blue and yellow ceramic pot.

"I spoke to your mother today," Dr. Shea said. "She told me you found a job at an advertising agency."

"They gave me a writing test. Thought I'd do well in account management," I said.

"Sounds perfect for you. You're back in school?" he asked.

"Loyola allowed me to register for spring semester. I'll graduate in June."

"Taking your meds?"

"Lithium makes me gain weight. When can I stop?"

"As we discussed, you've been diagnosed with bipolar disorder. Another name for it is manic depression." Compassion lit Dr. Shea's features. "You may have to take medication the rest of your life." He took in my reaction. I wasn't used to being scrutinized. I fended off attention by being quiet and withdrawn. People gave up when confronted with my silences. "What are you studying?"

"My senior seminar is on Virginia Woolf."

"I've never read her," Shea said.

"Woolf should be required reading for psychiatrists," I said. "She committed suicide."

He made a note on his yellow pad. "How about you? Do you have thoughts of harming yourself?"

"No. I like my new job. Commuting gives me time to finish my college assignments. The salary covers tuition. My final paper is an analysis of *To the Lighthouse*. A character named Lily Briscoe intrigued me, a single woman dedicated to her art."

"Anything else interesting going on?"

I shook my head, unwilling to divulge how Hugh Devlin had dumped me. Even though Dr. Shea had saved my life by putting me on lithium and stopped me from wandering the streets, details of my love life seemed too intimate. As I stood to leave, Dr. Shea said, "Call me if anything changes."

If taking my meds helped me work in advertising another couple of years and finish my degree, I could deal with the weight gain. After I graduated, I could enter a writing program at University of Chicago and become the writer I was destined to be.

FIVE

A BACKYARD PICNIC WAS HOW MY PARENTS CELEBRATED college graduation. Mountains of dark clouds rode the horizon, the only mountains Illinois could claim. Warm wet air meeting cool temperatures aloft guaranteed a thunderstorm later.

I cleared paper plates and a platter where a roast chicken had been. All that remained was an empty bottle of merlot, a dictionary, and *Bartlett's Familiar Quotations*. We debated opening a second bottle. The idea gained traction. Mom raised her almost empty glass. "Proud of you, Deirdre."

Pride sat uneasily with the knowledge I had yet to graduate into a normal life. My friends were married and having children.

"You worked hard, kiddo," Dad said. He held a copy of Loyola's literary journal featuring two of my poems. A third, called "Fear," had won a contest sponsored by Dial-A-Poem Chicago. I was asked to record my poem. During my lunch hour, I visited the Chicago Public Library on Michigan Avenue, a neoclassical building between Randolph and Washington.

My parents debated who wrote, "What is so rare as a day in June," which led to my retrieving *Bartlett's*. Mom was sure it was Shakespeare; Dad thought not. "You're the English major," he said, pouring me wine.

I combed through *Bartlett's* until I found James Russell Lowell. *And what is so rare as a day in June? Then, if ever, come perfect days.*

"A perfect day," Mom said, swinging her wine glass toward her rose garden. Apricot buds of the winsome tea party yearned toward Peace

Rose's sculptured petals. Ruby droplets sprayed as she extended her arm toward a vegetable garden planted with tomatoes and zucchini.

An engine backfiring announced Brad Larson's arrival. My brother's friend drove his motorcycle along slender cement ribbons of our long driveway known in January to fling a car against the house. Dad battled it every winter, salted and chipped ice until his fingers turned blue with cold. Brad, red bearded as a Norse invader, straddled his Honda CB 750 as he noted wine bottles, a dictionary splayed on the picnic table.

Kevin emerged from his basement room wearing jeans and a denim jacket. I worried our drunken egghead family embarrassed him.

The kitchen landline rang. My parents saw no reason for cell phones. Our landline sufficed. Mom went inside to answer. She returned cradling a new bottle of merlot. "Phone's for you," she said as she handed Dad a corkscrew.

I went inside and grabbed the extension, surprised it was Emma Mueller, my humanities professor. Lacing a twisty phone cord through my fingers, I sat on the basement stairs.

"Hope I'm not disturbing you." Her soft sibilant voice was tinged with a German accent.

Mueller taught a course on androgyny. The Austrian professor was a fan of Jung, not Freud. Our textbook explained males and females contained elements of both sexes, animus and anima. "Your dream fragment about Anaïs Nin was revealing." The word *revealing* made the fine hairs on my forearm stand. Mueller's classroom manner was formal. We mined symbols using Jung's book, *Dreams*. I wondered why she was calling.

My journal entry sprang from a dream of a shimmering lake appearing beyond Mom's garden. Leaving her mid-sentence, I dove into water so wide I could not see the far shore. A strong current propelled my body through undulating waves.

"Do you mind if we talk about it?" she asked. A professor had never called me at home. Nin's journals hinted her relationship with Henry Miller was rife with secret pleasures and illicit acts I had not experienced.

Brad joked with my parents while my brother retrieved his Kawasaki from the garage. I wondered if Kevin's friends found our family weird, or was every family weird?

Laughter crested over a roar of motorcycles roaring down our quiet street. I held the phone against my ear. "You don't have to stay with your parents," Mueller said. "You can swim away."

Besides writing, I hadn't decided what I'd do after graduation. I loved the city more than my job. Dad had introduced me at an early age to his old friends: architectural works of wonder, glass skyscrapers, vintage buildings. Chicago was alive. In a way the suburb I'd had grown up in could never be. People were always on the move. I mined a constant stream of conversation heard on the sidewalks for dialogue.

Deflecting further talk of my family, I told Professor Mueller her course opened my eyes to how the sexes relate. Talking while drinking wasn't a problem. I was experienced at being plastered and still articulate. When I partied with my friends, I was usually the last one talking.

"Professor Meuller," I said, "I'm going to finish my novel."

A long pause made me wonder if she were still there. "Review Jung on individuation. At your age, you have freedom to explore countless options. You wrote about your father's playwriting aspirations. Make sure you don't inhabit the shadow side of his dream to make him happy."

Mueller was getting too deep. I didn't care to contemplate my unknown dark side. "Thanks for calling," I said, unwinding the cord by swinging the receiver downward. On a whim, I called Hugh Devlin. "I graduated with departmental honors. Let's celebrate."

"Good news, Deirdre. I'm happy for you." A long pause was followed by Hugh clearing his throat. "I thought you might have heard I'm getting married. St. Ben's published the banns."

How would I have heard? I thought but did not say. "Congratulations," I said and hung up the phone. Sucker punched, I poured myself a shot from Dad's bottle of Jameson's.

When I returned, Nikki Adamos was straddling the bench, talking with my parents. I didn't remember inviting her. Nikki balanced her foot on the bench next to where Dad sat. "I was telling your parents how many writers live in New Mexico." She addressed Dad. "You remember our roommate Lizzy Monroe? I visited her on a Western work trip. She and her fiancé Justin Suarez are touring Europe with the symphony. Deirdre can stay at her place free while she finishes her novel."

Lizzy and I had camped in the Jemez Mountains. A broad expanse of sky without landmarks or buildings both thrilled and terrified me.

Mom ignored Nikki and addressed me. "You have a flair for advertising. They were talking about promoting you."

Foote, Cone and Belding was where I worked. It occupied five floors of the Equitable Building at Michigan and Wacker. Most employees were young. Easy to find a companion to grab a drink after work or visit an art exhibit. "I've had fun in advertising, Mom. The creatives burn themselves out making commercials. The copywriters I've met all have novels in progress under their beds they never finish. I won't write anything important if I stay."

Mom squared her shoulders. "I converted the spare bedroom into a study. Perfect place for you to write."

Dad watched, saying nothing. He was often silent. He told me while we were washing dishes that he gave up wedging a word in at dinner. Somebody always had a more pressing problem, a more compelling story. When I was in grade school, Dad devoted himself to writing a play.

Every Sunday after mass, he tapped his blue Selectric keys as cigarette smoke curled above black hair shot with fine gray strands. He listened to Dave Brubeck, as if he were layering his words with jazz. Dad's play was about a young man looking for his father. Mom told me Dad's father, a jazz band leader, had left his mother before he was born.

Dad stopped writing after Hull House Playwrights Workshop staged his play. Even though Robert Sickinger, the program director, complimented Dad's depression-era Chicago setting and dialogue, the play was not picked up by a New York producer. Mom explained writing at home was impossible, what with the kids making a racket.

Our house phone rang again. Dad sprang to answer. On his way inside he mumbled sotto voce, "A writer should live alone."

"Won't you be lonely?" Mom asked. Her gaze drifted toward the soft pink groove marking my right wrist. Heat lightning creased the sky. Mom covered her roses with a tarp.

Nikki leaned toward me. "Your parents are very cool, but they'll keep you in the backyard your whole life if you let them."

Casual and convincing, Dad told the caller, "I'm not sure where she's living. I don't have her new number." Dad returned. "I told Tommy you aren't available."

Tommy McBride was a distant cousin I met at his grandfather's wake shortly after Hugh Devlin went away. Lou McBride was so popular the funeral parlor line was three city blocks. Tommy called me the next day. Dating him meant drinking Tullamore D.E.W. at The Atlantic Bar and Grill with geriatric micks. At closing time, I was too tipsy to fight him off. He introduced me to his private detective friends as his fiancée.

I didn't want to marry him any more than I wanted him lying on top of me on his mattress set on the floor. When I ended our relationship, he followed me everywhere. I didn't tell anyone I had spotted him across the Ravinia Festival lawn. He scanned the crowd like a hawk searching for prey. I hid in a restroom.

Nikki whispered, "Meet me out front. There's a midnight flight. You can call your folks from Albuquerque."

Lightning zigzagged the sky. Droplets dotting the tablecloth turned into a puddle. "We're in for it now," Mom said as she rescued delicate Orrefors crystal wine glasses.

I tucked *Barlett's* under my shirt. As I passed Nikki, I whispered, "Meet me down the block." A stretch of prairie where neighbors walked their dogs, I still thought of it as my special spot where I parked with Hugh.

Not having time to pack a suitcase, I shoved *A Confederacy of Dunces* inside my purse as I snuck away.

Marriage banns had been published, Hugh said. He was getting married, but not to me.

Nikki finished her beer while driving. A six-pack lifted from Dad's cooler sat in the passenger well. She turned toward me.

"Watch the road," I said.

"Not everyone has your talent. My sacred duty is to spring you from your parents' basement."

Low flying planes signaled the approach to O'Hare. "I need a drink," she said. I followed her into Fools Rush Inn where their eponymous theme song played in the foyer twenty-four hours a day. An old couple danced on a postage stamp-sized dance floor. Another man, younger than the couple but still old, held up the bar. Hair slicked back from an expanse of greasy forehead, he wore creased dress slacks and a baby blue cashmere cardigan. Nikki claimed an adjacent bar stool and motioned me to sit.

"Would you ladies do me the honor of buying you a cocktail?" On his left hand where a wedding ring should be, he wore a pinkie ring, a gold band set with a red ruby. Dark liquid shimmered inside his heavy highball glass.

Nikki let the man who called himself Pete buy us another round. I sipped mine, not enjoying a medicinal top note fighting sweet maraschino cherry.

Tony Bennett launched into "I Want to Be Around." The old guy on the dance floor loosened a mustard-colored tie that clashed with his chartreuse checkered sport jacket. His wife's linen dress wilted in the airless room. She leaned her stiff coiffure against her husband's shoulder.

Nikki pulled Pete up to dance. Frank Sinatra was next. Bennet and Sinatra seemed to be the only singers permitted on the Fools Rush Inn juke box. Pete sang, "I saw a man, he danced with his wife," as if he had never heard the words before. Nikki pressed her body close. She spoke animatedly in Pete's ear, an act I had seen in Champaign when she ran out of beer money before her assistance check arrived.

As the song ended, Nikki settled on a stool next to me. "Pete has a prestigious job at O'Hare. Oversees international shipments." His pinkie ring glowed burgundy as an autumn sunrise. Nikki draped her arms over Pete's shoulder. "Turns out Pete's sister was a talented writer. I was telling him how we need to spring you from this dirty old town so you can write your masterpiece."

Pete's broad smile revealed silver fillings and a gold tooth set between yellowed incisors. Nikki trailed her fingers down his back. Pete turned his flushed face toward me. "Nikki says you've read every book in the library. My sister loved reading." He moved closer even though I could hear every word he said. "You remind me of her. She died young."

The couple who had been dancing took a seat at a small square table.

Nikki flashed her white-toothed smile. "Pete wants to help you," Nikki said. "You can pay him back when you publish your novel."

Pete drew a wallet stuffed with bills from his pocket and handed Nikki five hundred dollars. By the looks of it, five hundred ones.

Elvis sang "Fools Rush In Where Angels Fear to Tread" as we hurried down musty carpeted stairs. Nikki pushed me into the car. "Let's get out of here before Pete realizes we're not coming back."

O'Hare was an eight-minute drive. A buzz of anxiety invaded my relaxed drunken state produced by Pete's Manhattans. Nikki slid into a space in Departures. I wasn't ready to fly to Albuquerque. I didn't have clothes or even a hairbrush. "Aren't you coming?" I asked Nikki.

Spearmint wafted from her chewing gum. "Didn't I tell you? My company's sending me to California to finish engineering training. You can visit." She pocketed Pete's bills and gave me $300.

I was fairly sure New Mexico and California weren't visiting distance. Thinking about what I might need in Albuquerque, I rummaged through my purse. "Didn't pack my meds."

"Forget those beans," she said. "You'll be fine once you escape." She gave me a hug, then handed me a slip of paper. "Lizzy's address. She keeps a key in a fake rock under the porch."

Automatic glass doors slid open. I entered the airport. A lone man stood behind a United counter, posture erect as a bank teller. The glare of lights was excessive at 3:00 a.m. I lowered myself on a backless bench. Pete's bills were loose in my purse. I approached a lone service agent. The man sold me a ticket and told me to hurry. "Flight's leaving in two minutes. You better hustle."

I was the last passenger to board.

SIX

THE THUNDERSTORM THAT HAD BEEN THREATENING all night unleashed a deluge that delayed my flight. I was seated in first class next to a tanned tawny woman with long thin arms.

"My name is Sarah Wooten," my seatmate said. Sarah examined the book I was reading—*A Confederacy of Dunces*.

"Such an odd title. Do you recommend it?"

I told her how funny I found it. I omitted John Kennedy O'Toole's suicide when he couldn't publish his novel.

The captain announced complimentary drinks to compensate for the delay. A flight attendant served us red wine, and went on to serve everyone on the plane whatever they asked for. "We'll be on the ground a while."

As we sipped our drinks, Sarah and I gifted each other as women do with our life stories to establish a bond. Emboldened by my buzz, I told her about my plan to publish a novel.

"You are ambitious," she said, retrieving lipstick from her purse. "I majored in electrical engineering. My position is with Sandia Labs. What they're paying enabled me to buy a house in Nob Hill."

A constant flow of drinks and conversation shortened our three-hour flight and helped me forget I wasn't anywhere near to buying my own house. Darkness shrouded the Sandia Mountains as we landed. Sarah removed a card from her wallet and wrote her phone number on the back. "Let's catch up once we get settled. I'd love to buy your book."

Drunk and elated from beers we drank after the complimentary wine, I headed for car rentals. The last time I visited Lizzy Monroe, she'd lived in a tidy adobe in Corrales, a rural village west of city limits. Chile ristras decorated the entry. Sunflowers grew under the mailbox. When Justin proposed, she moved to his city neighborhood at Lead and Coal where Interstates 25 and 40 crossed. Mid-century houses as beat up as the inhabitants' trucks lined narrow streets. I parked at Lizzy's address, a dilapidated frame house separated into four rental units.

I searched for the house key on my hands and knees, finally locating it under the porch inside a fake rock that looked like the real rocks surrounding it.

The phone was ringing as I unlocked Lizzy's apartment. Keys clutched in my left hand, I answered. Mom was crying. "How could you leave without telling us? Let me talk to Nikki."

"She didn't come," I said.

Dad picked up the extension. "How do you do? How are you?" His voice was measured and pleasant as if it were a normal call.

"You sound out of it," Mom said. "Were you drinking on the plane?"

"Just tired," I said, trying to sound sober. "Lizzy left me a temp agency number. I can get a job to pay expenses. Living alone will give me a chance to finish my novel and sell it."

Mom still cried. "I'll send your father. You're too fragile to make it alone. You didn't pack a suitcase."

"Can you send me clothes?" I asked.

"You should come home," Mom said.

"I can do this."

She sighed. "Let me know if you need kitchen supplies. How will you get to work?"

"I rented a car. Maybe you can lend me money until I get paid. Lizzy's kitchen is fully stocked. Thanks for the offer."

Dad asked me what I planned to write in Albuquerque. I reminded him of the satirical novel I had started in college. "Remember, this week's satire lines next week's bird cages," he said.

Promising I'd call soon, I hung up and surveyed Lizzy's apartment. The centerpiece of the narrow living room was an oatmeal-colored corduroy couch. Opposite was an entertainment center constructed from two wood planks balanced on cinder blocks, turntable and speakers flanked by rows of classical albums. A rhododendron reached for the ceiling.

My friends were so arty they didn't have a TV in the living room. I needed to hear a human voice. A search of the kitchen revealed a tiny transistor Sony TV wedged between coffee maker and toaster oven.

Most of the furniture had been moved from Lizzy's one-bedroom apartment to a new home in Sandia Heights. I unrolled a futon propped against the wall. Lying under a sheet, I heard a bathroom faucet dripping and the murmur of expressway traffic. At 2:00 a.m., a man trod the rickety porch singing in Spanish: *Nunca podré morir. Mi corazón no lo tengo aquí.* A door slammed. Quiet returned. I identified with the singer. My heart always seemed to be where I wasn't. When I was in Chicago, I longed for New Mexico.

Doubt that I had made a good decision arrived with a predawn hangover. Sunlight creeping through blinds woke me before my alarm. I showered and selected a tailored blue dress from Lizzy's closet. Luckily, we were the same size.

I headed for a temp agency located on Lomas Boulevard. A sharp angle of light blinded me as if I were driving straight into the sun. My pupils took time to adjust in the cool dim lobby of Worthington Associates. After acing vocabulary and typing tests, a pleasant woman assigned me an admin job with a nursing home chain. "You should feel proud. Skyline is one of our most prestigious clients."

I bit my lip. No one was proud of me. I was a temp.

That night I slept well, awoke rested, and filled with hope.

As I drove to my new job, the sky was a shade of imperturbable blue, which had made me fall in love with New Mexico the first time I'd visited Lizzy. She said Chicago was too crowded, used up. During a Jemez camping trip, she showed me "virgas", streaks of precipitation falling from clouds, evaporating before reaching the ground. "When rain does fall," she'd said, "you can see it coming miles away."

Flowerpots resting on turquoise gravel lined the entry to Skyline Nursing Homes. The front office decor was southwest corporate, a combination of chrome tables and walls hung with paintings of Native American women draped in shawls.

A young Hispanic receptionist smiled from behind a white and chrome desk.

"Good morning, "she said. "You must be our latest temp. Josie Tafoya will be right out to escort you to Corporate."

Warning bells rang at the word *latest*. Josie's blue-black hair was styled in a chignon. She wore high heels matching her navy wraparound dress. "Worthington Temps assured me you have great typing skills."

I projected a friendly competence. "Will you be my supervisor?"

Josie shook her head without disturbing her elaborate hairdo. "No, I won't. I sure won't. I'm just a secretary. You'll support our two top executives. George Miner is the president, and Levi Solomon is head of acquisitions."

A mailman piloting a squeaky cart interrupted our conversation. "Hostile takeovers is more like it. I'm Carlos," he said, dropping two bundles of rubber-banded mail onto my desk.

Since Miner and Solomon were not present and Josie had no other tasks, she told me to familiarize myself with letters from patients and their families. "Make two separate piles, compliment or complaint."

My task was to mark negative or positive on a spreadsheet. I was surprised to find an abundance of compliments. Tom from Tucumcari praised Ivan the orderly. "We appreciate your wheeling Dad outside to listen to birds sing." Tears welled as I pictured patients dependent on the kindness of strangers. "I work two jobs and can't visit Dad as much as I should. I am thankful you take good care of him."

I turned to Josie. "I can craft stories of caring employees for Skyline's marketing materials. My background is in advertising."

Her expression hovered between pity and disapproval. "Please recycle letters after you complete the worksheet." She indicated the blue bin. Josie was polite. Everyone in New Mexico was unfailingly polite.

After work, I smoked a cigarette on the porch to celebrate my first day. A compact man wearing a short-sleeved guayabera parked his VW behind my rental car. Guitar slung over his shoulder, he approached whistling the same song I heard last night.

"Are you my new neighbor?" he asked.

"Temporarily," I said. "I'm staying in Lizzy Monroe's place. We were college roommates."

He stuck out his hand. "I'm Alex Miranda." A wide smile bisected his pock-marked cheeks. Bowed tanned legs ended in huarache-covered feet. "Welcome to Albuquerque. Mind if I get a beer and join you?"

Alex was a painter who taught at the University of New Mexico. I told him about the Skyline temp job, how my coworkers didn't understand my sense of humor. "If I say something funny, they accuse me of meanness."

Beer foamed his moustache as he lifted a Corona to his mouth. "I was raised in Miami. Different manners in different parts of the country." Alex explained the Spaniard Francisco Vázquez de Coronado arrived in New Mexico in 1540, long before New England was settled. "Most locals claim they are descended from the conquistadores. Their old-world graciousness is charming, if provincial." He rested his palm on my thigh. "New Mexicans don't get sarcasm," he said. Aware of the pressure of his touch, I shifted my weight to create a distance. "People who grew up here are insular. They tend to socialize with family and friends they've known for years. Don't take it personally."

The next weekend, Carmen Sanchez, Alex's neighbor, hosted a block party. Alex contributed a bottle of wine. Bringing a dish might help me make new friends. Every restaurant I had visited since I arrived in Albuquerque served enchiladas smothered in red or green sauce.

As I had no idea how to cook with chili peppers, I made Grandma's German potato salad. Vinegar, bacon, and potatoes were available. A local mom-and-pop grocer did not carry green onions, so I visited Albertson's across the river. Back in Lizzy's kitchen, I peeled five pounds of potatoes, diced them, and boiled them to flaky perfection. Bacon sizzled in a fry pan. I added vinegar, a pinch of sugar and green onions. I drizzled bacon dressing over the potatoes I'd mounded in a bowl. I found a roll of foil to protect my dish for transport.

Carmen's yard was strung with white lights, a table set with chips and salsa. Cut lemons floated atop a punch bowl filled with sangria. I drank a cup and mingled with Alex's neighbors. One was an adjunct professor at the University of New Mexico, another a car mechanic. Carmen supplied a boom box. She offered to teach me salsa, gesturing toward a group of dancing women.

Alex kept my glass full. As the evening unwound, he played guitar. "What do you call that haunting song you always sing?" I asked.

"Cuando Salí de Cuba." Sad and romantic chords made me glad for the drunken courage that had landed me in an exotic land far removed from the flat Midwest. The night air cooled.

Carmen replenished bowls of chips and guacamole. No one had touched the potato salad. Carmen added a dollop to her plate. "Needs a little green chili," she said, smiling at me.

I felt embarrassed, as if I had been personally rejected instead of my potato salad. Alex slipped his arm around my waist. Sex would only complicate matters, or worse, separate us. Alex was the only person I'd talked freely with in New Mexico. Since I'd moved to Albuquerque, I had been feeling weightless, moving through the world like a child's balloon let loose at a birthday party.

I let him pull me inside his apartment, hoping his touch would moor me. Alex guided me toward a large mattress on his bedroom floor. His lips were dry, his kiss sharp, not soft like Hugh's.

I closed my eyes, let my thoughts drift as Alex rolled on top of me. A distance kept me from enjoying the sex that followed. I worried depression would make a return.

Alex hugged me. "Thank you for that." His casual thanks made me feel like a cashier bagging his groceries. He fell asleep humming his sad song. My heart went out to the singer. I couldn't die in Albuquerque. My soul resided in Chicago.

I dressed and let myself into Lizzy's unit. A vinegary bacon smell made me miss Grandma's kitchen. For the Fourth of July, we peeled ten pounds of potatoes for a family barbecue, and for Christmas we turned butter, flour, and sugar into light, feathery cookies.

My mood spiraled downward as I realized I missed more than the food. In Chicago, I made friends wherever I worked. My office mates at Skyline Nursing Homes were polite but distant. They couldn't pronounce my name. In the cafeteria they sat together, not inviting me to join them.

Shame washed over me that I had slept with Alex. Lizzy had warned me that Alex was not a good prospect. His wife had divorced him after she'd caught him cheating with a graduate student. I lay on the futon until morning sun made the bedroom too hot to tolerate. Heat messed with my sense of time as it unbearably expanded the hours.

A post office notice let me know a package was being held. I drove to retrieve it, unwrapping layers of brown paper sitting in my car. A handwritten note said, *Wear the dress to your writer's convention. Let us know how you do. Miss you, Mom.*

A photo album was nestled among work pants, my best blouses, and a black dress I'd worn to the Christmas party where I'd met Hugh Devlin. Curious, I opened it to find family scenes from Christmas and Easter during my elementary school years. I wondered why Mom had chosen this album. On the third page was a photo of me holding a blue ribbon for my first poem, which had been published in the school newspaper in second grade. Homesickness lurched through my body.

Alex occupied the porch swing when I returned. I accepted a beer and sat next to him.

"Big news," he said. "A gallery in Las Vegas hired me to manage their space and teach drawing."

"Congratulations." Happiness for Alex mixed with sadness for my loss. He was my only artist friend. Everyone else I had met through work was an acquaintance.

As he described his new job, I realized he was moving to Las Vegas, New Mexico, not Nevada. "You should visit. It's only a two-hour drive." He described the town's setting along Gallinas River. "Very quaint. Feels like you're entering the old West."

Returning to Mary's unit, I made a cup of tea. To comfort myself, I paged through Mom's photo album. Second grade friends gathered in party dresses to play pin the tail on the donkey.

As I flipped through the pages, vague memories tugged at me not memorialized by photographs. All I knew was life changed between my seventh and eighth birthdays. I flipped to third grade to find a picture in front of the Chicago library at Michigan and Randolph. Grandma and Mom took me to Marshall Field's every year to buy my spring wardrobe. A saleslady directed us to an alcove where she brought dresses to try. Much to my delight, Mom bought new school clothes. Grandma selected a white eyelet dress for schoolmates' birthday parties.

The next page showed lunch at the Walnut Room accompanied by a classical pianist. A frothing raspberry kiddie cocktail for me. We ate Mrs. Hering's 1890 original pot pie, created by a saleswoman who served shoppers lunch in the millinery department to keep them in the store.

After lunch that day, we'd visited Grandpa's office in the Insurance Exchange at 175 W. Jackson, where Dad was an underwriter. Grandma and Mom caught an early train home, leaving me to enjoy time with Dad.

We walked north on Michigan Avenue and west on Wacker; Dad pointing out famous buildings like The London Guarantee. "Can't believe they stuck a Burger King where the best jazz club in the city used to be," he said. I couldn't tell whether his eyes were teary because of the cold, or if he were crying. A strong wind almost knocked me off my feet. Dad steadied me. "The tall buildings create wind tunnels," he said.

He steered me toward the Bismarck Hotel. We stood outside, watching well-dressed people alight from cabs. Holding my hand, Dad led me into a dark hotel bar, so dark my eyes had trouble adjusting. Black letters on a white sign announced the South Side Rhythm Boys. A silver-haired man with my father's aquiline nose wore a white dinner jacket and played piano.

The other Boys were a drummer, a bassist, and a man playing a horn that looked like a backwards "J." When the drummer played by himself, the others kept time, shaking their heads and snapping fingers.

During a break, we approached the piano player. Dad told him my name and said I was taking piano lessons. We stayed to hear the band play "When the Red Red Robin (Comes Bobbing Along)." The man's fingers took command of the keyboard playing in a jaunty style Mom never employed. Dad called it stride piano.

On the train home, I asked Dad, "Who was that man?"

"My father," he said.

"Why doesn't he come to our house?"

Dad shook his head. "It's complicated. Remind me to tell you the story later." The conductor collected our tickets. "Do me a favor. Don't tell your mother I took you to a bar." He never told me the story.

Pouring more tea, I tried to fit the pictures with stories overheard from my parents when I eavesdropped on their late-night conversations, which was the only way to get information in my tight-lipped family. Grandma and Grandpa rarely told stories about their West side neighborhoods, except to say they had met at a dance reached by streetcar. It was as if the older generations had abandoned their origin stories when they'd left city neighborhoods to move to the suburbs.

From what I could piece together, Dad's father, Jerry, hit the ground running, working from the time he was ten. His family of eleven children needed the paycheck. He ran errands, cleaned O'Callaghan's after closing time, and washed dishes at local tea rooms. He married and divorced Dad's mother soon after Dad was born. He let everyone believe it was the drinking, that Dorothy couldn't stand his late hours playing piano with the Southside Rhythm Boys. He didn't mention how difficult Dorothy was and how jealous. Jerry taught himself Spanish and French in case he could book European dates for his band.

The night he came home and found she had boxed his books and sold them—because she couldn't stand the time he spent with them—was the last straw. He packed what he could find in the little apartment, taken over with Dorothy's dishes and porcelain knickknacks, the plunder from their wedding he believed she loved more than him.

The day after our downtown trip, Dad came home from work in a funny mood. He entered through the front door instead of the back as he usually did, removing his fedora. "How do you do, how are you?" he said, his voice light and rapid as music.

At the dinner table, conversation was music, voices ascending and descending the scale. Dad talked like his jazz records, an unexpected emphasis, a surprise lilt bouncing a sentence up instead of down.

That night, he looked so tired, I offered to dry dishes. Dad washed glasses first, then plates. His lips twitched like he was talking but he didn't say anything. A dish dropped from his soapy hands.

"Don't like it inside," he said. His blurted phrase clanged with his usual rhythmic tone. Shadows clouded his face. White flecks dotted the corners of his lips.

Mom guided him to a chair. "Hard day?"

Color returned to his face. "I'm fine. How are my girls?"

"Why don't you change into your pajamas, honey? We'll make it an early night." Dad walked toward the narrow hall that led to our bedrooms.

Mom took the plate I was drying and placed it in the cabinet. "Your father has a condition called epilepsy. He had an absence seizure."

"When he talks but doesn't make sense?" I asked.

Mom nodded.

"Do I have it, too?" I asked, feeling guilty for worrying about myself when Dad was in trouble.

"No, it's congenital. That means a birth defect. His mother was advised to schedule a caesarean section at the hospital. She insisted on giving birth at home."

I worried about my busy brain. My brain never rested, even when I was asleep. Always a running conversation, a soundtrack, a railroad track, wheels clacking on the Chicago and Northwestern three blocks from my childhood bedroom, a constant stream of music.

Like so many of my early childhood memories, I was never sure if the next part of the story was true, or a vivid dream. I awoke to the sound of Dad yelling outside my bedroom. I watched through the window as Mom in her nightgown chased him around the yard. I heard Dad say, "I'm finished with those pills. They don't help."

"You have to stop this and be the man of this family," Mom said.

Dad's next words were anguished. "No one taught me how to be a man."

Grandpa appeared, alighting from his large sedan wearing a topcoat over dress pants at 3:00 a.m. He told me to go back to bed. "I'll call the doctor," Grandpa told Mom.

In the morning, Dad was gone. Grandma made toaster waffles for Kevin and me. She said Dad was in the hospital. From the look on her face, I knew it wasn't the regular hospital where babies were born.

After Alex moved, I visited different Albuquerque neighborhoods to keep a creeping depression at bay. The *Weekly Alibi* newspaper advertised a writer's group at a bookstore in North Valley. I drove there after work. The boutique shop was small and inviting, providing comfy chairs in nooks. Two women and three men occupied a round table surrounded by bookshelves, at least a generation older than I. A shaggy-headed man with an Irish accent welcomed me. "Have a seat. We're sharing work if you're so inclined."

I slid into an empty chair. "I'll listen, if you don't mind." The man who had welcomed me read a story about a woman who waits for a man who never arrives. His soothing voice coaxed me toward sleep. Depression was limiting my sleep to two hours a night. I fought back by working harder, convinced publishing my book would solve my problems.

A woman with tight curls shared a poem about her poodle. The Irishman poured coffee. "Are you attending SouthWest Writer's Conference next month?" He detailed their offerings: speakers from top publishers, craft seminars, agent pitching sessions. I drove to Lead Street dreaming of finding an agent and publishing *After Lunch*. All I had to do was finish it.

Friday nights I was happy, knowing I would have two days to write. The upcoming conference renewed my hope by giving me a purpose. Every night after work I wrote at Lizzy's kitchen table. My new manuscript *After Lunch* was a satire about corporate politics, complete except for a final edit. Excited, I called my parents and told them Lizzy's landlord had agreed to let me stay an extra month.

"You sound tired. I'm worried about you." Mom said. "Finish the book here with us."

Dad wished me good luck. "I know you're seeking an agent. Might be more important to find an editor. Think of everything Maxwell Perkins did for Fitzgerald and Hemingway, not to mention Thomas Wolfe."

During the week, no matter what time I went to bed, I awoke two hours later and stayed awake. Exercise was supposed to help. Dogs barked from behind wire fences as I walked the neighborhood after dinner. Stars lay flat against a denim blue sky. I missed talking about art with Alex. I missed anyone who knew me before depression stole my personality.

After my walk, I searched the photo album for pictures of my parents when they were young and happy. Easter Sunday of my third grade year I posed with my brother in front of honeysuckle bushes so lush I could practically smell pink flowers and hear the buzz of bees in the branches. Kevin sported a topcoat and tie. Grandma had bought me the prettiest dress at Field's, a pale blue organdy topped by a white lace bib. Lace gloves to match and a picture hat ringed with daisies. Behind Kevin's feet an amber pill bottle was nestled in a bed of geraniums.

Dad was not in the picture. Grandpa was at the house every day, making sure Kevin and I were eating right, and I was going to school. Mom wanted to keep me home, but Grandpa insisted we fulfill our obligations. Grandpa and Grandma took us to fish fries on Friday night and brunch after Sunday mass. I wandered the house, sitting in Dad's chair. Kevin was a toddler. He kept me company standing at the window, waiting for Dad's return.

The day of Dad's discharge finally arrived. I stayed after the bell rang to clean blackboards for Miss Dotson, an older woman with a large bosom. "Don't you want to go home and see your father?" she asked.

I dawdled on the way home, kicking a stone with the toe of my patent leather Mary Jane shoe.

Dad sat in his favorite chair, small as a boy, dark hair newly flecked gray. We ate ground beef and potato casserole and went to bed early.

The next day, everything went back to normal. Dad returned to work at Grandpa's insurance agency; I went to school. When I came home in the afternoon, my brother was napping. I had Mom all to myself.

I lay on the living room floor, writing a poem for a school contest. Mom sat at the piano bench, back straight. A metronome clicked to the rhythmic beat of songs written by men with names like barking dogs: Bach, Mozart, Schubert.

 "What are you doing, Mufflet? Mom asked.

"Trying to win a contest."

Mom called me Mufflet, a muffled Miss Muffet.

Outside, a storm brewed. I traced a black geometric pattern threading the gray living room carpet, straight lines springing from circles. As Mom played a Chopin ballade, I inched toward floral drapes floating over white sheers.

I stood at the bay window, conducting the rain in time with swaying elm trees. Unnamed troubles danced with utter joy. Drops of water slid down my neck. I looked up. The ceiling was dry. I had sprung a leak like when parade bands made me cry.

She patted the bench next to her. "Come here Mufflet," Mom said. She removed a tissue from her sleeve and wiped my tears. "Music helps us feel our feelings. It's okay." Her eyes were lit with joy. I stopped crying. "Listen." Mom turned off the metronome. "A song about the moon by Claude Debussy." Even his name sounded like music.

A spare tune, more whisper than music, let me wander like I wasn't expected anywhere, my body lighter than a cloud in a painting Mom showed me at The Art Institute of Chicago.

I titled my poem "Here Comes the Rain."

Mom ran her fingers through my hair. "The man who sees the sun shining red on your hair will fall in love with you."

We never spoke of Dad's time away. Weekends, he sat on a square of cement he called Daddio's Patio, transistor radio tuned to a South Side jazz station. Horns soared over an insistent beat.

The grass roared with cicada song. I cartwheeled from the patio to the flower garden at the end of the yard.

An overwhelming tenderness filled me for my parents' unfulfilled dreams. I had always blamed Mom for a lifetime of uncertainty once I saw my father break down in front of me. Even if I knew my feelings weren't rational, I thought it was her job to keep the family intact.

What I hadn't understood was they had been young parents dreaming their own dreams. Opportunities stolen by errant brain chemicals. Understanding they were flawed didn't make it any easier to reconcile.

Exhausted by sleepless nights, I shuffled through my days at Skyline Nursing Homes. Levi Solomon paced his office, negotiating a takeover of his fiftieth family-owned nursing home. Skyline was the West's fastest growing chain. President George Miner still had not shown. Word was Miner was gravely ill. I took a break midmorning outdoors. Gray shapeless clouds circled the white wigged Sandias. I lit a cigarette, trying to understand how the big sky that sheltered me when Lizzy and I camped mountainside now swallowed me whole.

Carlos, the mailroom supervisor, joined me. "You're George Miner's temp," he said. "Where is he?"

"Out sick, or so I've been told."

"Miner wouldn't be caught dead in one of his own nursing homes."

At noon, the sky was so black, staff gathered at the window. New Mexico skies were such a reliable blue, a stretch of days without sun produced worried headlines.

The mail cart wheels squeaked to a stop. Carlos dropped bundled letters on my desk. "Monsoon coming." I pictured people drowning in India.

Rain pounded the roof, smeared dusty windows.

Workers abandoned their desks to crowd the parking lot. Carlos whispered to Josie, "Deirdre never talks anymore. Do you think there's something wrong with her?"

"She's from back East," Josie said. "That's how they are."

Carlos climbed atop his car. Goaded by his mailroom pals, he removed his shirt. Rain slid down his chest.

Back at my desk, I sorted letters from patients' families. Skyline had recently acquired its nine hundred forty-fifth nursing home.

No one read letters written by grieving adult children. If I were my old self or had even an ounce of energy, I'd protest. As Miner was on indefinite leave, there was no one to inform.

I wondered if I should forward heartfelt letters to the employees mentioned. That I was a tender of dead letters, a modern Bartleby the Scrivener, deepened my depression.

My eyelids fluttered. Sleep hovered. The day before, I had blacked out turning left on San Mateo, a four lane, fast moving boulevard. When I opened my eyes, I had no memory of traveling through the intersection.

Sharp cornered manila folders pricked my fingers. I hated filing, but standing at the steel cabinet kept me awake. By 5:00 p.m., my car was a tube of hot metal. Heat radiated from my steering wheel. Native Albuquerqueans employed cardboard windshield screens. I smoked to stay awake. The sharp attack of the "Get Down Tonight" opening piano chords rang through the parking lot. Levi Solomon sat two spaces over in his red convertible, volume cranked. A double speed guitar solo rattled the pickup truck crowd.

The full-time office girls were jealous of the attention Solomon paid me. They whispered, "He's Jewish," as if he belonged to a cult. They didn't like that he instructed me to answer his phone. They laughed at my accent, flat vowels, quick clipped tones, which they took as an insult to their slow, lilting speech patterns. I knew which calls were important, when to walk right into Solomon's office. His New York sarcasm translated as meanness to New Mexican ears. The girls swore they didn't understand a word he said. "I can't, I sure can't," Josie said.

Solomon's body was tight, his face angular, his tone even. He wore expensive cowboy boots with designer suits. His negotiations were surgical. He grinned when he executed hostile takeovers of family-owned businesses.

I eased my rented Ford Focus into the exit line.

Get Down Tonight! Sheer sound vibrated as Solomon angled his cherry red convertible through a pack of pastel pickups. Polite smiles turned sideways sneers as funk overspread the plinking guitars of Western ballads. I laughed for the first time in days.

Droplets dotted my windshield. Turning on Montgomery, a torrent of rain obscured my view. I located my wiper button. Rotting unused blades dragged across windshield glass. As the traffic signal turned red, a pink Impala low rider rolled past on wire spoke wheels. The car sported hand drawn portraits of Elvis on the trunk and Jesus on the hood.

I killed my overdrive air conditioning, lowered my window to get a better look at a rose border. The car bounced on fender skirted wheels as water rose in gutterless streets. Unsure if the change in the weather or sheer exhaustion was making me giddy, I laughed again.

It would be just like me to drown in the desert.

SEVEN

THE WRITER'S CONFERENCE BEGAN WITH A KEYNOTE speech by Tony Hillerman. His humor and humility brought the crowd to its feet with a standing ovation. After Hillerman, a panel of literary agents discussed writing a successful query. Submitting work was the ultimate challenge. Writing a one-page letter asking an agent to read sample novel pages was more challenging than writing a novel. Important to know what to include and what to omit.

Afternoon pitch sessions drew a crowd. Most agents were bright, dark-haired, bespectacled women. I marked my program to approach a New York agent who mentioned during the panel she had relocated to Santa Fe.

Box lunches were provided as part of the conference package. I ate a turkey sandwich while avoiding coleslaw, afraid of spilling mayonnaise on my clothes.

At 1:00 p.m., staff opened the grand ballroom, where agents waited at café tables. Folding chairs extended from each station. Four writers waited for the agent I had picked. Swamp coolers rattled but did not cool the room. Sweaty and anxious, I watched my competition talk about their work, hoping to get clues about her personality. She wore a tailored dress with dangly turquoise earrings, half New York and half Santa Fe.

When it was my turn, I froze. "My novel is a social satire," I said, then attempted an ill-conceived sentence, rote as a robot.

The agent folded her hands. "Satire is not something I represent. Did you attend the agent panel?" Trying to hide my misery, I nodded.

"Panelists discussed how important it is to find someone who will champion your work. Keep trying," she said.

She had rejected me. "I have a relative who's a famous writer," I said. I wondered whether or not to name-drop my grandfather's cousin, a Catholic priest, who wrote racy novels that had landed on the bestseller lists. I did. "He said the book had some great moments," I said.

"No doubt. But I'm afraid I'm not at all interested in what you're writing."

She summoned the next writer. I joined another line to pitch an agent who specialized in contemporary novels. My wait was long. By the time I reached her, I was so nervous my description came out jumbled. The second agent was kind. She advised me to memorize an elevator pitch. Two hours of waiting on a series of folding chairs resulted in three rejections and no sample chapter requests. No one wanted my book. I left the conference without hearing the closing speaker.

My car was parked behind a cement pillar underground. As I followed Second Street toward Paseo Del Norte, I reviewed my pitch sessions and cringed at how I stumbled describing my own work. Not selling my book had not occurred to me. I turned left on State Route 550 past the Coronado Historic Site. *Not at all interested.* The words ricocheted like pinballs hitting flippers. Underlying my anger was a fear agents knew I was no good and never would be. Impossible to return to Chicago with only a temp agency pay stub. A feeling of utter worthlessness bore down. Better not to return.

Thirty-five miles from Albuquerque to Jemez. No landmarks except an occasional filling station. Pink sandstone bluffs rose at the approach to Jemez Pueblo, easing lonesome empty brown miles. Highway 550 was the state's deadliest. New Mexico traded places with Utah for the most

DUI arrests. If I drove the dusty roads often enough, I might die in a fatal car accident.

Rejection is part of writing. Still, I needed success to validate the time I had devoted to my unpublished books. Approaching forty, I was hardly an enfant terrible. Some days I felt like such a failure I wished God would take me. He remained silent about my mortality. Being unable to commit to suicide made me feel gutless.

Bright red cliffs sprouted pine trees. Trailer homes dotted Jemez Pueblo outskirts. I passed tribal offices, a grocery store, and a gas station. A longer stretch lined with red cliffs followed before I reached the village.

Before Lizzy had met her husband Justin, I'd camped with her on the side of a bluff outside Jemez. Lizzy had brought her cello so as not to miss her practice time. After roasting kebabs over a fire and drinking a six-pack, she played as we sang Beatles songs.

Highway 4 was the village's main drag. I passed a grocery store, Jemez Mountain Inn, a tiny library, Laughing Lizard Cafe, and Los Ojos Restaurant and Saloon. At the far end of town was an historic site. I parked there and rooted through camping supplies in the trunk. I found a camping knife and stuck it inside a canvas satchel.

A bell jingled over the door. Standing behind a desk, a middle-aged native American man flanked by two boys collected a modest admission fee. The taller boy was about ten, the smaller brother a bright-eyed miniature.

Between the gift shop and ruins of an ancient cathedral was an exhibit hall displaying photographs of the mission compound. Placards detailing site history were mounted to the wall. When Spanish soldiers arrived in 1621, they asked people what they called themselves. Native Americans replied, "We are Jemez; we are the people." Spanish priests forced the Native Americans to construct a limestone church with sandstone and volcanic tuff. The sharp anger I had felt while driving intensified as I read details of Spanish persecution.

Hanging between pictures of the site in various historical stages was a quote: "We are concerned about Anglo intentions. There is a design in living things. We must not let ourselves get caught up in the results of an over efficient society, rapidly moving at a rate and in a way that to most Indians represents panic."

I copied the quote on my conference program next to the names of the agents who had rejected me. I was fooling myself, never excelling at work, taking shitty jobs to keep my mind free, ignoring normal life acceptable to everyone else. Making my way outside, I rested my back against a four-hundred-year-old wall opposite a crumbling altar, absorbing sunbaked stone the Jemez had used for construction.

There was no other way but out. Checking the knife was still in my pouch, I climbed a stony trail lined by pinyon pines. A sharp incline stole my breath. I was out of shape, smoking a pack a day. A clearing beyond the ridge was where I would kill myself. I searched my backpack for a pen, contemplating whether I should leave a goodbye note.

Pounding feet on the trail announced the arrival of the boys I had met earlier.

"You are on pueblo territory," the older one said, a stern expression on his face. "You can't be here," he said to underline his point. His little brother smiled, unable to stifle his happiness at an odd white woman disrupting their day.

The older boy pointed to a near ridge where an animal prowled, larger than a dog, smaller than a lion. "See the bobcat?" he asked.

"Is he special to your culture?" I asked.

The older boy shook his head. "Eats our chickens." He removed a rifle from his gym bag, took aim, and shot the animal.

The boys' father called them. The knife fell at my ankle.

"You forgot something," the elder said as he returned it, his expression a mix of pity and curiosity.

The little boy took my hand. "Let's go."

Glad for their company, I scrambled downward with the boys.

Realizing they would have found me if I completed my plan, I drove back to Lizzy's apartment filled with shame.

Insomnia visited every night. Sitting in the Skyline offices, I stared at my computer, wondering why none of my coworkers noticed how much I had disintegrated. Health center psychiatrists were booked three months out, so I scheduled an appointment with an internist, hoping for prescription sleeping pills.

Dr. Shea knew what to do, but I was afraid to call him. I was afraid he would be mad I had stopped taking lithium. No matter how much I exercised, I could not lose weight. I blamed the drug.

My doctor was pregnant, pretty in a girl-next-door kind of style. She introduced herself as a part-time doctor and full-time mother.

In a tiny voice, I described my problem. "An article I read claimed Prozac restores patients' lives. If I sleep, I can move mountains." The doctor wrote a prescription without discussion.

My hope I would soon be normal was short-lived. Prozac robbed me of the one or two hours of sleep I had been getting. I called the health service and begged for a psych referral. When the receptionist said she had no appointments, I went in person planning to request lithium. Instead I met a chirpy social worker who insisted I join a support group.

She asked everyone to introduce themselves, give a reason for why they were present. When it was my turn, I spoke so self-deprecatingly that everyone laughed. By session's end, everyone felt better except me.

A psychiatric appointment finally opened. The shrink dismissed my idea it did not get dark enough in Albuquerque to sleep.

"A trick of your insomnia. Dark is dark," the shrink said.

I doubted his words as I doubted God heard my prayers.

Claiming lithium was not recommended for my condition, the shrink wrote a Tramadol prescription. The pills put me in an unrefreshing sleep where I lay bleary-eyed, a heavy hand pressing my body into the mattress. At our next appointment, the shrink switched me to Wellbutrin, which left me so severely dry-mouthed I accomplished nothing at work between drinking water and leaving my desk to pee. My hair fell out in hunks on the bathroom floor. A call to the internist's office revealed my doctor was on maternity leave.

Depression had me in its clutches. Knowing I had no one to confide in made it worse. I walked after dinner past dogs barking from behind chain link fences. At home I jumped rope but still could not fall asleep. At 3:00 a.m., a hallucination of sleep overtook me. I prayed to my grandfather, who had kept me alive when I'd attempted suicide as a teenager. Light fading behind my eyelids signaled sleep's approach. The blue knot of Grandpa's tie hovered over his smile. Waking at 3:05 a.m., I prayed for three hours of sleep before work. My request was not granted. God had disappeared over the Sandias, if He existed at all.

The night was so long I called a psych hospital. A woman with a soft voice answered.

"I want to kill myself," I said.

"Come in as soon as possible, dear."

I opened the curtain. Fat flakes of snow-covered sidewalks. Snow in Albuquerque usually limited itself to coating mountaintops, seldom appearing in town. Not trusting myself to drive, I called a cab. The driver confessed he did not know how to drive in snow. He wanted to wait until it melted. "Albuquerque doesn't own snow removal equipment," he said. I sat at the window counting each flake until my cab showed two hours later.

My cab headed toward the northeast quadrant. I slumped in the back seat so no one could see me. Not that anyone in Albuquerque knew me. Instead of giving me freedom to write, temping made me lonely. Days passed when I talked to no one.

As I awaited the doctor on call, a young man signed himself in. A frazzled woman wearing a heavy jacket suitable for real winter fussed with his collar. Tall and fair skinned, the boy's clothes hung off his slender frame. His hand shook as he signed admission forms. Hard to gauge his age as the lilt of his voice and a shaky hand as he wrote put him between sixteen and thirty.

A doctor bounded into the room. "I'm Dr. Isaacs." He shook my hand. "Good to meet you." Boots with a rugged tread hugged his insulated bib pants. "Don't mind my outfit. I was snowmobiling." Pointing at me, he said, "Let's talk in my office." He reviewed my records, then grabbed a yellow pad. "I wrote a list of meds Health Services prescribed—Haldol, Wellbutrin, Tramadol—let me know if I missed anything. I can't believe they prescribed Prozac. Dangerous for bipolar patents."

"Can you give me lithium? It works. It's the only one they wouldn't prescribe."

Dr. Isaacs stopped writing and looked at me. "I'm prescribing lithium and a first-generation antidepressant with a simpler composition than meds the health service docs prescribed. Lithium will stabilize your moods. The antidepressant will get you back to sleep."

"How long do I have to stay here?"

"Until Monday," Dr. Isaacs said. "We'll evaluate how your medications are working. Your father hasn't returned our call yet."

"You called my parents?"

"They're your emergency contacts. We must talk to someone who knows you."

"I didn't bring clothes." All I had with me was a large purse. A large purse stuffed with manuscript pages.

Closing my file, Dr. Isaacs said, "Give the meds a couple of days. Once they start working, you will feel human again. Hopefully you'll never have to see the inside of a place like this again."

A place like this. A chemical smell of institutional cleanliness woke me to where I was. Had I really signed myself into a mental hospital? A uniformed man guarded the exit to make sure no one left. My hope they could fix me like a car with a faulty carburetor was ridiculous. How could a place so barren of life heal me?

Dr. Isaac shook my hand and directed me back to a square beige room behind admissions. No magazines. Time stretched like Silly Putty. I was glad when the young man I had seen earlier approached.

He sat down next to me. "I'm Max Fletcher."

"Short for Maximilian?"

"More like Mad Max. What's your name?"

"Deirdre."

An orderly entered. He was a large man, not fat, with a wide back. "Doctor says you two aren't allowed to eat with the general population." He straightened a badge pinned to the hem of his scrubs. "I'll bring your dinner here."

Time passed without the natural markers of breakfast, lunch, and dinner. The only sign of normalcy outside the room, unfurnished except for two chairs and a table, was a crackle of announcements. Boxed games were piled on a beige cart.

Max selected a chess set. "Let's play."

"I'm not very good," I said.

"I'll teach you. You're smart. I can tell by how you talk. Naturally pretty, like my mom, Santa Fe style."

Touched by the way he saw me after months of feeling invisible, I smiled. "What do you mean? I should wear fringy jackets and silver earrings?"

"Means you don't wear tons of makeup, 'cause you don't need to." Max's words suggested a grown man's swagger. His eyes revealed a scared boy. Halfway into our second game, our orderly returned with two trays.

We balanced chicken fricassee and wobbly dishes of Jell-O on our knees. Max confided he'd flown from New Jersey to Albuquerque on a whim to visit his high school girl friend, a student at the University of New Mexico. He found her at a Halloween dorm party kissing a vampire.

White bandages circled Max's slender wrists. His eyes followed my gaze. "I'm sorry they found me."

"Don't say that." Words trickled like pure rain into the dry well of my throat. My job was to salve this sweet boy's wounds. We talked about nothing in particular, our voices a lifeline.

I visited a restroom off admissions. When I returned, Max was reading my manuscript.

"Pages fell on the floor." He balanced my purse on his lap awkwardly as a husband safeguarding his wife's belongings. "I would kill to write like you do." He read, "'Depression is a complete lack of energy punctuated by intermittent periods of suffocating anxiety.'"

He opened a package of Saltines from his dinner tray and slid a cracker into his mouth. He replaced the pages inside my bag. "You described exactly how I feel when I get low. Never know whether my mood will flow out with the tide or pull me under."

When we tired of playing chess, Max selected a thousand-piece Starry Night puzzle from the game cart. I groaned. "I'm bad at puzzles."

"You say that about everything. Have confidence," Max said. He handed me pieces of deep blue sky. In our silent sanctuary, I snapped swirls of cloud while he pieced together a cypress tree. Night sky spread before us. His hand brushed mine as he fit together golden pieces of a lopsided crescent moon.

There was a comfort in his touch. I reminded myself how young he was. "Did they forget about us?" I asked. The anxiety of not knowing what happened next crept into my voice.

Max squeezed my hand. "Let's stay here as long as we can."

Clouds sailed past Van Gogh's steepled church pushed by curlicued currents of air. The village we built made me forget where we were. Our dream of inhabiting a blue-roofed house was shattered by a loudspeaker announcing evening meds. The orderly who brought dinner escorted us to separate rooms.

I was scared, alone except for dinging machines and staff talking at the station. Afraid of sliding off the narrow mattress, I called a nurse. "It's so noisy," I said.

"We must leave your door open," she said. "It's the rules. You are on suicide watch."

A sleepless drugged night left me agitated. "Please let me leave," I told a day nurse. "I don't get paid unless I work." I was afraid of spending another night on the slippery plastic-covered mattress. My nurse promised to call Dr. Isaacs. I avoided the professional mental patients who populated the dayroom. They knew how to work the system for disability insurance, free rides to doctor appointments.

I paced the courtyard outside, smoking a cigarette that tasted like dirt. When the nurse finally returned, she said, "Doctor says sit tight. He wants you to attend a social worker talk in the day room."

A plump earnest man perched on the back of a couch. "You need to take personal responsibility," he said. "Depression doesn't just happen."

Mine did. I never invited it in.

"Do you know how lucky we are to live in a place where God paints the sky different colors every day?"

I wondered what God the counselor worshipped. I never found a church that got God right. My stern and distant Catholic God wanted me to sit down, shut up, and adore him from afar. A high school friend invited me to play volleyball in her church parking lot and introduced me to a kind Methodist God. On TV, I watched a huckster God who promised great riches if I deeded my soul. My personal God had given me a good start in life and then abandoned me at graduation when spirals of depression destroyed my early promise. My bipolar God gave me the gift of words then buried them under heavy moods. He did not answer when I called out perished, wrecked tired. God granted me an illness so erratic every time I found a job, a love, a groove, He knocked me down to see if I could get up again.

The social worker was emotional. "Did you drive home last night surrounded by a vivid sunset? Did you tell God, 'Nice, but not what I wanted?'" His admonition was a truth I hated hearing.

Max was not in the day room or cafeteria. I read old magazines and smoked. On Monday morning, Dr. Isaacs released me.

I asked an orderly to find Max. He was dressed in the same clothes he wore Saturday, his expression slack. The orderly left us alone. Max removed something from under his sweatshirt. "Remember me," he said as he handed me a moon made of snapped together puzzle pieces.

The orderly returned to tell me my ride had arrived, a taxi ordered by the hospital.

When I turned to say goodbye, Max was gone. I felt a tug knowing I would not see him again. That he had seen me as a fellow human in my darkest hour helped more than he knew.

EIGHT

MOM WAS SITTING ON THE PORCH SWING WHEN I AR-
rived at Lizzy's apartment.

"How did you . . . ?" My voice trailed off.

"Know?" We finished each other's sentences. It was too boring to connect the dots. "I'm your emergency contact," she continued. "Every time I called, the hospital said you were in a group meeting. Your father and I were very worried."

"Where's Dad?"

"He has an important interview."

Grandpa had passed away on Labor Day and Grandma in early fall. After Grandpa's insurance business was sold, Dad spent months searching for a new job with the help of a group called Forty Plus that helped older job seekers.

"Can we go inside?" Mom asked.

I unlocked Lizzy's apartment, surprised it was neat, no physical disturbance to betray my mental anguish.

Mom surveyed watercolor sketches of New Mexico skies brightening the wall behind a squat oatmeal-colored couch with collapsed cushions. Adjoining faded walls were unadorned. Lizzy had packed her favorite paintings to move into her new home when she returned from Europe.

Mom took a folding chair from the kitchen nook and sat. "Do you feel like talking?"

I organized mail into piles, dropped a rejection from a literary magazine in the waste basket. "I stopped sleeping. Still worked every day." No need to tell her about the day I fell asleep in the middle of an intersection. I expected Mom to redouble her efforts for me to train as a dental hygienist. Instead, she walked across the room and hugged me.

"Things got scary," I said.

Mom stroked my hair. "When you get home, you can see Dr. Shea. He wished you had called him."

"What could he do from Chicago?"

"He told me he would have found a way to get you back on lithium."

A window envelope contained a check from Worthington Temporaries. The possibility of full-time employment with Skyline evaporated when I missed work the morning of my discharge.

Mom drew her finger across her forehead. "My head hurts. Let me rest. When I get up, I'll treat for dinner."

By the time I sorted mail, wrote checks for urgent bills, Mom was breathing softly. Her naps lasted hours.

Staring at walls was not an option. A lithium/nortriptyline cocktail swam through my system. Not trusting myself to drive, I set out on foot. Afternoon heat kept residents behind cement block walls. The only creatures stirring were dogs lolling on cement patios. A German Shepherd eyed me as I passed. My legs trembled, a lithium side effect. Even though no one could see the tremors, I was self-conscious. I hoped no one was watching. Still, it felt good to move. Carmen Sanchez, the woman who had hosted a block party soon after I arrived in Albuquerque, watered an explosion of pink bell-shaped flowers climbing a trellis.

"Beautiful," I said. "What are those pink flowers called?"

Carmen turned off the hose. "Mexican evening primrose. Why are you walking so fast? Sit with me," she said.

No human was braving the heat. Neighborhood dogs ceased their incessant barking. I chose a brown wicker chair with a hand-stitched pillow. Carmen disappeared into her adobe house, returning with two glasses of lemonade.

"Have you talked to Alex since he moved?" she asked.

"No," I said. "He must be busy." To cut off further questions, I bent down and retied my shoelaces.

When she finished her lemonade, Carmen turned to the craft table at her elbow. "My church is hosting a bazaar Sunday. Want to help me make dried flower shadow boxes?"

I stood. "My mom's in town. I should go. Appreciate the lemonade."

When I returned Mom was applying lipstick. "Pack your bag, Deirdre," Mom said. "We're going sightseeing." A *Frommer's* guide sprouting sticky notes lurked in her purse. "Let's leave Albuquerque. Everyone says the best of New Mexico lies north of Santa Fe."

We loaded our rental car trunk with suitcases and left Albuquerque's concrete sprawl, traveling north on I-25. Our first stop was Bernalillo, home of the County Detention Center.

Preoccupied as I had been with my problems, I hadn't noticed October turning toward November, warm days stretching like a blanket over a hardening hearth. Groves of yellow quaking aspens lit shortening days. Jacket chilly but not Chicago cold.

"How do you feel?" Mom asked.

The smell of roasting pinyon drifted through an open window. "I'm looking forward to lunch. Everything tastes good again," I said.

"Maybe we'll buy a painting you can take home."

Finding a piece of artwork to remind me of my time in New Mexico was Mom's attempt to make me happy. I was grateful she didn't make me talk about my hospital stay.

As I exited, my purse fell from my shoulder. Wallet, brush, lipstick, tiny notebook and pen spilled to reveal my vanities. My hands shook as

I retrieved my belongings. I leaned against the car until my trembling legs quieted.

"Are you all right?" Mom asked.

"A side effect of lithium. Don't worry, it wears off in a week or two; the same thing happened last time. I'll catch up with you." I lit a cigarette. My plan was to contact a hypnotist to help me quit. Right now, I needed a nicotine jolt. Sun on my back felt like the comforting hand of God.

The Range Café was crowded with tourists and locals. Chili ristras garlanded adobe walls. Mom reapplied her lipstick, something she did frequently. "Since I'm here, I thought you could show me New Mexico. Our return tickets are Saturday."

After an enchilada lunch, we followed signs to a low beige building housing an art fair. The gallery displayed wood carvings of saints called "retablos". I lingered near a handwritten card which explained how saint makers, called "Santeros", fashioned the pieces. I rolled the word Santero over my lips, loving its simple elegance.

I wondered whether to bring home St. Jude, the helper of the hopeless, or St. Therese, the little flower of Jesus. In a small room off the main gallery, a tree trunk rose from the floor. My stomach lurched in amazement as I registered life thrusting toward Heaven. Faces representing father, mother, sister, brother, friends, and angels were carved into the trunk. Their expressions were so vital, they looked like they could have been sitting next to us at lunch. God the Father topped the imposing structure. I trembled with a tiny joy as a dormant energy reawakened.

A man with soulful dark eyes wearing a tracksuit appeared from behind a narrow wooden door. He stuck out his hand. "I am Felipe Lopez. How do you like my work?"

His humility surprised me. "Your faces are so alive I expect them to speak."

"I used a chain saw and then sanded the piece."

"What inspired you to sculpt from wood?"

"I was a tour bus driver over twenty years. When workers went on strike, I drank so heavily I lost my wife to another man. Getting sober helped me comprehend the temporary nature of life."

Perhaps it was time I got sober. I didn't drink as much as I had in my twenties, yet I still wasted weekends hungover.

Lopez's jeans were pressed with a tight crease, his plaid shirt starched. He moved with vigor to show me other pieces. It was only when he stopped talking that I detected age lines striating his eyes and mouth, temples turning gray, a fleeting woundedness in his dark eyes. "I was called to do my art," he said. "I still feel like I have more to learn so I can attain everything I visualize."

Most art I had seen before New Mexico was housed at Chicago's Art Institute. Artists venerated in textbooks, untouchable as paintings protected by uniformed security guards. A bus driver creating such splendor cracked open new possibilities.

Seatbelted into our rental, we discussed whether to follow the low road along the Rio Grande or take the high road to Taos. I read from *Frommer's* guide. "The High Road winds through scenic villages known for silver work and weaving."

Mom started the ignition. "If we take that route, we won't get there in time. Let's take the low road so we can make Taos before attractions close. An adobe church Georgia O'Keefe made famous is top of my list." Even though Mom had stopped attending mass every Sunday, she loved visiting historic churches.

North of Santa Fe, a juniper-dotted plain stretched to colorful badlands. I read from *Frommer's*. "Oceans flooded and drained over centuries, leaving coastal plains." The thought of ancient mountains thrusting from the earth only to be worn down by ceaseless erosion made me feel comfortably small. "Nature cares nothing about our flyspeck concerns," I said.

"Millenniums rolled through this landscape," Mom said. A faint smile played around her lips. We were quiet as we passed tiny villages along the Rio Grande. Mom treated me as her travel partner, foregoing further questions about how I had landed in the hospital. Emotional stoicism was the best and worst of our family dynamic. My parents never discussed their feelings, deflecting them with wit or drowning them in drink.

The Rio Grande current was low and slow, keeping rafters away. We reached Taos a half hour before the church closed. Gift shops ringed the square. San Francisco de Asís Mission Church was simple and stunning, a large adobe structure flanked by beehive-curved buttresses.

Standing outside an idling bus in the dusty parking lot, a driver bedecked with a turquoise belt buckle and a matching bolo tie greeted boarding tourists.

Mom disappeared into a gallery.

I slipped between a pair of bell towers into the church to escape late afternoon heat. The cool dark interior smelled of dried pinyon and missal paper. I submerged my fingers into a holy water font and genuflected as I entered a wooden pew. A slender old woman leaning on a cane traveled the aisle. She picked a pew opposite, her movements graceful despite her cane. As she lowered herself on a kneeler, she made the sign of the cross. Her gaze as she turned toward me was full of light and curiosity, hazel eyes flecked green.

A young boy exited a confessional. The old woman, white abundant hair caught in a silver clip at the nape of her neck, took his place. I felt ashamed of my self-centered prayers, more like complaints. I faced forward and thanked God for my life. I wanted to believe He had stayed the hand trying to pull me under a second time.

The interior centered around a wooden altar covered by embroidered white cloth, simpler than the stained glass and marble statues adorning the church where I worshipped as a child. Priests at St. Paul of the Cross celebrated mass distanced from congregants. As a child, I liked how bells ringing pierced the silence, but I never thought much about Christ. I blamed my status as a public school student for keeping me from forming a relationship.

A niche contained eight oil paintings on canvas. Two depicted the agony of Christ. My anguish mounted for my wreck of a life. Shoulders shaking, I genuflected and exited the pew, hoping to leave behind emotions I didn't know how to tame or release.

Our rental car sat empty. I found a shop selling mass cards and figurines of saints. Lack of overhead lighting and a comfortable musty smell made me feel like I had stumbled into a private museum. Backlit individual cabinets housed retablos and hand carved wooden sparrows. A male voice greeted me from a dim recess behind a cash register. "Feel free to browse."

A collection of saints fashioned from tin sat in a bowl. St. Christopher kept company with Mary and Joseph. St. Anthony of Padua, patron saint of finding true love, sat in the middle. As I leaned over to select him, my purse knocked the bowl over. Saints went flying. Expecting a reprimand, I descended to my knees and quickly gathered Bernadette, Gabriel and Therese.

The shop owner kneeled on the floor to help me retrieve scattered replicas.

"I'm sorry," I said, "so sorry."

His voice was low and gentle. "Let me help you." His kindness calmed me. I had forgotten such gentle souls lived in the world.

I emerged with three books and a small paper bag jingling with tiny saints. Mom leaned against our rental. Her expression was calm. She was good at hiding her worry and aggravation over my missteps. She brightened when she saw me, pointed toward a painting in the trunk. "Look what I found."

Taos Mountain wreathed in pinkish gold fronted by a ribbon of cool blue stream mirroring the sky. A perfect painting to remind me of New Mexico.

The Sagebrush Inn & Suites corridors were hung with art. I carried our suitcases, stopping to look at the artists' names. Sandoval painted vivid landscapes, an adobe home an afterthought in the vast landscape. R. C. Gorman's Navajo women hid secret worlds under shawls draped over their full-bodied figures.

Mom plopped on the bed reading a guest guide. "Georgia O'Keefe lived here. Scenes from *Easy Rider* were shot behind the hotel." She closed the guide and lay back. "Turn off the light. I'm going to shut my eyes." Mom's breath evened as she escaped into sleep.

Even with the air conditioner's hum and a blanket swaddled around me, I couldn't relax. My hand trembled as I reached toward the nightstand for a glass of water to take my medicine.

A woman taking towels from a cart waved as I followed a dim hall toward the back exit to see where *Easy Rider* was filmed. Nothing moved. A hawk traced circles overhead. Silence smothered echoes of Dennis Hopper and Peter Fonda tearing up the field on their motorcycles.

I was tired of fighting my treacherous thoughts. Anxiety beat a familiar arrhythmia. I walked to the field's far end. Recalling the hospital counselor's advice to replace negative thoughts with positive, I took a hotel notepad from my pocket and wrote two positive events. Nortriptyline helped me sleep. Lithium evened my moods, even though it made me shaky. Taking the right medication restored life in all its color to senses shut down by depression.

If only the trip away from our troubles would last forever. As wonderful as it was to recover, another unknown future lay ahead. While my friends bought houses and welcomed babies, I had to start over again. Questions mounted a new attack: *Will I be okay? Will my medicine work? How long will this period of peace last?*

Mom stirred when I reentered our hotel room. I pulled a blanket around me. She propped herself against her pillow. "You look like R. C. Gorman's women. Let's get dinner."

Art was everywhere in Taos, from galleries on the square to The Sagebrush bar walls. Painters captured mountain landscapes, symphonic sunsets hung next to art of weavers, potters, and silversmiths.

Clusters of dark wood tables surrounded a series of nooks. We ate chips and salsa, watching the bar fill with so many people we couldn't hear each other. Our waitress directed us to an outside patio occupied by two young couples and a family of four. The young parents fussed over a boy who joked with his father and a girl who drew placemat pictures. Their ordinary interactions filled me with longing for my own family.

"Another round for the lovely sisters," the waitress said as she placed two margaritas in front of us.

Mom didn't correct her.

We drank in silence, tart lime pursing our lips. Tequila exacerbated my rising anxiety. I groaned. "What will I do next?"

Mom had always looked ten years younger than her real age. Slender and active, not matronly like my friends' mothers. She returned reluctantly from her tequila high. "Come home. We miss you."

"As much as I love you, I don't want to live with you and Dad."

Mom gripped the stem of her margarita glass. "We have an idea. I need to tell you that your Great Aunt Katherine died last month."

"Why didn't you tell me earlier?" Katherine was my favorite relative. She took me to plays and galleries, celebrated every poem I published.

"Considering what you were going through, we figured her death would make you too sad. Katherine left you her summer cottage near Antioch."

"In Wisconsin?"

"Her house is on the Illinois side. If we add insulation, you can live there year-round. Your own private Walden, a wonderful place where you can write. As a little girl, you loved playing near the pond. Her big back yard is filled with walnut and oak trees, extending toward a native grass prairie. No neighbors to bug you."

The young family gathered tote bags and coloring books as they shepherded their children into the hotel.

"Your responsibility is to pay the real estate taxes. A part-time job should cover your expenses. You'll have uninterrupted hours to write."

With the return of sleep, I could write again. New Mexico was where I wanted to be, not Illinois with its memories and failures. If I went home, I would disappear into my family and never have my own life. I would tell Mom at breakfast I was staying.

At 4:00 a.m., I found Mom standing in front of the lighted bathroom mirror. Her face was wet, whether from tears or tap water I couldn't tell. "What's wrong?" I asked. "You're sleeping during the day like you used to." When I was a child, Mom spent afternoons alone in her room. I wondered why, but never asked. "Are you and Dad all right?"

Mom wiped her face with a rough cloth. She turned to face me. "Those afternoons I spent in my room before Grandpa and Grandma died, I was mourning them, knowing how empty life would be after they were gone. I didn't confide in you because you were so depressed after high school. I had the world's kindest parents. They forgave my mistakes. All of them."

I put my arm over her shoulder. "I miss them, too. Makes me sad. Our favorite people cannot be replaced."

"It's early," Mom said. "Let's go back to sleep."

We visited Blumenschein Home and Museum, a single-story adobe built around a central courtyard. Mom gravitated toward a painting of Eagle Nest Lake. In the foreground, billowing blue water relieved stiff mountain ridges. A collection of diaries spread on a long wooden table attracted me. Ernest Blumenschein, a painter from Pittsburgh, described his first sight of Taos in 1883. When his wagon broke an axle, he was greeted by a vista of unimaginable beauty. "The color, the reflective character of the landscape, the drama of the vast spaces, the superb beauty and severity of the hills, stirred me deeply. Never shall I forget these first powerful impressions. My own impressions, direct from the new land, thru my own eyes, not another man's. Not another's adventure." Mom watched as I finished reading diary entries, her expression a mix of worry and hope.

We drank wine at lunch. Emboldened by a buzz of intoxication, I leaned across the table. "What if you and Dad fix up Aunt Katherine's cabin for *your* summer home? I feel like myself again. What do you think about my staying here to write a new novel? Rentals are cheap. I can find an office job."

"Please come home," Mom said.

Under the table, I dug my nails into my palms. "I like it here," I said. My voice was a squeak, barely rising over surface noise of diners chatting, cutlery clacking.

Mom reached in her purse to pay the tab. I contributed a tip. Our hands touched as we lay down bills.

"I'm worried about your father. He's losing weight. His skin's yellow."

"The scan didn't find anything."

"Dad isn't here because of an interview. I didn't tell you right away because I didn't want to worry you. His doctor ordered more tests." Mom grasped the stem of her glass as if someone were going to take it away. "In my dream last night, the three of us were driving in the Sandias. A cloudburst separated us. You and I were safe. Dad didn't make it."

Suffering from lifelong vivid dreams, I did not question the truth she had received in the night. I fell back asleep. Mom was sitting next to me when I awoke. She touched my forehead. "Oh, Deirdre of the Sorrows," she said. "Your red hair made me name you Deirdre. I never wanted you to suffer."

I opened my eyes and thought I was looking into my own face.

Mom tried a smile. "Please, Deirdre, I need you."

Aunt Katherine's wind-weathered Victorian house sat on three acres featuring a spring-fed pond. Local history claimed the original owners bottled water and sold it circa 1900. As a child, I played among orange day lilies and flowering pink crabapple trees that ringed the pond and roamed the prairie.

As much as I hated leaving New Mexico, making the house my home fulfilled a dream I did not know I had. A chance to change course. My parents' house was over an hour's drive away. Living far from anyone who knew me gave me a chance to stand strong as the artist I needed to be. Not bow with every changing wind, not let every encounter with a friend or lover knock me off the path. Here where no one knew me, I would make a new name for myself.

To earn money for property taxes and living expenses, I temped for a law firm. When the assignment ended, I joined an employment group at a local church. The leader said the schools needed substitute teachers. Sick of office life, I obtained a certificate. To my surprise, after I became acclimated to school life, I realized working with kids was a good fit. The pay was poor, but I was able to fashion my own schedule.

Consulting pictures from Aunt Katherine's photo albums, I recreated her garden. During a late autumn afternoon, I prepared her garden for winter by composting spent annuals and vegetable plants. The only flowers still alive were bright burgundy chrysanthemums bought from a local farmer. My phone rang. Even though everyone loved their smartphones, I refused to yoke myself to an electronic leash. A pay-as-you-go flip phone covered emergencies.

"How do you do, how are you?" Dad said. His tone was friendly and buoyant, but the timbre of his voice was weak and reedy. "I hate to take you away from whatever you're doing, but I was wondering if you could pick me up at the hospital. Just finished my latest test. I'd walk, but they won't release me without a ride."

After Grandpa died, his business was sold. Dad became an underwriter for a downtown insurance agency. I suspected he loved commuting more than his job, riding the train with a group of wiseacres. Jewell, a banker, Majewski, a chemical engineer, and Flavin, a PR man, stood in the vestibule making jokes while fellow commuters sat inside and rattled their newspapers. When that job ended, Dad aged quickly.

I folded a yard waste bag and set it between two garbage cans. "Shouldn't take too long this time of day," I said.

"Swell," Dad said. "I will wait for you."

It didn't dawn on me the slight stooped figure waiting outside was my father until I recognized the umbrella I gave him last Father's Day. When he saw me, his lips curled upward in an approximation of a smile. His sagging shoulders didn't hold their end of the bargain. As he approached, my heart sank. His former quick step had turned to a slow shuffle.

"Thanks for picking me up," he said. He paused. "I wanted to ask you something."

I took a detour past the forest preserve. Late afternoon light drenched an oak grove with a golden hue as hazy clouds dotted the sky.

Dad looked like a child belted into his seat. "How was your day?" he asked.

"No sub jobs, so I had time to work on my novel."

"I was wondering if you'll be my literary executor."

"You have plenty of time." It was impossible to imagine a world without Dad in it. I stared straight ahead, unwilling to acknowledge how pale his face appeared. "Do you have other work besides the play you wrote at Hull House?"

"Started a series of stories about the South Side neighborhood where I grew up. I even thought of a title."

I didn't tell him I'd seen a sheet titled "When the Darkness Falls" rolled into his old blue Selectric. Nothing followed. "If you record your stories, I'll type them." I turned on our street, pulled into the driveway.

"Appreciate the ride home, Deirdre." He leaned his back against the car seat as if contact hurt.

"Dad?" I asked as he tucked a newspaper inside his briefcase, "are you afraid to die?"

"No," he said. He gathered his strength and smiled. "Just the process." He walked up one of the long thin driveway ribbons he'd fought like a suburban gladiator. Pausing halfway, he turned and waved.

After I dropped him home, I tried to write. I fell asleep lights on, manuscript pages like fallen leaves surrounding me. Darkness fell. In the night, I dreamed he died. Dad's pale, still face stared from a satin coverlet. Knife sharp pain on my left side made me bolt upright in bed. I looked out the window. An animal ran through the field, shape shifting in shadows created by moonlight.

Some dreams were ordinary as a clerk sorting papers to be filed. This one was a vision.

Dad's surgery was scheduled for December 15. He insisted on completing his chores, bagging leaves as fast as they fell, chipping ice from the driveway.

In the yellow glare of the corridor outside his hospital room, Mother appeared diminished. I held her hand as we greeted Kevin, who had just arrived from Colorado. We kept our vigil. When Mother left for a cup of coffee, Kevin and I talked about trivial matters to keep the room from filling with silence. "I'm trying to remember the gas station owner's name. You know, where I worked in high school," Kevin said.

Dad had been silent, his bright blue eyes following the ping pong of conversation, despite an IV pumping morphine and machines beeping. "Giannopoulos. George Giannopoulos was his name." Kevin and I laughed, forgetting where we were. Father turned calmly to me and said, "My gym bag is under the bed. If you would be so kind as to hand me my pants, we can get out of here." He tried to swing his legs over the metal railing. The effort was too much. He collapsed against his pillow.

Surgery was supposed to remove whatever blockage made him lose weight so fast. His pants drooped like a little boy wearing his father's clothes. We believed he would be home for Christmas. Mom, Kevin, and I watched a medical show in the family waiting room. Surgery lasted two hours longer than expected. The doctor gathered Mom, Kevin, and I in a tiny airless room. "Cancer has spread throughout his organs. Spend all the time you can. Your father will not be leaving the hospital."

I sobbed in the lobby.

"You have to put on your game face," my brother said.

During an earlier trip to Mexico, we watched a middle-aged man soar from a cliff. Dad said, "Find me here. I always wanted to glide like a bird."

Mother returned. Her eyes were red. Kevin turned to comfort her where she stood at the foot of the bed. I squeezed Dad's hand. "I will write your stories," I whispered.

Words were our connection. A boy during the Great Depression when wakes were the only affordable entertainment on Chicago's South side, Dad had cultivated an ear for speech patterns. Walking through the Loop was a master class in sensory detail. Dialogue wrote itself as we eavesdropped on fedora-wearing men rushing to work. "Hi Bill, what's new? Let's stop for a cup." Add the lilt of train wheels clacking, taxis honking, and words became music. When I walked with Dad, jazz pianos played from downtown rooftops.

The hospital room was so silent we heard the clock tick. Dad pointed toward the door, as he did when he was late catching the train. He always said, "I gotta run." His lips moved, but no words emerged.

Hands of an institutional clock over his bed moved to join each other at straight up noon. He closed his eyes, and he was gone, his body inert, his spirit flying toward the station, heaven to Father being the platform of a city-bound train.

Part Two

NINE

Clairmont, Illinois
October 2010

AS I ATE A BOWL OF OATMEAL BEFORE SCHOOL, A GUN-shot made me drop my spoon. A second shot erupted from a cluster of oaks. Hunting season had not begun. Walking outside, I opened a rickety gate to investigate. A freshman-sized boy wearing a Hidden Springs hoodie cradled a shotgun. "Did you see the sign?" I asked. "No hunting on private property."

The boy shifted his weight, his stance alternating between defiance and surrender. His dirty hair was chestnut brown. Sun poking through budding leaves highlighted reddish cowlicks curled at his temples. Azure eyes. Straight nose, freckled cheeks.

"Shouldn't you be in school?" I asked. "What's your name?"

"Benjamin Babcock." His shoulders slumped. "No point. I'm failing everything." He pointed toward a backpack abandoned at the base of a tree.

His tears, like a surprise rain shower in full sun, made me gentle my tone. "There are people at Clairmont High who can help."

Benjamin packed his shotgun inside his backpack, looped it over one arm. "I gotta run home before my brothers wake up."

"Where are your parents?"

"Mom's at work, I hope. She manages the laundromat. I don't know where my father is."

"Promise you'll go back to school tomorrow." Before I could ask more questions, he ran west through the woods toward Clairmont.

At the outskirts of town sat a motel that housed families teetering on homelessness. I wondered if Benjamin lived there.

With the help of a local contractor named Clem Varner, Aunt Katherine's summer cabin had become habitable year-round. Clem had built a sunroom where I watched the seasons change. He brought in a crew to update electrical wiring. Renovation proved an endless project completed in spurts whenever money was available. My next goal was to replace drafty old windows.

A friendship of sorts evolved. Clem's advice on how to restore Aunt Katherine's garden yielded spring blooms of red and pink peonies. Her garden was my pride and joy. Flowers for beauty, an array of healthy vegetables. Keeping the garden as colorful and lush as it had been in my aunt's day necessitated hours of work. I planted, weeded, and watered. A fountain was installed to disperse algae that when untreated, formed a skim of sludge. I relaxed, watching water cascade over the pond.

Indoors, Aunt Katherine's red velvet Queen Anne's chair was my favorite reading spot. Her hand knit afghans and mohair throws decorated a new couch I bought the year I'd coached girls' soccer.

Living alone without partner or child was lonely at times. To prevent depression from returning, I kept busy. Teaching satisfied my maternal instincts.

Every time I felt walls closing in, I added an extracurricular duty to my schedule. Over time, I had been sponsor for the yearbook, student newspaper, poetry club. When the Comedy Club formed, I volunteered to assist the teacher in charge of turning comedy nerds into performers.

My demons were chased away by hard work. I never officially gave up alcohol. The less I drank, the less I felt like it. Old friends lived so far away our weekend drinking get-togethers faded into memory.

Clairmont High was a twenty-minute drive. Patches of burgundy peeked through a colonnade of white ash trees lining the approach to the village's three-block downtown. Cool air rushed in through my open car window as I drove to school. Broken chords in a minor key playing from a jazz station lent a note of mystery to the lightening sky.

A slight man crossed on yellow two blocks ahead, a stiff breeze ruffling his navy windbreaker. He looked so much like my father I sped up to catch him. My grief still played tricks on me. As I turned left toward teacher parking, I realized the quick moving figure was not Dad, but a student I had helped write a Gatsby paper.

The old building was faceless as a stockade. A space was open between a Ford-150 and a rusty beater. I parked and listened to piano jazz before killing the engine. Asleep in the beater was a man with tangled graying blonde curls. His wrinkled cheek rested against driver's side window; the back seat overflowed with various-sized pieces of pipe and sheets of foil. I remembered him as a substitute teacher famous for falling asleep in class. A shortage of subs made him a logical choice when Clairmont's art teacher went on maternity leave. He relieved me for lunch.

I knocked on his window. He acknowledged my presence and righted himself. As he exited the Honda Civic, a sketchbook fell, open to a drawing of a stage in a forest clearing. Yellow aspens quaked in a dawning orange sky.

"Love your colors," I said.

"I can show you the installation if you're interested." He tucked a crumpled plaid shirt into the waistband of tan cargo pants. His small stature and gamin features made him look like a sprite.

Teachers were already manning their classrooms except for stragglers delayed by a long parent drop-off line. As we entered school, we were swept into two-way traffic rushing toward classrooms. The sub gave me a backward wave as he ran downstairs two at time toward the art wing.

Principal Greg Nowak was outside greeting arriving students. I described how I met Benjamin Babcock.

Nowak, a fit tall man in his thirties with a dimpled smile, looked nothing like the stern principals of my youth. "Let's talk in my office." He waved me toward a visitor's chair. "Benjamin enrolled earlier this month. He needs intense tutoring to reach grade level. Bright, good test scores. Rough home life. Oldest brother of three boys being raised by a single mom. Benjamin needs someone to care about him."

I had been planning to pitch a creative writing magazine. From Nowak's intent expression, I knew he meant me. I owed him.

Greg leaned forward, stretching his hands as if in prayer. "Let's clear your schedule fifth period. Daily tutoring paired with after-school sessions should bring our boy up to speed."

Benjamin Babcock was sure to rub teachers the wrong way. He needed an adult in his corner. There was something familiar about him, endearing. If I'd had a son, he might resemble him. Sad, sweet, and ornery, his drowned azure eyes betrayed the prevailing weather of his mood.

My purse strap was twisted around the chair. As I unraveled it, I caught Nowak's hopeful expression. "Whatever you need," I said.

Clem's latest project was to convert an upstairs bedroom into a yoga studio. I found him on his hands and knees removing carpet as I arrived home from school. "My daughter practices meditation at that Buddhist temple in Woodstock," Clem said. "She says silence calms her. More likely an excuse not to talk to me."

I stifled a laugh. "Can you install a mirror over the powder room sink?"

We walked downstairs. Removing a nail from his mouth, Clem said, "See if the height suits you." I paused in front of the mirror. My auburn hair was shoulder length, colored to cover gray strands. Laugh lines had claimed territory around my eyes. My rounded chin was turning bony. Gravity was doing its work.

Clem cleared his throat. "Don't think I'm fresh, but the boys who work for me were talking. They wonder why no one's snapped you up. Must get lonely living in this old house alone."

Attempting to keep my tone light, I said, "Sometimes I wonder, too." I walked him out. "Say hi to your wife for me."

A blue heron alighted on a wooden bridge spanning the pond. What a long wingspan. Prehistoric.

As Clem drove away, I thought of dating strategies I'd tried when I first moved to Clairmont. Churches were no better than bars. Everyone was married, many with large families. Single men were in short supply at Meet-Up Hikes. Conversation on the trail revealed them to be bitterly divorced or avid hunters who found my devotion to writing odd. A fellow aide named Linda Boyd suggested Match.com or SilverSingles. Computer dating did me in. I had no patience sending notes to strangers. Linda made fun of me. "I thought you were a writer," she said. I hired a dating sherpa who promised an appealing profile would attract winners.

A potential match named Jeff Chamberlain responded. Smart, handsome, and kind, he seemed too good to be true. A CPA with a prestigious firm, he took me to wonderful restaurants, trying a different cuisine each week. We got to know each other slowly. For Christmas, he gave me a silver necklace, hinting that next would be an engagement ring.

I asked about his ex-wife. "She was impulsive, life of the party," he said. "Spent money like it was going out of style. Her doctor diagnosed her as bipolar." He asked the waiter for champagne. "That's why I'm so happy with you. You're the sensible type. Quiet and considerate."

To Jeff and my present associates, I appeared normal. I didn't have the courage to explain my past to Jeff. A therapist—or a close friend— might have helped me poke holes in that thinking. Fear convinced me it was too late to walk back my early missteps.

My self-esteem couldn't take the blow of another rejection. I backed away from the relationship, refusing to tell Jeff why. Eventually, he stopped calling. I threw myself into my work with at risk kids and my ongoing effort to write a novel.

Jeff refreshed his profile on Match.com with a new picture. I deleted my account.

On October 14, I showered and dressed before making coffee. It was my fifteen-year anniversary at the high school. Bringing a box of donuts was a good way to thank my colleagues for their friendship and support. Paperwork awaited me on my desk.

Dawn was brightening the sky as I drove toward Clairmont. I contemplated how much I had changed in fifteen years. My first months as a teacher's aide were shaky, as I was adjusting to lithium in my system. The other aides were standoffish. They saved me tasks they hated. My second week, I balked when Linda told me to clean desks sticky with spilled pop.

I had been assigned to the Shield Room, a respite area designated for behaviorally challenged high schoolers. When I entered, students were sprawled on couches watching videos, eating subsidized cafeteria lunches. A whiff of rancid grease and unwashed bodies greeted me.

Linda surveyed crumpled napkins and ketchup-stained carrels. "You have to clean before next period starts," she said, handing me a tube of Clorox Disinfecting Wipes.

Anger corroded my already shaky mood. "I don't think so," I said and handed back the wipes. I didn't come here to be a maid." My chest tightened against my rapidly beating heart. I hurried to the exit and drove home blinded by anger.

Principal Greg Nowak visited me at home. "Try another week," he said.

"The work doesn't suit me."

"Really?" Nowak said. "You were right about Benjamin Babcock. Based on what you told me, his English class was changed. He's thriving in a co-taught class. Remedial was boring him so badly he tuned out." Nowak's sincere Midwestern manner touched me.

"One week," I said.

On his way out, Nowak handed me a social worker's card. Weekly appointments with a seasoned female therapist named Dr. Gottlieb helped me adjust to my new life. With her encouragement, I selected weekend classes to complete a master's degree. The process took two to four years of study.

Although I fell into teaching at a time when erratic moods kept me from making measured choices, working with difficult kids proved my favorite job. I fell in love with the rebellious outliers. Our mutual eccentricities fit like puzzle pieces. Their faces haunted me as I walked the prairie behind my house. I strategized how to introduce them to fellow oddballs like Holden Caulfield.

First period, Spencer Graham lay under a Chicago Bears blanket in Shield. Students rose for the national anthem and Pledge of Allegiance.

I let him be, as district policy allowed students to stand or not. After the pledge ended, Spencer drew his blanket over his face to block overhead lights.

His semester grades were four D's and an F. "You have work to do, Spencer."

"I'm good." Spencer spoke from under his blanket.

"You're failing English."

Spencer shifted on the couch. "My teacher hates me."

"You were assigned a speech a month ago. Why didn't you get help?"

When I earned my teaching certificate after working as a paraprofessional, I had dreams of helping children love books. I was surprised how many resisted reading, said they hated books. I mourned when a student accepted a low passing grade so they could graduate.

"Meet me in the Credit Recovery Room," I said.

No other scheduled students had arrived for online course work. Spencer took a seat next to me. His Chromebook was shut and his posture was rigid as the hard metal chair supporting his body. His dark eyes were expressionless. A three day stubble on his chin.

"How long should your speech be?" I asked.

"Five minutes." He retrieved a crumple of papers from his distended backpack. The essay was a variation of the hero's journey, student as hero climbing rocky paths, summiting in sunshine.

"Can you read everything you've written so far?" I asked.

"I'm supposed to base it on an essay I didn't write—what 'apotheosis' means to me." Spencer slouched in his chair. "I've hit my morning wall," he said.

No ember burned within him. The essay revealed his mother belittled him because he didn't like reading. Compounding his misery, a girl who showed him kindness last semester had stopped talking to him. Spencer's eyelids closed. I jiggled his chair. "Don't check out on me now," I said. "Tell me what 'apotheosis' means."

"A high point. I only know because my mother is a writer. My teacher said we should explain how we can elevate ourselves to a divine status."

He looked so sad I felt compassion. "What does apotheosis mean to you?"

"A job where I don't smell like French fries. Girls hate it."

My challenge was to raise Spencer to a godlike stature. "Let's take a walk," I said.

Students clutching neon-colored passes fled classrooms for bathroom breaks. The smell of ground beef browning wafted from culinary. Spencer revived at the sight of Eli Nowak, a student who had recently transferred from a therapeutic school where he received one-on-one assistance. Eli walked the halls when he couldn't concentrate in class. Spencer waved.

The first time I met Eli, he'd screamed, "Hello," with his mouth curled in a Jim Carrey-esque rictus smile. Soon after I settled him with an algebra worksheet, he muttered under his breath, "Can I scream? Can I leave right now?"

He interrupted me when I was working with other students, banging a fidget bar on his desk with an untied shoe. If I didn't acknowledge him right away, he raised his volume and repeated in five-second intervals, "Can I walk out?" A dedicated paraprofessional sat with him in class, removing him to the breakout room when he had a meltdown. When he was quiet, which wasn't often, his elfin ears and pointy chin rendered him momentarily adorable.

I had been supervising the Shield Room one day when Eli arrived so distraught, it took two teachers using a safety harness and a cushioned blocking pad to keep him from hitting staff. Today Eli appeared calm. Large headphones dwarfed his features.

Linda was showing a student how to brown ground beef. "Can you spare a sandwich?" I asked. She nodded. "Grab a bun, Spencer. Plates are in the cabinet."

Spencer added hot sauce and ate his sandwich in four bites. A full stomach lightened his mood. He walked beside me back to our classroom. "Can't wait for this weekend. We're camping at Coger's Bluff."

"Sounds cold," I said.

"Winter camping is awesome," Spencer said.

We returned to the Credit Recovery Room. "Let me see what you wrote." I took three index cards from him. The first was titled "The Mad Hatter."

"You a Lewis Carroll fan?"

"No," Spencer said. "Mom was smoking Mad Hatter the day my grand-parents took me to live with them. I'll never forget the strawberry-colored package. I was four."

My silence prompted an outpouring of detail. Spencer abandoned his folding chair, closed the door. He shook off his early morning torpor and paced the eleven by fifteen-foot room. "She smoked a bowl of it, which you're not supposed to do. Made her shake. She was crying, said she couldn't take care of me anymore."

I searched "Mad Hatter" on my Chromebook. A green-faced hatter tipped his hat, offering three grams of Strawberry incense.

"I was in my car seat, wrapper on the floor. The Hatter wore a bowtie over a checkered vest. Green letters dripped off the page. Mom parked in front of my grandparents' house. They came out. Mom was yelling. I opened my car window. A brisk wind whipped words right out of their mouths. Grandpa put his arm around Mom. Said it was the best phone call she ever made."

"Are you still with your grandparents?" I asked.

"Mom took me back after she quit drugs. She's doing great now. Her latest book was made into a movie."

I had read Eleanor Graham's short stories. Was Spencer her son? "Did your mother win the Pulitzer Prize?" I asked.

He nodded. Tears wet his straight black lashes. "She made me play Scrabble instead of catch."

Twenty minutes remained in the period. Spencer used five index cards to create bullet points for his speech.

"Let's time it," I said.

Spencer's speech clocked in at four minutes and forty-five seconds.

The bell rang. "Speak slowly and you'll hit five minutes, no problem."

As soon as he left, I googled Eleanor Graham. Her literary pedigree was flawless. Iowa Writer's Workshop, Pulitzer Prize, Columbia University professor. I wondered if she would attend Parents' Night.

At home, I weeded my garden. Afterward, I settled on the porch swing with a Chicago newspaper. A front-page *Tribune* arts section article showed a picture of my college housemate, Jamie Nordberg. The caption stated she won a Pushcart Prize for flash fiction. Nikki Adamos had called her a little girl who wouldn't say boo to a goose.

Jamie's room was across the hall from where Nikki and I stayed at the University of Illinois. When we returned drunk and raucous at closing time, we heard Jamie crying in her room.

A stab of jealousy traveled my torso from collarbone to gut as I read about Jamie's prize, her job as editor at a New York publishing house. My writing earned me a stack of rejections.

Nothing calmed me, not a long walk through deep woods or washing the kitchen floor. I sat down on my porch rocker, closed my eyes, and counted my breaths. I breathed in, expelled each breath with an audible whoosh.

"Be careful or you'll hyperventilate."

A tall woman wearing a tan duster coat over a starched white shirt stood before me. "Didn't mean to startle you. I'm Eleanor Graham, Spencer's mother."

I stood, trying to regain my composure. A person with less presence wearing such a long coat would have looked ridiculous. Graham's lanky limbs and laconic manner gave her authority. She wore no makeup. Her angular face was more weathered than tanned, the skin on her hands peeling. "My son needs you. I tried calling you to arrange tutoring sessions."

"I don't work with students privately," I said.

"Unfortunate." Eleanor Graham took a seat on the steps as if we were old friends. She removed a crushed pack of Marlboros from her pocket and lit up. "Spencer likes you. The speech you helped him write saved his grade."

I bit my lip to hide my amusement that the son of a renowned writer was flunking remedial English. "He did it himself."

Eleanor kicked a walnut shell into a bed of hydrangeas. "Spencer wants to drop out of high school and work at the grocery store with his friends. No matter how I paint it, he says he's not interested in college."

"Not every student is cut out for college or college right away," I said.

A squirrel retrieved a walnut shell. "My son cannot be a dropout. We didn't get anywhere with the school social worker. I sent him to the most expensive child psychologist in the area. Spencer won't confide in anyone. He likes you. I'll pay you to tutor, threaten, cajole, whatever it takes to drag his ass across the finish line." She ground a cigarette butt under her boot. "Forgot my manners. I didn't even ask if you minded."

Smoke floated over our heads like ghosts of parties past. "Feel free." I did some quick mental calculations. Tutoring money would finance a writer's conference in Greece. "Let's make a deal. I'll get your son across the stage if you provide standard tutoring fees and notes on my novel-in-progress."

Eleanor Graham pulled herself from a slouch to her full height. "Can you start tomorrow?" She handed me a card. "Send your manuscript to my email."

She unlatched the back gate without making a sound. Footprints etched in prairie grass were my only proof one of America's greatest living short story writers had been sitting on my porch. Requesting notes on my manuscript had required every ounce of nerve I had.

It was hard to picture Eleanor Graham as a mother, especially Spencer's mother. Spencer was volatile but kind, protective of any student who was bullied. Eleanor's manner was guarded, as if her soul lived behind a bookcase in an uninhabited house. I had read her stories after college, wishing I had a knowledgeable professor to guide me through them. Sentences byzantine in their intricacy relieved by a tang of noir. Plot lines were constructed with a geometry I didn't understand but hoped to, someday. Her protagonists never rose to the occasion, addled by drugs and regret.

Spencer needed someone to care. His English speech made that clear. The mother in his story had thrown him away as casually as a drug wrapper. Had Eleanor done that? High schoolers often confessed the most terrible truths in their essays. I pictured his toddler self, seeking his mother's attention as he sat immobilized, strapped into his child seat.

I rocked to the rhythm of frogs chorusing from the pond. Eleanor Graham said Spencer needed me. Did it matter if my motivation was helping a struggling student or furthering my writing career?

Buoyed by Eleanor Graham's promise to read my novel in progress, I spent the weekend writing. Saturday when I finished, I sat in the garden reading a book called *Several Short Sentences about Writing* by Verlyn Klinkenborg, who advised every sentence had to justify its existence and flow smoothly into the next sentence. Sunday, I edited every sentence I had written on Saturday.

Monday after school, a silver Volvo full of boys pulled into my driveway piloted by Spencer Graham. Benjamin Babcock spilled out of the back seat followed by two little brothers.

"What's happening?" I asked.

Spencer's jeans were torn. Benjamin's shirt collar was blood stained. Spencer pulled me to the garden's edge. "I drove past the playground coming home. Benjamin was watching his brothers like he always does. Three guys from shop class were hiding in the bushes. They ambushed him and started wailing on him. Hope you don't mind. I brought him here."

"I'll call Benjamin's mother."

"I tried. She won't pick up. Either at work or the tavern. Let them stay."

I handed him *The Old Man and the Sea*. "If you finish your paper and Benjamin completes his math, you can stay. Your English teacher said if you don't submit your paper, you'll flunk. You can't graduate without four years of English."

"I'll get it done," Spencer said. "Before I forget, Mother sent you a message." He drew a tattered envelope from his backpack. Inside was a note written in formal penmanship. Eleanor had read my pages and made notes. She invited me to visit her at her writing cabin. I wondered why she hadn't texted. She was more of a Luddite than I was.

Spencer sat at the picnic table writing on a yellow pad. Benjamin joined him and worked on math. The little brothers, Blaze and Boyd, pushed each other into leaves I had gathered, scattering yellow oak and red maple into new geometric patterns. Satisfied Spencer and Benjamin were working, I raked. As I turned to check Benjamin's progress, the little boys scattered my orderly pile. They were laughing so hard, I raked a pile back together and jumped with them.

Saturday morning, I headed for Eleanor Graham's writing cabin. She had drawn a map showing her Fox River location accessible only on foot. Late October was warm and sunny, the perfect Indian summer, unlike last year when northern Illinois had gotten two inches of snow on Halloween. I took a wrong turn, snagged my sweater on a hazelnut shrub. By the time I found her, I was sweaty and anxious.

Eleanor Graham sat on an Adirondack chair drinking from a thermos. Her free hand rested on her knee; fingers curved in a mudra. "Thoreau meditated long hours. That's why his writing is so clean." She wore a long floral print dress. Her feet were bare.

I stood awaiting an invitation to sit, willing my heart rate to slow. "My college professor never mentioned Thoreau meditated."

Graham's curled lower lip showed what she thought of my education. "HDT, as my son calls him, sat in front of his cabin from early morning to noon watching sunlight change across the sky. Non-doing is the essence of meditation. No multitasking. Those hours without anxious thoughts invading his brain put space around his ideas." Graham's knees cracked as she levered her long torso from the chair. "As Thoreau put it, 'It's not what you look at that matters, it's what you see.'"

I followed Graham into her tiny cabin. A bust of Thoreau sat on a ledge above a wooden table, doubling as a desk. We bumped heads bending down to examine it. I rubbed my head as Graham continued to talk. Her tone was academic, like a docent giving a museum tour. "My space is built to the exact dimensions of HDT's cabin, ten feet by fifteen feet. I used recycled and hand cut materials. Cost me $28.12."

I wondered if Clem Varner could convert my aunt's potting shed into a writing studio. "Do you mind if I build my own tribute to Thoreau?"

Graham continued as if I hadn't spoken. "Thoreau had three chairs in his house: one for solitude, two for friendship, three for society. One chair suits my needs."

She talked to me as if I were one of her students, a slow one. If she didn't have so much to teach me, I wouldn't have tolerated her superior tone. I took a breath. "I never would have figured Thoreau as your inspiration," I said.

"Making assumptions will flatten your work. To write good characters, respect paradox. Humans are a complexity of flaws and foibles mixed with flashes of wild perfection." A blue heron landed on the fence. "I reread Walden every year," Graham said. "Thoreau knew being tethered to time was one of modern man's biggest problems. It's healthier to let the sun measure the length of day, let seasons cradle the year."

I followed her outside. We walked along the Fox River banks. "Your story entitled 'Seesaw' intrigued me. A sympathetic protagonist. You could expand the content into a novel."

Pride swelled my chest. "There's an attractive oddness to how you view the world."

I was glad we were walking face forward so she could not see how happy her words made me.

"I only read a bit of *After Lunch*," Graham said. She stopped to watch adult Canada geese surround their goslings as they bounced along. "Hints of satire," she went on, "but mostly predictable fluff. To publish it, you must learn craft."

Like every writer, I wanted to hear my work was brilliant, nothing needed to be changed. Graham had dispensed all the praise I was going to get. She continued, unaware her comments were crushing me. "If I were you, I'd throw out *After Lunch* and work on 'Seesaw.' However, if you're dead set on publishing your satirical novel, edit one chapter at a time until you get the hang of scene setting, pacing, and transitions. Five or six passes should give you an editable draft." Graham threw a handful of pebbles into the water. "Your first assignment is to edit prepositions. Your manuscript is pockmarked with them."

"I thought prepositions were like sentence tags," I said. "The reader sees them, but they don't register."

"Used excessively, they're like potholes. They destroy the suspension of your sentences." She scanned my first paragraph. "More like stage directions than prose. Under, over, up, down. Are you a writer or a traffic cop?"

I felt the need to defend myself. "Everyone uses them."

"Listen to your first paragraph pared down." She was right. Her version was like walking into a freshly painted room. Ideas popped. Sentences flowed. I left Graham at her cabin. The sky turned a deep rose at sunset. At least she hadn't told me my plot didn't make sense.

I didn't mind editing. After dinner I eliminated excessive prepositions. Using "Find and Replace," I identified 1,178 uses of the word "to" in my manuscript. By midnight, I'd only revised three pages. It wasn't a matter of removing offensive words. Whole sentences needed rewriting. The exercise was wildly tedious. Easier to change the plot.

I fell asleep and woke up at dawn. I reread my edits as light pooled under bedroom curtains. Graham was right. Policing prepositions improved my writing at the sentence level.

TEN

AUNT KATHERINE'S ANTIQUE GE WASHING MACHINE died one Saturday morning. I gathered clothes and a pile of throw rugs. My destination was the Clairmont Laundromat. My only clean clothes were leggings and a smock. Without makeup, I looked like a child. The building was locked. A laminated sign indicated an attendant was on duty from 7:00 a.m.-9:00 p.m. It was 7:30 a.m. I peered through a smudged plate glass window. The place was dark.

Handee Mart was open. I cruised empty aisles, loading my cart with canned tomatoes and fresh produce. I paid and returned to the laundromat. Female Laurel and Hardy, one tall and thin, the other short and squat, waited outside, clothes piled in wheeled carts.

"Deb must have had a rough night," the squat one said. Her laugh held no mirth. She wore a sleeveless top. Even though her forearms were burned by the sun, her muscular shoulders were pale.

At 8:10 a.m., a twenty-year-old Camaro jerked backward as it stopped at the curb.

"Here's Deb," said the first woman.

The attendant, face imprinted with an odd combination of childlike excitement and wrinkled exhaustion, exited a moving car. She gave a backward wave to her boyfriend peeling away. Wear and tear made it hard to gauge her age. She marched past us, jangling a key ring. A whiff of last night's alcohol emanated from her pores. I loaded my comforter into the nearest machine.

Deb raised her hands like a referee calling a foul. "Didn't you read the sign?" A list of rules hung over my head. "You can't wash comforters in the small GE." She pointed a cracked fingernail toward a Hotpoint. Around her neck she wore a lanyard. Her ID picture resembled Benjamin. Deb Babcock had delicate features, pretty eyes over a small straight nose.

"Sorry," I said as I deposited my comforter where it belonged.

Deb pulled an empty Marlboro pack from her work smock. "Damn, I'm out."

"I got you," said the short woman clad in pajama pants. She and her taller counterpart sorted and loaded their clothes. They dragged metal folding chairs to a small yard behind the laundromat ringed with plastic crates.

The hefty woman with a two-toned tan lit a cigarette and expelled a smoke ring. "You want to join us?" she asked.

"I don't smoke," I said, ruining my chances for camaraderie.

A damp *People* magazine abandoned on the dryer occupied me as my laundry did its bumps and grinds through the spin cycle.

Deb told the ladies her boyfriend had kept her out until dawn. When my machine stopped, she shifted her attention to me. Her appraising look made clear she knew I sat home alone.

As soon as my comforter was dry, I loaded two baskets of clean clothes into my car. On the way home, I stopped at the village library to borrow graphic novels Benjamin Babcock might enjoy.

Monday afternoon was our first tutoring session. Benjamin appeared after school in a good mood, chatty and friendly. The weather was mild enough to sit in the garden.

"Why don't you show me your homework?"

"Can't find it," he said.

"No wonder, when everything you own is crammed in your backpack." A morass of crumpled and tear-stained papers sprang at madcap angles from a crumb-filled bottom. "Just as I thought," I said, assuming the manner of a doctor speaking to a patient. "You have freshman backpack syndrome." Benjamin picked at the laces of his grass-stained sneakers. "What are you reading in English?" I asked.

"That book about kids with cancer. Everything our teacher makes us read is tragic. My grandpa died of cancer. He took me fishing."

A tattered copy of *The Fault in Our Stars* was wedged between a fistful of math assignments and a biology textbook. Benjamin looked so sad I dropped my chirpy teacher voice. Softly, I said, "You like history. Why don't read this book I checked out for you? We'll tackle your paper tomorrow." I handed him *Maus,* a graphic novel I had borrowed from the library.

He scanned front and back covers, opened the book, turning pages quickly as his eyes roved over text.

Friday at 3:00 p.m., I was locking the Shield Room, ready to go home when the Special Education Division Leader, Josh Hartman, stopped me. "Can you join us in the principal's conference room? We're doing an unscheduled IEP check-in for Spencer Graham. His mother is threatening outside lawyers. Ten minutes?"

I wondered why Eleanor hadn't talked to me before calling a lawyer.

An IEP was an individualized education plan agreed to by teachers and parents. Meetings were usually scheduled in advance. I hurried to the conference room. The meeting seemed to be wrapping as I arrived. A spring storm raged outside the floor to ceiling windows. No one spoke. Spencer sat with his mother. Across the table was Josh Hartman and Chloe Zigler, district social worker. Chloe smiled as I took a seat opposite Spencer.

Eleanor Graham sat rigidly in her chair. A black-and-white geometric patterned scarf didn't completely cover her wrinkled skin, which extended from her chin to the top of an ecru tank top. The severely cut black jacket added to the effect. She did not regard or touch her son.

"We called a check-in meeting as we are concerned about graduation," Josh said. "Spencer is in danger of failing English unless he receives full credit for his creative writing project. He asked you to be included in the meeting."

Chloe Zigler tapped her laptop. "Spencer's teacher flagged certain themes in his paper. We're concerned about drug references. Spencer cut English three times this week and missed all day Monday."

Eleanor Graham crossed her arms over her chest. Her speaking now might cause more harm than good. Spencer's eyes pleaded.

I folded my hands. "The assignment was to write a story based on a scene imagined from the perspective of a small child," I said. "While working with Spencer, I discovered an active imagination and creative writing talent he hadn't shared as an underclassman. From what I understand, his character was created from a conversation he overheard at the grocery store, not an experience from his life."

My boss pushed his chair back from the table. "We'll assign Spencer detentions to cover his absences," he said. "Miss Collins will help him complete assignments during in-school suspension." Josh put his arm around Spencer. "Graduation is on the horizon, buddy. We want to applaud as you accept your diploma."

I gathered my briefcase and purse. Eleanor Graham followed me to the parking lot. "Spencer is working. Grab a bite with me?"

Even though I was exhausted, Eleanor's eagerness for company melted my objections. We stopped at Clairmont Café. We did not talk as we ate, both hungry. Eleanor ordered a gin and tonic.

"We don't serve alcohol," the teenage server said.

"Give me a cheeseburger and fries," Eleanor said.

I ordered a salad.

Eleanor blotted her lips with a paper napkin. "I wish I could eat like you do. Jealous of your garden and the fresh vegetables you consume. We're the same age, yet you look ten years younger."

Shocked Eleanor Graham could be jealous of me, I bit my lip to hide a smile. Her skin appeared sallow in the fluorescent light, her fingernails brittle and cracked. "When I'm writing, I forget to eat. I tend to calm down with a couple of cocktails," Eleanor said.

I thought of Spencer's story about his mother high on Mad Hatter. Despite what I had said in the conference, I guessed it was true.

"Don't worry," she said. "I cut out drugs years ago." I wondered if it was the writer in her that enabled her to intuit to my thoughts.

A group of young girls commandeered a large table.

Eleanor snagged the check. "My treat. You should teach me your healthy ways." She stood at my shoulder while I fumbled for my car keys. "Look Deirdre, while I'm working, I'm a wizard with access to every part of the world—physical or metaphysical. I can see everything, touch everything, feel everything. When I finish, I become normal sized. My insignificance chokes me." She looked at me intently. "Do you want to grab a drink?"

"Sorry, but I'm too tired."

"Do you drink?"

"Not as much as I should," I said. We laughed.

I sat in my car and watched her walk toward the tavern.

ELEVEN

DOWNTOWN CLAIRMONT WAS DARK BY 7:00 P.M., EXCEPT for the tavern and grocery store. No light burned from the butcher shop or the doctor's office. Deb's laundromat must have closed early. I didn't frequent the tavern, not wanting to run into any parents of my students. Not ready to confront an empty house, I stopped for staples.

Spencer helped an elderly woman load groceries into her trunk. We waved at each other.

Once inside, exhaustion overtook me. I rushed through my list, eager to go home. Becky, the girl I had seen Spencer working with last time I visited Handee Mart, asked me, "Need help loading your groceries?"

I shook my head. As I pulled from the parking space, my phone rang. My glasses were in my purse. I answered without checking the number.

"What're you doing? It's me, Max."

"You must have a wrong number."

"Don't tell me you forgot your old pal Max Fletcher from Albuquerque." The voice took me back to the intake room stacked with games.

"I found you on Facebook." His tone was as casual, as if we had met at a college mixer. "Your phone number is listed."

Panic fluttered like a bird in my chest. I turned off the ignition. A lifetime had passed. I never expected to hear from Max Fletcher again.

"Are you still there?" Max asked. "I'm at my friend's apartment in Chicago. Nothing to eat or drink here. His living room is square and empty, painted beige. Reminded me of the room where we pieced together puzzles."

Dusk drew low over the pond, illuminating yellow leaves clinging to an ash tree. In Thoreau's time, a person could erase all traces of a former life by moving mere miles. Social media allowed people to visit the past at will, like travelers without passports, to open doors better left shut. Max Fletcher had seen me at my absolute worst.

"Meet me at The Second City tonight," Max said. "My friend Eddie Greer is performing."

"You know him?"

"We went to grade school together."

Greer was a rising star, a comedic actor who starred in a romantic comedy panned by critics, loved by moviegoers.

"I live fifty miles away. Probably won't make it in time."

"We need to talk."

"I'm listening," I said.

"I really need to talk to you in person," Max said. He sounded sincere. "If you can't make the show, meet me at Butch McGuire's afterwards."

A night in the city sang a lost song. I had gotten used to living like a nun, but without friends I was lonely. I wondered what Max wanted.

No way I could navigate expressway traffic. I drove to the commuter station, caught a local, making seventeen stops as it meandered through a series of suburbs before aligning itself with the Kennedy. Expresses didn't run after rush hour. Tucked in my wallet was a piece of the moon Max lifted from our Van Gogh puzzle.

On the train I contemplated why Max wanted to see me. Our age difference ruled out romance. Max and I had been comrades sharing a foxhole. Perhaps he was in some kind of trouble and needed my help. Always a siren song.

I did not reach Second City in time. "Show's over," a security guard said. I walked to Butch McGuire's. Crowded sidewalks gave me a feeling of security. Under a green awning, a pod of lacquered women who had taken a wrong turn from a bachelorette party took selfies. Max was nowhere among a throng assembled at the bar. I grabbed a stool and ordered a gin and tonic. The bartender asked me if I was waiting for someone.

"Have you seen a group of comedians?" I asked.

A loud crash was followed by drunken laughter. "Those assholes are at it again," the bartender said. "They kick doors open, think they're funny. I'll show them funny." He charged the men's room, bar towel flying. A tall handsome man who starred in action movies was caught in the middle of kicking a stall. Metal cracked. A knot of men gathered around a sink hanging from a wall.

Eddie Greer emerged first, his posse trailing behind. He listed a bit. Even drunk, his smile was as silly as a little boy pulling a prank. Max was last, looking nothing like the shy boy I'd met in the hospital. He lurched forward, left shoulder higher than right. His gait reminded me of my father's when he was tight. Max's grin was crooked, his eyes unnaturally bright.

A flicker of recognition passed over his face. "Deirdre, I knew you'd come." He slung his arm around my shoulder. "Do you know of a quiet place where we can talk?"

Certain it was a bad idea, but curious what he had in mind, I showed Max the way to Moe's, a 4:00 a.m. joint I had visited with Nikki. Over a tiny, deserted bar hung an oil portrait of Moe Howard. A discarded pack of Jay's potato chips lay on the counter.

Max ordered straight gin. I asked mine be mixed with soda water. "Good to see you, Deirdre. You look great. How's your writing going?"

Gin made me woozy. Maybe I did look great. I told him I was planning to self-publish my satire about a digitally addicted social media influencer.

Max rested his arm on my chair. "We could write a screenplay about two bipolar patients meeting on suicide watch. Think *Girl, Interrupted* meets *One Flew Over the Cuckoo's Nest*. Your writing skills combined with my moxie equals Academy Award."

My idea we had a special connection died. Blindsided by his proposal, I pushed my drink away. Every muscle in my body knotted at the prospect of exposing my illness. I escaped to the ladies' room to collect myself, splashing my face with water on my face before registering there were no paper towels. I grabbed a wad of toilet paper to dry my face.

When I returned, Max asked, "What's wrong? Did you see a ghost in the bathroom?"

"Look, Max, your idea makes me uncomfortable. I'm a teacher. No one would trust me with their kids if they knew about my past."

He patted my back. "Don't take it so seriously. Think of mental hospitals as the new singles bars. A little crazy sparks creativity. Don't you know most geniuses are certifiable?" I inched toward the far side of my chair. He leaned closer. "We could make real money. Let's talk at my friend's place."

We walked four blocks to a northbound L, joined by a last call army invading streets awash in spirits. Frat boys yelled their way to parking garages. They emerged driving their parents' Mercedes, so impaired they prayed to guardian angels to steer them to a place where they could lay down, preferably not alone.

We sprinted down dirty stairs and secured two vacant seats on a northbound L train. My hands were cold. Max held them as we sped past windows lit against the night. "Write our story."

"What story?"

"How we saved each other's lives." He removed a crumpled bit of ruled paper from his wallet. He had kept my poem "Fear" I had shared with him in the hospital.

I conjured an image of that night. How we sat in the beige room trying to create a temporary home with cardboard puzzle pieces. A shared bowl of wobbly Jell-O topped with a blob of whipped cream slid off my tray. Hospital disinfectants combatting a stale smell of defeat emanating from dirty hair and unwashed clothes. Soldiers who had returned from the lost battle of fighting long afternoons sat in silent rooms.

Our train sped toward Fullerton. A silhouette of lovers was framed in a window at Clybourn. Max squeezed my hand.

"I don't want to be known as mentally ill," I mumbled as the L screeched into a turn.

Max leaned close. "What did you say?" he asked. A prerecorded announcement smothered my anger and shame. All I wanted was to pass as normal. "Have some guts," he said.

Lights flickered, throwing the passengers' faces into odd angles like a funhouse ride. He kissed my forehead. His gin-soaked breath brought me to places I didn't want to go. Memories of drunken men who loved alcohol more than me crowded my brain. I already knew how our night would end. A bottle, crumpled sheets, me riding home hungover and alone.

The L screeched to a stop. As a pneumatic door opened, I patted Max's hand. "You take care," I said as I escaped. I bumped a man carrying a briefcase. Instead of yelling at me, he grabbed my arm and steadied me so I was facing the train as it pulled away. A dejected Max sat slumped against a soot-streaked window.

No cabs were available. I walked to Clybourn Avenue to catch a commuter train inhabited by late revelers. Feeling empty and alone, I called my mother. Debussy's "Claire de Lune" played in the background.

"You're still up?" I asked.

"I started playing again after I stopped drinking wine. Kevin bought me a piano."

"I'm so sorry you never got to be a concert pianist," I said.

Mom sighed. "Don't you know you're my work of art? Where are you, Deirdre? You sound off."

"Just excited," I said. "I was meeting with a man named Max who will collaborate with me on a screenplay."

Her voice shifted to a warm timbre I remembered when I sat on her lap bathed in the golden pink light of late afternoon. "Tell me more. What has this Max person written?"

"Jokes. He's a comedian. A handsome comedian."

"Oh, Deirdre. Not another temporary Heathcliff. Why don't you come to Colorado? You don't sound good."

"I have to finish second semester."

"Then do that. Forget about this Max character."

The train pulled into Clairmont. "I don't know how to be successful," I said. "He has connections."

I moved to the vestibule, waited for the pneumatic sound of the door opening. My phone fell from my hand. As I picked it from the platform, I heard Mom say, "Follow your talent. Don't punish yourself for your mistakes. Don't hurt yourself for mine."

A crescent moon hung cockeyed overhead. My car was alone in the lot. I sunk my hand in my pocket as I followed a narrow lane toward Aunt Katherine's house. Instead of my key, I retrieved a puzzle piece. Birds singing at dawn filled me with shame for my wasted day ahead.

I hadn't had a drink in months and now a hangover was announcing itself with tiny hammers to my head. Music played from my phone. I pressed it to my ear. Mom was playing "Claire de Lune."

TWELVE

A CANADIAN COLD FRONT BROUGHT RELIEF FROM LATE summer heat that had enervated students the first weeks of school. Sweaters and hoodies were dug from closets as temperatures dropped.

Back to school energy helped me institute a six-week boot camp where I let nothing distract me from finishing my final edit of *After Lunch*. Early to bed, awake at sunrise, I worked before school and all day on weekends. I didn't rest until I sought and destroyed every extraneous preposition.

With my editing completed, I decided to appeal to Eleanor Graham. Landing a powerhouse agent was preferable to marketing my book myself. Graham was represented by one of the oldest literary agencies in New York.

I retraced my steps to her writing cabin, listening to wind thread fronds of dry prairie grass. Eleanor Graham's spot along a western Fox River bank was more remote than I recalled.

Graham was seated in an Adirondack chair, bare feet planted in tall grass. Three fishing poles extended into the river. A straw hat shaded her eyes. "How's your work coming along?" she asked.

"Better, now that I've committed."

Graham seemed so relaxed I thought it might be a suitable time to ask the question I had wanted to ask since I met her. "Do you think I can query your agent?"

She rose to bait a pole. "My agent doesn't handle debut authors. Besides, he wouldn't be interested in your subject matter."

Tears pricked my eyelids. "I thought you saw something in my work."

"You aren't serious enough to produce what I thought you had in you." Graham steepled her fingers. "You chase fads."

"I have a passion. Writing is a calling, *not a job*," I said.

"That's where you're wrong. Writing is demanding work. Marquez called it carpentry. People think ideas fall into writers' heads like an apple hitting Newton. I had to relinquish everything normal people deem necessary." Her candor was so unexpected, I didn't dare interrupt. "Think long and hard about the life you want to create," Graham said. "Dream editors in tweedy jackets who will recognize your genius died with Maxwell Perkins. These days publishing is big business no different from tech or sports. Competition is brutal. A thousand new MFA graduates every year. Add a swarm of aspiring writers who compete for fewer and fewer book contracts and prizes. Corporate publishers are acquiring smaller houses. Agents need to make a score with material they know will sell." Her smile was equal parts condescension and pity. "Look, Deirdre, there are many other things you can do besides write if you value happiness."

My smile cracked like dried plaster. "Who said I wanted to be happy?" I hurried away from Graham's cabin, hitting the trail hard to suppress anger rising like a geyser. Not only had Graham refused a referral, she'd suggested I quit writing.

Two trails intersecting required I make a choice. Going east would take me back to town toward neat rows of houses where normal life unfolded through endless cycles of breakfast, lunch, and dinner, the only life Graham thought I was capable of living. A sign pointed west toward Settler's Grove, a stand of ancient white and scarlet oaks.

A lone wolf oak commanded a curved trail. Wild waving branches, coarse as an old woman's hair, extended from a trunk five feet wide. From a distance, a tree sparkled with clear baubles. I blinked, amazed someone had hiked so far into the woods to decorate a massive tree.

Worried for the state of my mind, I pulled up a memory of the hospital counselor's advice to appreciate ordinary beauty. As I drew nearer, I realized what I thought were ornaments were trembling droplets of water illuminated by an angle of sun. Awestruck, I wondered if it were a mere trick of light, or a sign from my usually taciturn God. I chose to believe the apparition was a call to capture the brilliance hovering around the edges of my imagination or die trying. I followed a path I had never taken home.

An unfamiliar SUV was parked on my gravel driveway when I arrived home. My brother Kevin and my mother were sitting on the front porch swing.

"Surprise, surprise," Mom said.

"Wow, I can't believe you're here," I said. "What brings you to this neck of the woods?" I was glad to see them, truly glad. My mind inventoried how I had left the house. Luckily, I had cleaned the night before to rid myself of nervous energy after a particularly challenging day with my students.

"Mom came with me on a business trip. We had a layover at O'Hare. Weather in Denver or some such nonsense delayed out flight," Kevin said. "The airline offered free tickets for a later flight."

"I wanted to put flowers on your father's grave," Mom said. "We realized we could see you if we drove fast." She punched Kevin's arm. "You know your brother."

"If I had known, I would have prepared lunch." They followed me into the house.

"You must not have had your phone turned on," Kevin said. "I kept calling."

My phone sat on the kitchen table. I had not taken it along when I visited Eleanor. "I'll make coffee," I said.

"Don't bother," Kevin said. "We only have half an hour." Carrying extra weight, my brother looked older, more settled. He wore tan dress slacks, a starched white shirt, and a tie. He caught my gaze. "Had a business meeting this morning."

"You clean up well," I said.

Mom was moving around the living room, picking up knickknacks, straightening couch pillows. "Love how you display Aunt Katherine's keepsakes." Mom shook a snow globe. "She brought this from her trip to Iceland years before it was trendy."

Family stories reminded me Aunt Katherine was her own woman. Never married, she worked in an accountant's office to make money to travel the world. She had a pottery kiln in the shed I had restored into my writing space. Katherine fired and glazed dishes, bowls, and coffee cups. A beautiful engraved ceramic box she created had been displayed at the Smithsonian.

"You kept all her old books," Kevin said. He removed *The Sun Also Rises* from an antique walnut cabinet where *Sister Carrie* kept company with *The Man with the Golden Arm*. Dust arose from yellowed pages, making Kevin sneeze.

"You should dust once in a while," Mom said. "Should we gift her a cleaning service for Christmas?" Mom asked my brother.

Kevin disappeared into a downstairs bathroom off the kitchen. "Your plumbing is antique. Do you know a local handyman who can replace it?"

"On my list," I said brightly, seething inside that they were subjecting my house to a white glove test. "My salary is modest, so completing renovations takes time. I did replace the electrical wiring."

Kevin consulted his phone. "We have to run if we're going to make our flight."

Never a family who showed physical affection, they were out the door and seatbelted in their rental car before I'd registered that they had visited. Mom rolled down her window. She caught my hand. "I'm glad you're doing so well," she said. "You have color in your cheeks, the house is coming along. Aunt Katherine would be proud of how you've preserved her garden. I'll call you when we get home so we can talk more. I want to hear about your writing."

I stood in the garden, bright with orange and yellow chrysanthemums, emanating a thick dense smell reminiscent of back to school. Kevin was proud of my grades when we were kids. I couldn't shake the feeling I had disappointed him with my lack of success. Since I had nothing as tangible to show as my colorful thriving flowers, I hadn't mentioned my novel was almost finished.

A new variety of mums from a local nursery needed deadheading. Donning gardening gloves, I pinched tips of six-inch magenta plants, removed leggy shoots from quilled white blooms.

More determined than ever, I plotted the last chapters in my head.

Six weeks later, I completed *After Lunch*. The discipline of early writing, work, and long walks in the woods made life nearly perfect. Loneliness descended late afternoon after I closed my laptop on my characters and confronted silence. Fitzgerald and Hemingway frequented Parisian sidewalk cafes.

I needed writer friends, especially a beta reader to evaluate my final draft of *After Lunch*. Bars were out since I had quit drinking. I searched local writers online. The closest group met thirty miles away. Too far. An invitation to join Virtually Literary appeared in my email. Billed as an online salon, it met once a week and was free. They required a writing sample. I sent them "Fear," a poem about childhood. A moderator named Charlotte approved my application and forwarded meeting details. As sunset produced a scarlet sky, I walked around the pond, hoping to find my tribe.

Friday night, two writers appeared in their Zoom boxes. Charlotte apologized with a written message that she was having technical difficulties with her camera and audio. *I will lead the meeting through posted comments in Chat,* she typed. She asked a volunteer to read. A thin woman wearing large glasses read a poem by Wallace Stevens and then one of her own, a tribute to "Thirteen Ways of Looking at a Blackbird." The other participant was an elderly man, who read an account of his first date with his wife of fifty years. When it was my turn, I selected a passage from *Seesaw.* Charlotte typed a thumbs up emoji.

Afterwards, my phone dinged with an apology from Charlotte: *So embarrassed about the technical difficulties.*

No worries, I texted back.

I saw reflections of my own moods in your imagery. Wondering if you might like to exchange work privately if the Zoom group doesn't fly, Charlotte typed.

She seemed so sincere, I sent her another passage. Darkness fell as we texted. Nocturnal creatures emerged from the woods including a green-eyed raccoon whose neon eyes flashed from atop a trash can.

I went inside. Even though I had not seen her face or heard her voice, Charlotte's wry intimate tone made me feel like I knew her. I illuminated Aunt Katherine's Tiffany tulip lamp and retrieved a new poem entitled "Wolf Oak" and sent it to Charlotte before I went to bed.

She replied, *Takes guts to write like that. So good I almost hate you.*

Her words echoed Max's admonition: *Have some guts.* Although I thought of him from time to time, I had not contacted him since our westbound L ride.

Spencer waved from his checkout stand at Handee Mart when I drove into Clairmont for groceries. He radiated happiness working with Becky, a dimpled, ponytailed checker. Two inches taller and leaner from biking and camping, Spencer's demeanor signaled a change beyond physical. He was confident, with no trace of the chaotic energy that had made him vibrate in his chair when we struggled through English assignments in Credit Recovery. The older version of Spencer seemed so content, I wondered why I had worried so much about him.

He helped me stow groceries in my trunk.

"How are you enjoying your gap year?" I asked. "Thinking about college?"

He closed my trunk lid. "Mother keeps pushing me. I don't want to attend college. I don't love reading and writing like she does. I want to be a father. I mean, I'm going to be a father. Becky's pregnant. We're getting married."

I arranged grocery bags neatly in an insulated box as if order would restore the world back to where it was before Spencer's statement. "Are you sure you want a family at this age?"

He nodded. "I've never been surer of anything in my life."

I tried to listen without forming arguments or counterarguments. "You're only seventeen."

"Listen, Miss Collins, all I want is a normal family. I love Becky. I don't want to save the world or write a book. If I apply for emancipation, will you write a letter stating I'm mature enough to manage my own affairs? Joseph did it, and he's fine."

"He had no other choice," I said. Joseph Moore's mother had died in a car crash, leaving the child with an absentee father. "Your mother loves you."

Spencer squared his stance. "You can't talk me out of it. Promise not to call Mother. Becky and I will tell her at her birthday dinner. Hopefully, she won't have a fit at the restaurant." He collected carts as he turned to reenter the store.

My heart melted at the sight of a boy trying to make himself into a man.

He stopped in front of me. "I know Mother loves me. She just loves her books more. Can't help herself."

"I'm proud of you," I yelled over the engine roar, and pulled out of my space.

The week was uneventful. No major meltdowns in the Shield Room. Three *Catcher in the Rye* and two *Cuckoo's Nest* essays completed. Friday night I went to bed early, so I could spend Saturday editing my social satire. When I finished, I weeded a border of yellow and orange chrysanthemums. Hands covered with dirt, I remembered the prairie which extended from Mom's garden, a vast wild place where I escaped after pulling weeds. A neighbor girl and I pretended we were Indians walking silently in moccasined feet through tall grass. The image inspired me to grab my phone and write a poem. On a whim, I sent it to Charlotte.

She replied immediately with her own poem: *Full sun at noon you stoop to pick a dandelion. Butter cup it under your chin. The wind freshens as you dance over grass. A voice calls you inside but you can't stop dancing, twirling, creating an energy that reaches a black hole I'm digging to China. Come up you Morse code me. Escape your pit and raise your arms sunward.*

I went to bed with a smile on my face, knowing someone understood me.

Around midnight, a sound of metal hitting concrete interrupted my sleep. I went downstairs, expecting to find a raccoon rummaging through garbage. I opened a blind over the kitchen window.

My heart clenched with fear when I saw a dark figure righting an upended planter. I illuminated a flood light. Caught like an animal in the glare, Eleanor Graham turned to face me.

I walked onto the back porch. When I extended a hand to help Eleanor stand, a sour wine smell drifted from her mouth. Her signature starched white blouse bloomed with a red stain shaped like a flower. She snatched her hand from mine and stumbled to her feet. "I want my money back," she said. "I gave you my son to teach, and you returned a grocery store clerk." Her voice ascended an octave. "Spencer gave me three weeks' notice. He's applying for emancipation. He said you vouched for him."

"You're scaring the critters," I said. I ignited my keychain flashlight. "Let's walk."

A raccoon who had been rocking a garbage can lid skittered away. "Spencer's girlfriend is pregnant," Eleanor said.

I didn't reply, hoping quiet and exercise might calm her nerves. As we approached a prairie meadow, Eleanor tripped over a tree root. She fell and I toppled over her. When I didn't rise right away, she decided to stay where she was.

"Everyone goes gaga over a full moon," I said. "The quarter moon is underrated."

Prairie fronds bleached by moonlight swayed above our foreheads. "A quarter moon hangs lopsided in a velvety sky," she said. "I won a Pulitzer Prize, dammit. Spencer doesn't even want to attend college. He said you offered him a place to live."

I picked a piece of grass from my hair. "Temporarily. He can live in my writing shack while you're on your book tour. Unless he would rather stay with his father."

Eleanor braced herself on her left elbow. "I don't know if Frank is alive or dead." An owl hooted from a walnut tree. Webs of dew dampened hair cushioned my neck. Eleanor continued, "We met on the dance floor of a blues club. We were madly in love, or at least I was. When he found out I was pregnant, he left town. Took me five years and a stint in rehab to get myself together."

I thought of Spencer's speech about Mad Hatter. The child in his story was four. "Where is Frank now?"

"Never attempted to find him. I can't bear to look at Spencer sometimes—he looks so much like Frank." Eleanor sighed. "Closest to love I ever came."

"You have Spencer."

"I was a terrible mother. I don't get kids. Never knew what to do with him." Eleanor rose to her feet and brushed dirt from her shirt. "Spencer can stay with you while I'm away," she said. "Don't forget— he's my son."

"You should get to know him. While the adults in his life are drinking and fighting, seeking titles and awards, Spencer spreads love. Do you know how kind your son is, how he puts others first, supports underdogs?" I braced myself with my right hand and sat. "You should be excited about the baby. A new person is coming into the world for you to love and who will love you."

A silent Eleanor Graham followed me from an open meadow through dark wood to the driveway. Her truck engine backfired as tires crunched gravel.

Term papers were due. Most Shield program kids had not started writing or even outlining projects comprising a significant percentage of their grades. No matter how I threatened or cajoled, kids refused to work, staring mutely at flashing cartoon images on their devices. Poor monkeys. I drove home craving a nap. A silver Mercedes was parked in the gravel driveway. As I approached, a woman in oversized designer sunglasses, tapered slacks topped by a linen tunic, emerged. I didn't recognize Nikki Adamos until she flipped back the brim of her floppy hat. Outside of Christmas cards, we had no contact since the night she stuffed me in a cab and sent me to Albuquerque. She handed me a slim book, entitled "Downtime".

"Somebody ripped you off big time," she said, instead of hello.

I flinched as if to ward off a blow. The author was "anyone" in lower case.

Nikki hurried inside, plopped on the sofa. "The story is different, but it contains lines from that book you were working on in college, *Seesaw*. You read me excerpts when we were roommates." The loss of her beer weight revealed a svelte figure. "Bet it's Jamie Nordberg. Remember how she hung around our room?"

Jamie, a fellow English major, was our roommate in the Champaign house. A girl so depressed she couldn't get out of bed to attend class. She dropped out of school before first semester ended.

"She won a Pushcart Prize for flash fiction under her own name," I said. "Why would she publish a novella anonymously?"

Nikki extracted a slim volume titled *Downtime* from her purse and threw it at me. I scanned the story. *My depression took on the status of a character defect,* I read. *When it got too bad, it scared me because I couldn't remember life before depression.* Both were sentences I had written.

My old roommate's look had changed from flannel wearing college student to a stylish suburban matron. She lit a cigarette. "I know you hate confrontation. But maybe you should sue whoever stole your work." She pointed to a back cover squib. "Soon to be a major motion picture."

I was so stunned, I took a puff from Nikki's cigarette, even though I had quit years ago.

She scrutinized her phone. "My husband knows people."

"The mechanic?" Did she want to hire a goon to work over the plagiarizing SOB with a tire iron?

"I married Chad Marshfield, the trader we met at Moe's." She waved her phone in my face. Her husband was a blonde-haired blue-eyed WASP. Her two children resembled him more than her, as if she were erasing any trace of Greek ethnicity. "Chad has a seat on the Exchange. His brother is a partner in a top law firm. The Marshfields are connected from here to next Sunday. I'll text you a referral." As Nikki clicked her lighter, her phone buzzed. She gripped it with perfectly manicured fingers painted blood red. "On my way."

She squeezed my shoulder. "My daughter's new Jeep blew a tire. Will you be all right?"

I shrugged.

Nikki backed past a colonnade of trees lining the driveway and blasted her horn when she reached the main road.

Laptop open at my side, I read a Kirkus Review: "A bright new talent shines a light on the inner recesses of an original, if troubled mind."

I thumbed random pages from the novella. *Downtime* wasn't exactly my story, but it was near enough. Certain phrases seemed familiar. I grabbed a pad of sticky notes and marked every phrase lifted from *Seesaw* to describe the male protagonist's suffering. Phrases I'd written in college when I'd experienced my first depression, like: *My mirror revealed an impassive mask of a face. Internal thermostat set to bare maintenance; my heart beat slower.*

Anger clawed my chest. I had invested long hours learning my craft. Early rising, invitations declined so I could stay in shape to become a better writer, one worthy of my subject matter. Instead of wallpapering my bathroom with rejections as Steinbeck had, I ground my teeth over form letters saying, 'Thanks for sending, not for me, not a fit for my list.' I had neglected my personal life so badly I had no one to call in an emergency.

Pain traveled my left arm from shoulder to wrist. I threw one of Aunt Katherine's needlepoint pillows. It skittered off a ceramic umbrella stand. Returning to the dining room table, I braced my feet against the curved legs of a fragile upholstered chair. I tore 198 pages from the book spine and shredded them, creating a paper snowstorm. When I had finished, I paced, not feeling cleansed but foolish. I had to order another copy from Amazon to show Nikki's lawyer.

My phone dinged with a text from Charlotte. She had a sixth sense when I needed bolstering. My feelings were so raw I described Max's plagiarism and Nikki's suggestion I that file a lawsuit.

Have you made an appointment? Charlotte texted.
Not yet.
Let me know when you do. I can give you moral support.

I went to bed and slept, exhausted by my rage, yet happy there was one person I could call if I needed help.

I was finishing an article on drug store prescription errors when I heard someone knocking. Freelancing helped cover repairs needed to keep my old home habitable. Heating bills were atrocious. Drafty windows needed to be replaced before winter. Notes regarding my lawyer visit were spread on the floor.

Spencer Graham's face was red, his shirt escaping from his belt as it did during high school days when he calmed himself in the break-out room. "Becky and I told Mother," he said. "She surprised me. If I complete my associate degree, she'll give us a down payment on a house. The problem is I don't want to attend school."

"Your mother is trying to help you live a good life. Without a degree, you'll have a harder time providing for your family. You might have to work two or three jobs."

His expression showed truth was sinking in. "If you help me write my papers." He pointed at papers fanned around me. "Your novel?"

From our tutoring days I was so used to treating him as a friend, I told him the truth. "These notes are research for a revenge lawsuit."

"You don't go after people with a sledgehammer. What did this person do to you?"

"Stole my idea."

Spencer laughed. "You have plenty of ideas. Why waste your time?" His words rang in my head long after he drove away on his motorcycle. Physically he had changed from boy to man in the brief time I had known him. His words carried heft.

I didn't go after people with a sledgehammer, I thought as I vacuumed my couch and dusted coffee tables. I should forget Max and concentrate on my life. Removing the vacuum cleaner dust collector, I hit my hand on a side table and spilled dust all over my freshly-vacuumed rug. The sharp impact renewed my anger. Max had stolen from me by pirating my work, as surely as if he had stolen my wallet. I called the lawyer, then texted Charlotte.

I missed an express train, which doubled my travel time. Sufficient time to reread the novella beribboned with Post-It Notes indicating phrases lifted from *Seesaw*. Nikki offered to accompany me. I declined. She would dominate the meeting. I needed to advocate for myself.

On my second reading, I realized the anonymous author had spun a much different story from my own. Only five phrases were directly lifted from *Seesaw*. Maybe Spencer was right. Perhaps I was overreacting.

The story of a boy raised by his mother's college roommate while his mother traveled the world kept me reading all the way downtown. The roommate raised the boy as her own, never telling him about his birth mother. A woman he knew as Mom's friend attended his birthday parties and soccer games. The boy didn't learn the truth until he took his driver's test. Searching for his birth certificate, he found his mom's friend's name listed as his mother. Despondent and betrayed, he attempted suicide. He told no one his secret, letting people think he was depressed about a failed romance. My heart went out to the character. We shared an ability to harbor a secret, even when it stung like a pest burrowing under skin.

The conductor announced the Clybourn stop. Once an industrial area, the neighborhood teemed with trendy loft apartments. I considered canceling my legal appointment to wander Chicago's Art Institute's marble floored galleries, but I had promised Nikki. We were on the verge of rekindling our friendship. I needed a friend.

On the platform, I joined a stream of commuters hurrying to their morning destinations. Chicago's vitality shocked through the soles of my shoes. In Clairmont, I had to generate my own momentum.

Nikki's contact maintained a suite of offices in the Opera Building two blocks west of Elliott Partners, where I worked in college. *Chicago Magazine* was open on a low table to an article about a #MeToo case won by a partner. Power emanated from the lobby's sleek design of carefully curated chrome furniture gleaming in low light.

When I told Mom I had no interest in becoming a dental hygienist, she'd suggested law school. Instead of being angry, I understood her desire for me to have agency in life instead of hovering at the outskirts as a secretary or a temp.

Samantha Brown was a young woman in her early thirties. She shook my hand. "Nice to meet you, Deirdre," she said. "Nikki's husband mentioned plagiarism. Fill me in over lunch."

We took the elevator to a wood paneled restaurant where the murmur of conversation crested over silver clinking against fine china. Our table overlooked the Chicago River.

Between bites of chopped kale, Samantha said, "Hard to prove plagiarism. Five different writers might choose the same phrase to describe depression."

I took a sip of iced tea. "Isn't it considered copyright infringement to make or sell derivative works without permission from the original owner?"

The lawyer put down her fork. "Where did you learn about derivative work?"

"I was a legal secretary in the intellectual property unit at Elliot Partners."

She gave me an appraising look. "I can recommend you for an admin job here, if you're interested."

Visions of fine clothes, lunches with coworkers perched high above the city, and a healthy bank balance danced before me. "Thanks, but I'm pursuing other projects right now."

"How did the person in question get a hold of your work, if it's not published?"

"Lifted it from my Word files?"

Our waiter returned with a check. "Computer hacking is a federal offense. If you provide proof, we can make a case." She wrote a phone number on her business card. In the elevator, I read the name of a private detective. I texted Charlotte from the lobby. She promised to meet me on the LaSalle Street Bridge.

After the appointment, I strolled the riverfront plaza. A trio of sharp-dressed office girls laughed and gossiped. Fifteen years in ex-urban Clairmont had not erased my love for city rhythms. Fifteen years was a long time to write with no success. Fear of failure might stop haunting me if I abandoned my dream of writing the great American novel.

Without missing a step, I rejoined the anonymous crowd.

THIRTEEN

THE MERCHANDISE MART ROSE LIKE A STERN FORTRESS from the banks of the Chicago River. Shadows spliced by metalwork hid the face of a figure walking toward me on the LaSalle Street Bridge. I didn't know what Charlotte looked like, as our communication had been by text. The edginess of sharing my writing with a stranger now seemed stupid on every level.

Clothed in black, the approaching silhouette resembled a cardboard cutout from a child's coloring book. I ransacked my purse for prescription sunglasses. As I balanced them on my nose, the face of Max Fletcher came into focus.

"What are you doing here?" I sidestepped Max's attempt at a hug. "You're Charlotte?"

"Excuse the prank," he said. "You mentioned you needed a writer's group, so I formed one." Wanting to punch him, I raised my fist. Max danced out of range. "At least give me points for creativity." He pointed toward the Riverwalk. "Does this path lead to Michigan Avenue?" I followed as he scrambled downstairs two at a time, finally catching him at the Jetty. A school group gathered near a wetland garden.

Max's features were haggard, as if he had not slept for weeks, his eyes bright pinpoints of green. "There was no other way I can spring you from your self-imposed exile," Max said. "Listen. You're not Henry David Thoreau. Not even close. I will lead you out of the woods. Your life won't be complete until you write our story."

We walked east. A warm breeze settled our mood, turning confrontation into a surprise holiday. Max bought two Italian ices from a vendor. My paper cup was wet and cold. "How do you know what's best for me?" I asked.

"Not me. Call it God, the universe, or spirit guide. Our story will make a brilliant screenplay."

Tart raspberry explosions puckered my tongue. "I don't know how to write a movie."

His smile exposed teeth tinted red. "You'll learn from an expert. Follow me back to the hotel."

It was impossible to match Max's long-legged stride. His energy level neared manic. As we threaded our way through lunchtime crowds, he kept talking. "My backer prefers to remain anonymous. His bipolar son was a scholar and athlete beset by uncontrollable highs followed by crippling depression. Took his life during orientation at Stanford. His father is on a mission to educate people about mood disturbances. How many people struggle to find the right medications or combinations of exercise and therapy? How many commit suicide when they can't manage their moods. If we do this right, we can help people and make money."

We walked east. Reflections of the blue glass 333 West Wacker building shimmered in the river. Further east, The Wrigley Building's white terra cotta towers floated in blue sky. On the south bank sat the Carbide and Carbon Building's Art Deco high-rise, polished black granite exterior topped by a gold-leafed tower. Tourists floated like angels in a hot haze, features blurred by slanted bright sunshine. I anchored my gaze to a group of office workers eating lunch on the River Theater's stone steps. "What about you? Will you help?" I asked.

"I told you I can't write. Eddie needs my assistance launching a new show. Follow me. I'll introduce you to a teacher who helped thousands."

We ascended a circular concrete staircase to street level. Max proposed a quick drink at a sidewalk café. The server knew him, bringing two shots of whiskey without his asking. He upended shot glasses like vials of cough syrup. Lightning forked over the river. Max grabbed my hand and hurried me toward his hotel as a sudden storm-flooded sidewalks. He guided me into the elevator and punched "Penthouse."

"Where are we going?" I asked.

"You'll love what I'm about to show you," Max said. Elevator doors opened on an old ballroom that had not been remodeled to match the sleek modern lines of the boutique hotel. A chandelier dripping crystals gleamed diffuse light over dark wood floors, walls adorned with Art Deco sconces. Arched windows framed a glittering city. Being so high lent a dreamy distance to the backward-flowing river. Tugboats completed the look of a period piece.

"Picture *The Great Gatsby*," Max said. "Men in black tail and women wearing silky sheaths admiring themselves in gilt mirrors."

We inhabited the city from inside a cloud as we watched purple fade to pink. "I didn't know you were so literary," I said.

He danced me toward chest of drawers. A bottle of champagne sat in a bucket. "Still cold," Max said. A thrill ran through me that Max had engineered the scene. He handed me a glass. And opened the bottle and poured. I hesitated, as I hardly drank anymore. "Just a sip," he coaxed.

Bubbles hitting my throat made me feel giddy. I had forgotten how champagne unlocked my id. "Hot in here," I said.

Max finished the rest. Heat radiated from his neck. "Bet you had me pegged as some TV hack," he said. "Read tons as a child. Remember in *Madame Bovary* where she attends her first ball? Her husband is a boring country doctor from the super-sticks. Emma is besotted by exquisite music and the guests' expensive clothes. When dancers complained they were perishing in the heat, a servant climbed a chair and broke windows." Max hoisted a metal folding chair stacked against the wall and swung it.

I half-hoped he'd break a window. He replaced the chair and steered me toward the elevator with a hand hugging the small of my back. We stopped on floor thirteen. "Come inside while I finish packing," he said.

A champagne buzz scattered my thoughts. Out of practice, a couple of sips intoxicated me. Through an open window, a Strauss waltz drifted from a tour boat gliding by.

My torso flushed with warmth as Max moved behind me. We faced the mirror. Pink highlighted my cheeks. Max's hands trailed my shoulders to my hips.

Sunshine illuminated the side of my face. Crow's feet traveled farther from my eyelid than last time I'd checked. There was a hint of crepe at my fifty-year-old neckline. I wasn't Emma Bovary at the ball. I wasn't even the young-looking thirty-eight-year-old who met Max in the psych ward.

"How old are you, Max?"

"Depends on the day. Older than time when I'm down. Right now, I'm feeling young and vigorous."

"Are you even forty?" I asked.

He brushed hair from my eyes. "Don't go spiraling into in-depth analysis, Deirdre. Enjoy the moment."

Max's license sat on the bureau. I squinted at his birthdate. He would be thirty on his next birthday, twenty years younger than I. I stepped forward to break our embrace.

"Are you sure?" Max murmured, looking toward the bed. "Amtrak has a later train."

Shaking my head, I smoothed my hair with my right hand and grabbed my purse with my left. "You didn't fly from New York?"

"Had an unpleasant experience. Never fly if I can help it." Max handed me *Save the Cat.* "Everything you need to know about screenwriting is contained in this book. You'll find a check inside with running around money." When I didn't answer, he said, "Check out a novel called *Downtime*. Haven't read it, but I hear it's an interesting take on mood disorders."

I neutralized my expression as we walked down the corridor. "Do you know who wrote it?" I asked.

"Wish I did," he said. "Critics call it brilliant."

The elevator opened on lower Wacker instead of street level where his Uber was waiting to take him to Union Station. "I forgot to ask how your appointment with the lawyer went," Max said.

A goateed young man wearing a frayed blazer over a dingy white shirt approached. Slung under his arm was a large portfolio. "Want to buy my last Van Gogh?" Inside the case was a reproduction of *Starry Night Over the Rhone*.

Beyond an expanse of water, a river bank extended like a wheat field. Still dizzy from what almost happened in the hotel room, Van Gogh's painting mesmerized me. To my unfocused eye, yellow daubs were stars or flowers or finger paint released from a child's sticky fingers. Homes nestled on a far bank beamed a security which transported me to the beige square hospital room where Max and I fitted together puzzle pieces. The night dark river mirrored yellow beams bright as any sun. A man leaned toward a woman. Their hats reflected starlight bouncing from the water to illuminate the shore.

"Delivered one too many to Best Western," the seller said. "Yours for twenty bucks."

Max removed a bill from his wallet as he clasped the framed work under his armpit. He turned his head, not quickly enough to hide an expression of sadness that ran deep. A sorrow I recognized but could not erase.

A shiver ran through me as he smoothed worried wrinkles lining my forehead. "You think too much," he said. I followed. Water taxis docked at Michigan Avenue loaded commuters for the trip to suburban stations.

We climbed to street level. Max shoved *Starry Night* in my hands as he opened the door of a blue Subaru. "Hang it over your bed."

Max waved. His driver joined traffic amid an ensemble of brass taxi horns harmonizing with deep tones of barges passing below.

I read *Save the Cat!* riding Metra. The screenplay formula was not complex. One hundred pages, compared to five hundred for a novel. I already knew my characters. All I needed to do was create set-up, conflict, continue to the climax and the denouement, as in any other story.

Struck by Max's grandiose ideas, I rested my head against the train window. Suburbs rolled by each with their row of bars and fitness centers clustered around stations. Nearing Clairmont, the scenery stretched into open fields between towns dotted with scrub trees, a manmade lake boasting a heron rookery.

A blue heron, wing span wide as a basketball player's arms, flew over the train. Max was a literary conman. That he might help me publish my book kept me tied to his schemes. Success was close enough to touch. Max promised my script could be turned into a novel. A book bearing my name on the spine was all I'd ever wanted. A book I could hold in my hands. A book a reader would remove from a library shelf on a rainy afternoon. A book I could dedicate to my late father. A book that would show the world I was special, not a backwoods loser hiding from my failures.

When I got home, I hung *Starry Night* over my bed.

Max called around midnight. Laughter cresting over clinking glasses and TV noise. "What's on your schedule tomorrow?" he asked.

"After school, I'll start drafting an outline à la Blake Snyder."

"Listen, sweetie. Can you hold the check until I deposit funds?" A high-pitched voice called his name. His voice was quiet when he spoke again. "I enjoyed being with you, Deirdre."

I slept uneasy. Money did not mean as much to me as it did to Max. The bar noises behind Max's voice constituted a song my father sang as his literary dreams crumbled.

The hell of it was that no one—until Max—had ever made me laugh like my father had.

As long as I was writing, my characters' chatter kept me company. It didn't matter whether Max had a backer or even if he was on board. Finishing the screenplay was key. I watched TV at the laundromat to gauge what was popular. Desperate to score a win, I edited my script to imitate a Lifetime movie.

When I finished my draft late Saturday afternoon, the house was so quiet I couldn't stand it. The weekend stretched out like an endless vista. As darkness fell, the weight of mortality threatened to suffocate me. Anxious dread stole my breath. Unanswered questions and unfulfilled longings sat on my chest. There were two places people congregated in Clairmont: church or tavern. Neither suited me. A text to Max went unanswered. We hadn't talked since he'd asked me not to deposit his check.

I lay on the couch and attempted a nap even though I wasn't tired. In a doze, I jumped when my phone buzzed with a text from Linda Boyd. She invited me to join her for a Wisconsin apple picking expedition. As I dressed, I remembered how much I disliked Linda when we'd first met. Months of working together had let me see her as an advocate for students with no voice.

The fall day was so perfect it was hard to imagine winter loomed. We toured a craft fair. Linda bought a hand-painted ceramic vase. A trailer ride circled a family farm. Sitting on a hay bale exacerbated my fall allergies.

A long line gathered around a wooden hut decorated with moon and star cutouts. "Think I'll have my cards read," I said.

Linda regarded me with amusement. "Find me afterward. I need to find cider doughnuts for the husband," she said.

The fortune teller wore an embroidered peasant blouse and a long skirt. *Cliché*, I thought. Her large hazel eyes flecked with green were kind. Our conversation made me feel so comfortable I described recurrent dreams. "Two figures appear in my dreams," I said. "One is a man whose face is always turned away. The other is a little girl in a white eyelet dress. Who are they?"

The woman shuffled her Tarot deck and drew three cards—a couple falling from a Tower, a bandaged man with a head wound surrounded by spikes, followed by The Lovers.

She clicked her tongue. A buzz of conversation arose from fortune seekers gathering outside. "There are dreams so powerful we call them visitations. Not ordinary ones where we sort and file daily events. Think of them as messages from God."

A woman yelled, "Hurry up in there," and banged on the door.

The tarot reader squeezed my hand. "I have to welcome my next client, or they'll fire me." She opened a silver locket hanging from her neck. A little girl with wide hazel eyes stared back. "My daughter. I'm her sole support. Can't lose this gig."

My purse fell from my lap as I stood. The fortune teller helped me gather manuscript pages I carried for free moments when I could edit. "Keep a dream journal," she said. "Key information will reveal itself."

I joined Linda, who sat on a hay bale. She offered me a doughnut and a glass of apple cider. "Look at the jewelry and potholders I bought. Perfect stocking stuffers."

My tarot reading held no secrets, but my dreams did. I bought a handmade book decorated with stars for my next dream journal. Linda and I moved through the crowd. After a long, hot summer, the cooler air was tinged with cinnamon and cloves.

FOURTEEN

LATE DECEMBER BROUGHT TWO FEET OF SNOW. BE-
tween bouts of writing, I strapped cleats to my boots and explored the
woods in their winter finery. The open prairie was a pristine expanse of
white. I hiked toward a circle of fir trees. A biting wind whistled as it
changed direction. When I could not feel my toes, I retraced my steps,
determined to finish the screenplay.

New Year's Eve temperatures dropped below zero. An ice storm
knocked out Clairmont's power grid. I fired up Aunt Katherine's gen-
erator and gave thanks when her antiquated fixtures illuminated and the
furnace kicked on. Standing at the window, I drank a cup of tea. The
rising sun reflected a splendor of ice-coated branches.

If I worked hard, I could finish the script. Winter break had started
after Christmas and extended into the second week of January, giving
me a gift of writing time. Loneliness did not have time to visit. When I
finished, I called Max. He told me to wait while he closed his office door.
An elevator bell dinged. My head fell back on embroidered lace pillows.

Exhausted from a series of all-nighters, I slept hard. In my dreams,
I flew between Chicago and New York, effortlessly catching a jet stream,
landing atop a skyscraper where *The Eddie Greer Show* was produced. My
dream switched gears. I was the sole woman sitting at a conference table.
Male voices crested over clinking glasses. It was impossible to distinguish
individual words amidst loud laughter. I had been so far afield in my
dreams I was shocked to awaken in Aunt Katherine's four poster bed.
How had I landed in her creaky old house alone?

I rolled over on a pile of manuscript. Poems, journal entries, pages of screenplay fluttered to the floor. A boyish laugh rose from a voice not Max's. I lifted my covers and saw a blinking light. Wishing I weren't so clueless about tech, I wondered why the camera was blinking. Was it possible I was being watched?

Max read the last line of my screenplay. "'Beyond that bright horizon lies the sea of heaven.'"

"You could do something with that," a boyish voice said.

Max spoke again. "Such an eager beaver. Does whatever I tell her. Not tech savvy. She doesn't realize I can see her through her laptop camera."

"Send me the screenplay," the boyish voice said. "My agent will let us know if we can sell it."

More voices. More laughter. My laptop went dark as I sat up straight.

Was the boyish-sounding man Eddie Greer? I pulled my nightgown to cover me. I had left my laptop open.

Under a hot shower, I tried to convince myself I had dreamed laughing men sitting at a long table. Vivid dreams had plagued me since I was a child. They woke me with a start and colored my mood. Dr. Shea explained sugar stimulated the amygdala, an almond-sized brain mass responsible for experiencing emotion. I'd been eating cookies to celebrate completing the screenplay. Curing my sweet tooth was harder than quitting drinking.

As a late adapter to technology, I learned only what benefitted my writing. Using a laptop was faster than writing by hand. I only used my phone to make calls or text.

The conversation I heard wasn't a dream. Max's voice was as plain as if he had been sitting next to me. I scrubbed every inch of my body as if a shower could erase dirty pictures flying through cyberspace. Shame and anger roiled through me. Most embarrassing was that he'd called me his "eager beaver."

Despite Nikki's warnings and my own common sense, I believed an invisible cord of understanding tethered Max's heart to mine. Scared and unmoored, we had shared a moment in the behavioral hospital. A featureless expanse of despair I had fashioned into a starry night. The truth was I had used Max as a prop much as I had used my dolls in childhood play.

Vanity had put me under Max Fletcher's spell. Compliments about my writing and his insinuation he found me attractive had me eating from his hand.

A call to Nikki's brother-in-law would bring detectives to trace the crime, and lawyers to prosecute it. Eddie Greer would transform overnight from family man to pervert as he was tried in the court of social media.

I dried my body with a towel damp from my last shower. As I dressed, I considered my options. If I called Nikki, she would take control. Advocating for myself was a matter of life or death. If I didn't, my life would swirl into insignificance.

There was no way I could lure Max to Chicago. I had to fly to New York. Under the guise of delivering the screenplay, I would confront him.

Driving to O'Hare, I listened to a confidence building podcast. Encouraging words enhanced my drive as I exited the interstate at Mannheim. Nodding and smiling, I located long-term parking. Self-doubt had derailed me too many times. There was no trouble getting a seat, as LaGuardia flights left every hour. Walking through throngs of travelers was disorienting after so much time spent alone. Greasy pretzel and sugary cinnamon smells nauseated me.

A young boy chasing his doppelgänger brother bumped into me as they chased a Frisbee. "Stop that," a man called. He grabbed the orange disk and stuffed it in a carry-on bag. "Sorry, ma'am." Grabbing a handkerchief, the man wiped his face glistening with sweat from running after his boys. "Say, Deirdre, is that you?" He peered at me. "Sure it is. Deirdre Collins."

"Sorry?" I said.

"Don't you remember seventh period with Mr. Grover, the dancing geometry teacher? I sat behind you." He grabbed my hand with doughy fingers and pumped it. "Gary Thompson."

A high school memory surfaced. I had spent first semester in honors geometry laughing at jokes the guy behind me told. When I flunked the midterm, my guidance counselor demoted me to regular geometry. Regular classes were a new territory where students snickered and yelled out when they felt like it. Gary was seated next to me at a long table in the back, pointing out how our teacher seemed to dance across the room as he moved gracefully in black patent leather shoes. Gary's whispered tales of boosting cars. Fascinated, I couldn't stop listening even though I was terrified of failing. I had never failed.

"Too bad about your nervous breakdown," Gary said. "Or was it two? I heard you had two. Must have been tough. You were a smart cookie."

The LaGuardia flight was called. I rushed to my gate without saying goodbye, my confidence shot.

My seatmate coughed his way to New York. Anger quickened my heartbeat as I thought of how Max had wronged me. Twenty years out of the hospital and thirteen hundred miles away, I had built a new life. I plotted how to avenge my name, my spirit, my body. Ridiculous ideas from movies flooded my brain—buy a gun, hire a hitman. Nothing I would ever do. Words were my weapon. Choosing my words, I would attack from every side, shame him, and shrivel his soul.

Flushing Bay came into view as the captain prepared for touchdown. All the righteous indignation I had been able to muster withered as I recalled Gary Thompson's words: "One breakdown or two?" Shame washed over me. Classmates remembered me as a failure, a hopeless mental patient.

At LaGuardia, lines of ragged travelers shuffled through dingy corridors. A cacophony of voices. And no one talking to me. I found my flip phone to let Max know I was on my way. The cab line snaked along the curb. I wished I had a smartphone to call an Uber as I dug my gloveless fingers deep in my pockets.

Max Fletcher's apartment was in Astoria. He answered wearing a plaid bathrobe. "Hi, Deirdre. You didn't have to make a personal delivery. Email works."

I felt foolish, more of a pizza delivery driver than artist. I lost my nerve. I didn't launch into the speech I'd crafted on the plane.

Blue terrycloth sagged around Max's shoulders. His dark hair was matted, his chin unshaven, a scene I had not imagined en route to New York. I tried to access my earlier righteous anger. Max's appearance reminded me of the lost boy I had met in the hospital.

His apartment was bare of knickknacks, as if he had recently moved in. An Indian blanket was draped over a couch, wedged close to a coffee table strewn with *Variety* and the *New York Times*. A galley-style kitchen housed an old Frigidaire next to an avocado-colored stove. On a narrow counter, a Nutella jar balanced next to a bottle of bourbon. His bedroom door was closed.

"Were you sleeping?" I asked.

He shook his head. Muted taxi horns sounded from blocks away. "I haven't slept all winter." A clock over the kitchen stove blinked 1:00 a.m. "You better stay here tonight. Hotel rooms are brutally expensive."

His bedroom was surprisingly neat. "I camp out on the couch when insomnia strikes," Max said. He gave me an extra blanket and a pillow.

The next morning, I awoke coughing. Max gave me a glass of orange juice and a bowl of cereal. He dragged his palm over my forehead. "You're hot. Hope you don't have the plague everybody's getting. I'm off to work. Get some rest."

Bands of strong sunlight woke me midmorning. My head felt as heavy as a bowling ball when I tried to lift it from the pillow. I fell into a state half sleep, half delirium. Every muscle in my body ached. Sleep overtook me until late afternoon. I listened for Max's return. The streets were quiet. How was it possible New York was quiet?

I called Nikki to hear a familiar voice. Her words were drowned by a screech of power tools. "My kitchen is being renovated," she yelled. "Call me later."

Through a cracked window, conversation drifted from the street. "No toilet paper at that store," a man with a Russian accent said.

"Chocolate," his wife said. "I need chocolate." A strong wind rattled the window. I closed it.

A strange quiet had descended over New York's teeming streets as if the world had run away and was hiding behind closed doors. Dark had settled like a blanket the next time I awoke. Max was not home. Streetlight crept in through window blinds creating angular shadows.

Across the street a single light burned. Not an electric light but a candle. A young woman fanned cards on a square table. Large rectangular cards, the size of a tarot deck. I wondered which cards she had drawn.

I wanted to warn her not to allow the colorful cards to shape her life as I had. How much precious time had I wasted coaxing stories from a deck of inanimate cards? The woman consulted a book of interpretations. Her hair swung toward a lit candle.

As I imagined burnt hair's particular acrid smell, a tall wiry man appeared behind her. He gathered her long dark hair in his hands and kissed her neck. Turning away, I let my head drop on the pillow and fell asleep until 3:00 a.m. I arose and peered into the living room to check if Max had arrived. A whiff of bourbon rose from a tumbler. Max lay face down on an Indian blanket, his left foot twisted at an uncomfortable angle. "Go back to bed," he said.

"I thought you were asleep," I said.

"I never sleep."

At dawn, I awoke to see Max standing over me. He shook an old-fashioned thermometer like my dad used and stuck it in my mouth. "One hundred four. You're not going anywhere."

I tried to sit but fell back on the pillow. "Hope I don't give you my germs."

He helped me out of bed. "Don't worry. I have enough Wild Turkey coursing through my veins to kill anything."

Soap scum dulled a ceramic bathtub. I opted for a sponge bath. Turquoise toothpaste dotted a small sink where I washed my face, ran a comb through my hair. I applied lipstick and returned to Max's bedroom. A small bookshelf contained college literary anthologies and a smattering of detective novels. I thumbed through a paperback copy of *The Big Sleep* and found a poem in Max's handwriting scribbled on a blank page at the end of the book. Feeling like a voyeur, I couldn't help myself from reading it.

> At her second maybe third wedding
> I brought her a perfect martini
> She placed it on a white-clothed table and
> Asked the waiter for white wine
>
> A large-brimmed hat shielded her eyes
> She stubbed out a cigarette
> As if she were crushing a flower.

The poem reminded me of something Max had said. I wasn't feeling well enough to trace back his comment.

Three days passed in a haze of sweat and sleep as fever burned through me.

Rain splashed my window. Watching patterns made by fat droplets dissolving into sidewalk puddles was fine entertainment.

Max was talking the next time I awoke. Usually, he talked so quietly I couldn't hear him. This time his voice rose an octave, then another. "Figure it out!" Those were his last words. When he finished the conversation, he knocked. "Feel like taking a walk?"

"I don't feel a hundred percent."

"Come on," he said. "Fresh air will do you good."

We walked down Ditmars Avenue. As we crossed the street to try a Japanese restaurant Max liked, a car raced through the intersection and hit a fire hydrant. The impact spun the car around so that it faced the opposite direction. The driver, head angled out the window, spoke on a cellphone.

Max put his arm around my shoulders. "Looks like that guy was trying to jump into his own blind spot."

"Can anyone see their own blind spots? I asked.

"Only in dreams or time warps," Max said.

"Like that Dalí painting of the melted watches," I said. "A fixed time that goes on forever."

"Writing-wise," Max said, "I see your blind spots and you see mine—together we are an unbeatable team. Let's go home and work on our script. I'll order from my favorite Thai place. You like Thai?" I nodded. He bought bottled water from a street vendor, took a vial from his pocket, and removed two blue tablets, which he popped in his mouth.

"What are you taking?" I asked.

"Just a little something to enhance my thought waves. I'm not creative like you, an endless stream of new ideas." We walked back to Max's apartment, where we settled on the couch with the screenplay. While he made a drink, I changed into my best black pants and a designer sweater, as if I were getting ready for a business meeting. I joined him on the couch.

I poured a glass of cranberry juice bought from the corner bodega and added sparkling water to make it look like I was drinking wine. Pretending to drink worked better than explaining to drinkers why I didn't. I had to keep my wits about me.

"You had a problem with my dialogue. Too rom-commie," I said.

Max balanced his forearms on his knees. His eyes bore through me with an intense expression I hadn't seen. His speech was rapid and clipped. His eyes darted around the room. "I know there's a temptation to copy popular movies. What you think works, or think will sell, like your social media satire. I read it by the way."

Fear and excitement twinged through my stomach. "You didn't like it. I can tell."

"An entertaining read. Your screenplay is in the same vein. Great if you're trying to write a Lifetime movie. I thought you had loftier literary goals." He read from *After Lunch*: "*It may not be your action to take; it might be his. The universe has brought Anthony into your life for a reason. Let your story unfold. Or are you smarter than the universe?*"

Hearing my words embarrassed me.

"You like magic tricks?" He attached a paper streamer to the ceiling and set it on fire. "Your poems are incredible. This is you setting words on fire." Flames expanded as they climbed twisted crepe paper. Fear clutched my chest as sparks flew, worrying where they might land. I pictured a stray spark igniting the couch. Max produced a fire extinguisher from a corner cabinet and sprayed. "This is you getting scared and throwing a bucket of water on your efforts."

He dropped a red extinguisher on the glass top coffee table. Shards of glass bounced around the room. I collected paper towels to retrieve glass embedded in the carpet.

Max removed the roll from my hand, angry I had interrupted his rant. "We'll clean up later." He pushed me toward the couch. "Don't you see? Your resentment is slowly boiling on the back burner you're afraid to turn up and use. Your desire to save lost souls is a distraction. If I had a nickel for every barfly who told me about their book, their song, their movie, I'd be rich." He paced. "You want to transcend. Be where you're not. Sometimes you must be here. Do your work." He threw open a window. Chilly air coursed the room.

"If you're such an expert, where's your masterpiece?" I asked.

His shoulders slumped. "You got me. Sometimes I'm all talk."

I put my shoes back on, grabbed the Indian blanket. "Maybe I can't give up my distractions."

"Admit you're like everyone else. Face your ordinariness."

Despite the fact his agitation was scaring me, I knew Max was right. Writing was my drug. Laboring over an idea like a husband tinkering in the garage to avoid his wife. Tightening a sentence until it squeaked. Walking away to enjoy lunch, a woodland ramble, returning to revisit pages familiar as an old friend glad to see me. I was amazed when my edited version conveyed my meaning.

"You crossed a boundary invading my space," he said. "At least it shows a little moxie."

He seemed a bit calmer. I decided to dig deeper. "What about those naked pictures you took?"

Max expelled an exasperated sigh. "You're such a Luddite. There are no pictures. An image briefly appeared on my phone, then gone. I wish I had your imagination. Besides everyone shares everything these days. The world won't come to an end if someone sees your ass." He jumped off the couch and threw open another window. "It's stifling in here." In his enthusiasm, he looked like a boy. He removed my blanket and dragged me into the kitchen.

A bruise rose on my arm where he had squeezed it. "Stop it, Max. You're hurting me."

Max pushed me onto the fire escape. "Let people know who you are."

Cold air raised goosebumps on my forearms. Tight-lipped, I murmured, "I'm not yelling, Max."

He pinched my upper arm. "Let me." He yelled, "Deirdre Collins is the best writer you're not reading."

I shifted my weight backward but couldn't loosen his grip. "Your neighbors," I said.

"Deirdre Collins can fucking write," he yelled louder as he pushed me hard against a metal bar. One more shove and I might tumble twelve stories down.

Using every ounce of strength I had, I broke free. I rubbed my arm and looked at him. "Come inside, Max."

"You go inside, Deirdre. Stay safe in your hidey hole." Without a backward glance, he ran downstairs and hailed a cab.

I sat by the window, watching. His words stung more than his erratic behavior. My hidey hole was a place I had constructed word by word.

Years of healthy living had tamed my unruly emotions. Max had not made similar progress. I'd thought we shared a wild strand of DNA—that bonded my heart to his. The old problems were a lure. I felt differently now. Ah, the old patterns.

A vial with no prescription label sat next to the microwave. Blue pills imprinted with the word "Sky."

I sat up until dawn, but Max didn't return.

Friday, my fifth morning in New York, I awoke wanting to leave the bed. I had been lying in this bed far too long. Windows needed opening. Firing up an empowerment podcast for courage, I stripped sheets to release the smell of my sickness, while thinking how I might address Max. I couldn't return to Chicago without confronting him.

The laundry room was well-lit and stocked with detergent, not stashed in an alley like my first Chicago apartment, a place I was afraid to venture into, until one manic night when I realized I had no clean clothes and snuck down at 2:00 a.m.

Another tenant arriving to collect laundry from the dryer saved me from following memory down a rabbit hole, where a stranger waited. A stranger I'd invited home.

No digression from my carefully considered routine had turned me into someone different but not completely new. No midnight strolls. No visiting bars alone to see what kind of trouble I might stir up. As much as my mental and physical health improved, lingering doubts revealed themselves in dreams and blocked my progress whenever it was time to stand up, step forward, and offer my gifts to the world.

Despite the discipline of a tight schedule, my cravings had not died. I tired the yappy little dogs of my desire with exercise until I fell exhausted into bed. Here it was different. Deep inside, I felt a thrum of excitement. New York was awakening me like Frankenstein from his slumber. I took a shower and washed my hair, glad to feel human again.

Max returned wearing a suit and a serious expression. "You didn't pick up my calls today," I said, tightening my core muscles as the podcaster recommended.

"Busy day," Max said. He reviewed his mail.

I removed a stack of envelopes from his hands. "Last night you almost pushed me off a fire escape."

"Don't be dramatic," Max said. He grabbed his phone, his face an emotionless mask. His smug confidence infuriated me so much I wanted to hit him. A purple umbrella hanging from a coatrack in the entry caught my eye.

Max reminded me of a third-grade bully named Tommy Krugholz. In class, I'd mocked his pronunciation. "Never seen you at the *li-bary*," I said.

After Girl Scouts, Tommy sprang from the evergreens muttering, "You think you're so smart." Tommy pushed me down, sat on my back, rubbed my face in the snow. I waited until spring for an opportunity to retaliate. As Tommy dismounted from playground parallel bars, I cocked my umbrella and beat him, rejoicing with each blow, knowing as a boy he wouldn't admit a girl had beat him.

Max's phone dinged with a text. He laughed as he read.

I thumped Max with his own umbrella to get his attention. "You could have killed me last night," I said.

Still laughing, Max said, "What are you doing?"

I dropped the umbrella and opened my palm. Even though I knew it was wrong, hitting Max was the only way to make my point. "Get over yourself," I said, and slapped Max hard.

He stepped back and regarded me as if he had never seen be before. "You have more gumption than I thought." He examined his face in his phone. "Anything else you wanted to mention?" He stroked his cheek.

"I should have used my words," I said. "That's how I counsel my students. But it felt good."

An intercom buzzer sounded. Max admitted a DoorDash driver delivering Thai food. Coconut and ginger smells filled the apartment. We started with Tom Yum soup. Between bites of Pad Thai, I asked Max, "How did you start working for Eddie Greer?"

"After I was released from the hospital, I moved into my parents' house. A play I wrote was produced off-off Broadway. Eddie attended with a handful of old friends who'd bought tickets. Afterwards, we went clubbing. Eddie offered me a good salary with benefits. I started working for him and never left."

"You make people laugh. Many would envy your life."

He piled rice on his plate. "My lofty goal was to write a twenty-first century version of *Long Day's Journey into Night*."

I scraped plates in Max's tiny kitchen. "Bring back more merlot." I poured him a glass, refreshed my faux wine before settling next to him on the couch.

"Did you read my notes?" he asked.

"How do you feel about me?"

"Why must you pigeonhole everything? I'm helping you bring an idea into being. Is it important you dress it in a suit and tie and stand it in the corner? Stop imitating everyone else if you want to be original."

"Guess I'm trying to find a place solid enough to make a stand."

"I gave up on stability a long time ago." Max looked downward. "No drug can cure my depression."

"Oh, Max," I said.

"You know the statistics. Let's say I don't expect to live to a ripe old age."

We strategized far into the night ways to communicate how mental illness shaped a person's life. After his third glass of wine, I asked Max again how he felt about me. "Why have you kept in touch?"

"The way you listened to me in the hospital was an enormous compliment," Max said. "No one else paid me such attention." He put down his drink.

"When we waltzed in the grand ballroom, I felt a connection," I said. "You visited Chicago twice. Quite an effort when you don't fly."

"I was working, scouting comics for Eddie's show." A jackhammer interrupted our conversation. Max laughed. "Only in New York do they do construction at midnight." He took my hand. "Maybe you're the mother I always wished I had. Soft and gentle. I know you came here ready to punish me, but it's just not in your nature."

He saw me as most people saw me. Quiet and unassuming. "I was worried last night you were spiraling into mania," I said.

"I'm a rapid cycler. My moods change in the space of a sentence. Look, Deirdre, I'm screwed up in ways they can't even name, but I care about you," Max said.

Around 2:00 a.m., we called it a night. As I got ready to slip under the covers, Max paused in the doorway. "Don't turn mental illness into something you can solve with a magic wand. Tell the truth."

Sleep did not come. Turning on a bedside lamp, I found Rumi poetry on the bookshelf. Probably left by a girlfriend. A strange mixture of distrust, worry what he might do to himself made me listen at the door. Max spoke in hushed tones. "I can't take off any more time. Can you take him to his doctor appointment?" He entered the small bedroom and removed the book from my hands.

"Did you tell your girlfriend you have someone staying over?" I asked.

"My ex-wife. Our oldest is sick. She's worried about that new virus."

"I didn't know you were married."

"Twice. Andrea loved me when I was depressed. She wanted to save me. Carly loved my manic spells. Spent my money redecorating. Not this place, as you can see." He laughed. "I could never find anyone brave enough to deal with whoever rolled out of bed. I don't blame them."

"Who did you love most?" I asked.

"My mother."

A smile twisted with pain warned me not to press, but I couldn't help myself. "Do you want to tell me?" I asked. "I care."

"Don't care so much. You're using your energy saving the world and getting jack shit done in your own life. My idea when I called you was collaborating on a story to open the world's eyes to what it's like to live with mental problems. How chronic illness separates you from normal people. How you walk away from people before they can reject you."

He opened a book of Rumi poetry and read a line: "*The breeze at dawn has secrets to tell you. Don't go back to sleep.*" Max was like no one I had ever met. That he could cycle between insufferable prick and poet in the space of a sentence fascinated me.

"I'll make coffee," I said.

Max shook his head. "I have an early meeting. We'll talk later."

Still fighting whatever virus had attacked me, I fell asleep. I dreamed Max and I were back in New Mexico, not in the beige intake room where we met, but hiking a mountain. Lightning flashed as we climbed Battleship Rock. At the summit, darkness descended as if God had turned off the lights. Rocks shifted under our feet. I grabbed a pinyon pine trunk to steady myself. Gravel shifted under Max's feet. He fell.

I woke in a panic, perched over the side of the bed as if it were a mountain we had been climbing. A sense of deep loss enveloped me. I had to see the living, breathing Max. Too late. An elevator *ding* signaled his escape. He was headed for the subway. I hadn't exercised in a week. Muscles slack, I walked unsteadily to the bathroom. My temperature was normal.

The living room was tidy, couch cushions replaced, coffee table straightened. A pile of manuscript lay on the coffee table, margins lined with blue pen. Clipped to the screenplay was an orange Post-It.

Good work, Deirdre. I'll finish reading and send you notes. My son needs to come and stay with me. A car will pick you up at 1:00 p.m. for LaGuardia.

Love, Max.

Just like that, he was kicking me out.

A light burned in the kitchen. Whiskey glass and coffee mug sat side-by-side in the sink. I noticed a blinking desktop computer, which had been covered during my other kitchen trips. A slip of paper was stuck to a drawer under the computer. Thinking it was from a fortune cookie, I unfurled Max's computer password.

The junk drawer below was slightly ajar. I pulled it open to find a jumble of birthday cards and take-out menus. A rubber-banded stack of paper was underneath. My eye was drawn to a letter clipped addressed to Max Fletcher from a New York literary agent whose name I recognized. Galleys labeled *Downtime*, a novel by *anyone*. My stomach churned. My first impulse was to trash his apartment or confront him at work. I gripped the counter. Shaking, I snapped a picture of the letter with my phone, another of his computer password.

An Uber waited downstairs. As we cruised along city streets, I reread the agent's letter: "If you change your mind and want to reissue *Downtime* under your name, I suggest we use this picture." In the headshot, Max's wry smile floated over a firm jaw. I saw no trace of a bewildered boy with bandaged wrists in the handsome man with a guarded gaze.

Anger and disbelief roiled through me. He had played me for a fool. I staggered back to the sink. I raised his whiskey glass over my head, intending to smash it on the floor. Leave him a mess as he had in my life. A bird chirping on the fire escape drew me outside. I stood on the landing, letting cool air soothe me.

Feeling calmer, I decided to return to Chicago and seek legal redress, revenge being a dish best served cold. My advantage over Max was that years of disciplined living kept my impulses under control while he raged through life.

FIFTEEN

NIKKI ADAMOS HADN'T CALLED IN SO LONG, I WAS surprised when she texted me. Her Aunt Cora had died. Nikki wanted me to attend the funeral. A service was being held at a cemetery on Chicago's northwest side. There was no way to decline. In Chicago, when someone died, you paid your respects. No matter if you were estranged or hated each other. You expressed condolences or at the very least sent a Novena. A sleeveless black cocktail dress hung in my closet. Honoring a long dead rule of etiquette, I covered my bare arms with a jacket and drove to River Grove.

At Elmwood Cemetery, a cenotaph on his parents' headstone memorialized John Belushi. An inscription read, "In Loving Memory of Our Son. He Gave Us Laughter." I remembered a generation's shock of loss when he died.

By the time I found Cora's service, Nikki's brothers were carrying their aunt's casket toward an uncovered hole. Wives and children formed a ring behind them. Nikki's mother leaned on Gregory, the oldest brother. "Pray for the eternal soul of Cora Hermione Adamos," the priest said. I remembered her as crazy Aunt Cora who never married. The priest praised her as a devoted daughter and proud aunt.

At my father's wake, a packed funeral parlor was quiet. Relatives and friends hid behind tight smiles, speaking quietly. Around Cora's freshly dug grave, handkerchiefs flew from pockets and tears flowed. Nikki's relatives were second-and third-generation immigrants turned teachers, insurance agents, and cops. They squeezed and patted me as if I were a tomato from a vegetable market in the old neighborhood.

Nikki's brothers, who as boys threw spaghetti at the ceiling to see if it stuck, now had small children playing around their feet. I tried to find my own footing. Everyone I'd known had grown up. The world had moved on without me. My grandparents, who were young and healthy for so long I thought they would never die, had passed. I wrote a eulogy to honor Grandpa. Two months later I threw flowers on Grandma's casket. I did not dwell on their deaths, preferring to feel their presence in my memories of them.

I wobbled on high heels navigating ground mushy from last night's rain. As Nikki's mother cried, I remembered how faint I'd felt at my father's service, slapped against the wall of a fun house ride, the floor disappearing beneath my feet. How many more hours and minutes remained until the rest slipped away? A sob erupted from Nikki's mother. Was she crying for Cora or herself? Did she wonder if she'd be sitting in a pew or laying in a coffin the next time her family gathered?

Nikki found me after the casket was lowered into a fresh grave. "So glad you came," she squeezed my hand. "Follow me to the restaurant."

Instead of heading to Greektown on Halsted where her family usually celebrated milestones, Nikki drove west, her destination a suburban banquet hall.

A procession of relatives pressed my hand as I passed through a receiving line. Aunt Athena hugged me. "Haven't seen you since the lamb roast after Nikki's graduation. You look wonderful."

At the luncheon, Gregory pushed a plate of dolmades in front of me. The first time I visited Nikki's house, her mother gestured toward her gang of sons and asked me which one I wanted to marry. I liked Gregory, the oldest and most serious. He was a Chicago cop, studying for the bar.

"Eat. You're getting too skinny," Gregory said. He poured me a shot from a bottle of Ouzo being passed around the table. I set it aside and drank water. It was time I functioned as an adult. Facing the moment sober was a first step.

Gregory whispered to his wife. She nodded. He turned toward me and said, "I need to escape these Greeks. Let's crash the Vanderhoeven wedding reception. Sounds swanky."

He led me to a small bar where he ordered scotch. The room was filled with WASPs, blonde beauties sporting a rainbow of honey, caramel, and bright yellow highlights. Their expensive couture made me self-conscious about my thrift store cocktail dress.

"What were you doing in New York?" Gregory said.

I described a screenplay I was developing with a New York producer, omitting details of how I met Max.

Gregory finished his drink. "Deirdre, I'm a cop. I know when someone's not giving me the full story." Wedding guests twirled around us. Gregory was safe. I told him how Max hacked into my computer and plagiarized my work. "You know that's a felony," he said.

I moved closer to the wall. Gregory stood beside me. "My sister told me you've had problems, how you left school two weeks before semester's end. Must've been tough. Doesn't give anyone the right to treat you poorly. Let me help."

"Nikki gave me the name of a lawyer downtown," I said.

Gregory's lip curled. "You need a shark on your side. I'll hook you up with someone savvy."

When we returned to the Adamos event, Nikki stood with a knot of guests gathered around her. "What's the best day school in Chicago?" Nikki asked.

A woman sipping from a champagne flute said, "Anyone who is serious will send their children to North Shore Country Day school." Nikki turned to address a man I recognized from the news as alderman. Gregory knocked my arm. "Get a load of my sister," he said. "Doors are opening, even if she pushes them open herself."

Not wanting to interrupt, I waved as I headed out. Avoiding the expressway, I took the long way home, taking time to mourn how my friendship with Nikki had changed from college days. We had little in common except our history. My breathing evened, driving through an expanse of corn and soybean fields surrounding Clairmont. Happiness settled over me as I followed a back road to Aunt Katherine's house.

With some surprise, I realized how much I loved my woodland retreat. My body had adjusted to the school year's rhythm of semesters, Winter Vacation, Spring Breaks, work and rest driving toward graduation. Critique sessions with Eleanor Graham had taught me how to work. Tending Aunt Katherine's garden in all its seasons brought joy. Shifting moods no longer tripped me. The ground was solid beneath my feet.

The lawyer Gregory Adamos recommended was a woman he'd dated before he met his wife. During our first call, she explained she had investigated using information I had forwarded, then drafted a complaint to be filed in the proper jurisdiction.

"Will he know it was me?"

"You can't file an anonymous complaint," the lawyer said.

As second semester progressed, I stewed about my decision. As angry as I was at Max, my gut lurched at taking so public an action. I was afraid that righting his wrongs might destroy more than my privacy.

Driving home after a particularly tough day, I pulled to the side of the road and called the lawyer. She didn't pick up, so I texted her that I wanted to withdraw the lawsuit.

As I approached Aunt Katherine's house my phone dinged. The lawyer texted: *Too late to withdraw. Max Fletcher was deposed today.*

An invitation to a christening party for Spencer Graham's baby arrived. Excited to meet his little girl, I rode the train downtown to find a special gift. After perusing merchandise at Macy's, I walked to Neiman Marcus on north Michigan Avenue. There I found a pretty lace dress bedecked with sky blue ribbons.

The party was held at Clairmont's Town Tavern. Spencer was parking as I arrived. His mother followed in a Jeep. Spencer removed a child carrier from his truck. A wide-eyed girl blinked brilliant blue eyes at sun streaming through sycamore trees. Eleanor Graham peered at the baby without touching her. Spencer unbuckled Alice from the car seat. Spencer beamed, comfortable in his new role. He cooed as he cradled the child, brushing fine strands of reddish hair from Alice's eyes.

We followed him to a private room where pink banners proclaimed, "It's A Girl!" A garland of pink, white, and gold balloons decorated the table. Spencer retrieved a bottle and a burp rag from a carryall. He extended a bottle toward me while raising an eyebrow.

"I'd love to feed her," I said.

Spencer handed me baby Alice, angling the bottle in my hand. A sweet scent wafted from the crown of her head. Alice and I did not break our gaze as she emptied the bottle sip by sip. My heart swelled as if I were falling in love. When she was finished, I handed Alice back to her father. "She is beautiful, Spencer. Such a pleasure to hold her."

Eleanor Graham ordered a Moscow Mule from the bar and brought it into our private room. "Take a picture with Alice," Spencer said. Eleanor leaned toward her granddaughter and smiled as she might for a professional photo.

Cake and champagne were served. Eleanor secured a bottle and refilled a shallow disposable cup at regular intervals. She touched my forearm. "I want you to send an excerpt from *Seesaw* to a new journal." She handed me a card. "They're seeking material."

When I arrived home, my mind was running fast with the thrill of conversation after not socializing in months. Unable to concentrate on Murakami's latest novel, I inserted Max's still undeposited check as a bookmark and turned on the television. Cable wasn't working. My only options were three network channels. I flipped between ABC, CBS, and NBC, landing on Eddie Greer's monologue.

Instead of his usual puckish grin, Greer looked serious, his eyes red. "Tonight we dedicate our show to Max Fletcher, a friend and coworker who passed away unexpectedly." Shock hit me like a hammer. I turned off the TV and Googled a report of a single vehicle crash westbound on the Pennsylvania Turnpike. Cause of the accident had not been determined. I wondered where Max was headed. Was he driving aimlessly, or headed west to Chicago?

Overcome with grief, I called in sick, something I rarely did. Insomnia was creeping back into my life, tapping me awake at 2:00 a.m., my brain a hollow gourd. I wanted to burrow under warm covers and sleep. Instead, I stared at the ceiling, then turned on my side to watch leaves falling. I couldn't stop wondering where Max was headed when he crashed. Had he fallen asleep at the wheel, or had he crashed on purpose? He had told me he didn't expect to live to a ripe old age. Was I magnifying the importance of our brief association? Perhaps his death had nothing to do with me.

Overnight, the northern Illinois temperature plummeted forty degrees overnight from eighty-five degrees to forty-five. I dragged myself from bed and drove to work. Drafts roamed Clairmont High, old windows no defense against winds chilling the plain.

Cyril Banks, the scruffy sub with crazy curls and hyperthyroidic turquoise eyes, occupied my Shield Room desk. He was deep in conversation with Eli Nowak.

"I'm the kind of individual who can't tolerate boredom," Eli said, his fingers texting as he talked.

Cyril showed Eli a picture of the Sistine Chapel on his phone. "Boredom creates great art. Michelangelo conceived ideas for his sculpture while lying in a Tuscan meadow. Ditch your headphones and appreciate what's going on around you."

"You need to call my headphones by their proper name," Eli said. "Electroacoustic transducers."

A snatch of music from an instrument I'd never heard played from Cyril's pocket. He silenced his phone. "Sorry, something I'm working on," he said. "They weren't sure if you would be back today. Are you all right?" he asked.

"I lost a dear friend," I said.

To prevent my grief from morphing into a full-blown depression, I threw myself into my work, meeting with students, supervising Homework Club after school.

Benjamin Babcock was reading *Old Man and the Sea.* "How do you like the book?" I asked.

He shrugged. "The relationship between the old man and his young helper was good. At least this book is short. Do you have water bottles in the fridge?"

"We've talked about how you stall when you don't feel like working," I said.

Benjamin buried in his face in his crossed arms. I tapped his shoulder. His azure eyes were wide with fatigue. "My mouth is so dry.

Doctor changed my antidepressant. All I do is drink and pee." Putting my arm around him was what I wanted to do. Instead, I chose the coldest water bottle in the mini-fridge.

While Benjamin found quotes for a paper he was assigned, I read an article about Ernest Hemingway's depression treatment at Mayo Clinic. Doctors let Hemingway wander Rochester, Minnesota, chat with inhabitants, have a drink when he wanted one. Even though I knew how the story ended, I grieved. Winning a Nobel Prize did not protect him from a cocktail of brain chemicals which felled him. As a tribute, I reread a Hemingway story where the protagonist chopped wood to tire himself. Every afternoon, I added firewood to the pile in my shed.

I kept no alcohol in my house.

A quarter of the student body played hooky opening day of hunting season. As Eli Nowak didn't hunt, he was underfoot, seeking attention from teachers manning the Shield Room.

I was glad to go home after work. A large brown envelope postmarked New York City protruded from the mailbox. Hands trembling, I slit it open using Aunt Katherine's pearl handled letter opener. A check of the calendar confirmed Max had mailed the envelope two days before he received a certified letter notifying my intention to file suit.

My screenplay marked with Max's notes slid out as well as several stapled stories written by him. I searched for a handwritten note but didn't find anything except his editorial comments.

Too upset to read script or stories, I took a long walk through the woods. When it was time for bed, I selected a calming book on Buddhist practice by Pema Chodron. Neither exercise nor meditation knocked me out. As a full moon progressed across the sky, I lay sleepless, wishing I had not hired Gregory Adamos' lawyer friend.

At 3:00 a.m., I retrieved my phone. Scrolling the Internet revealed no further details other than the private burial arranged by his family. If I hadn't retaliated, Max might still be alive. Even though he didn't foresee living to a ripe old age, I felt responsible. A thought I would have to carry the rest of my life.

Even though I was exhausted, staying home was not an option. Living alone with no one to distract me from my dark thoughts was too dangerous. A constant stream of activities helped manage creeping guilt and sadness.

Eight students were present in the Shield Room. One was marked home hospital, which meant she was completing assignments from her parents' house while under the care of a psychiatrist. Two other students were learning remotely. I was completing attendance when Cyril returned early from Metals class. His complexion was two shades whiter than his normal pallor. "What's wrong?"

I asked.

"Eli disappeared," Cyril said. "He left class when I had my back turned to help another kid. Searched the basement, cafeteria, the wrestling balcony where he hides behind mats, nothing."

My stomach clenched as he ticked off Eli's hiding places. "You stay here while I make my rounds. Will is completing his *One Flew Over the Cuckoo's Nest* paper. Jenna should be doing algebra." Jenna sat sideways in her chair, typing a text while curling a strand of dark hair around her finger.

I made a loop of the main floor past the principal's office, nurse, attendance clerk, and student services. Other students might pick up their backpacks and sneak out early. Not Eli. Every day whether he was scheduled in Shield or not, he stuck his head in the room and waved before he left the building. When he was wound up, he would scream "Goodbye!"

He wasn't crazy about going home where he was often alone. His father worked odd hours. Eli said when his father was present, he was either asleep or playing video games.

A veteran teacher named Mrs. Briggs, who had returned after retirement to supervise study hall, was one of Eli's favorites. She worked crossword puzzles with him when she found him wandering. The room was located downstairs past Autos, Woods, and Metal Shop. Loud laughter billowed from Autos, where boys of every size and two girls watched their teacher demonstrate how to change the oil in an Impala.

I willed Eli to suddenly appear before me with his Frankenstein monster gait, hair sticking like a brush from under the bar of his hard-shell headphones. No luck. Halls were deserted. I was tempted to run my hand over lockers decorated with banners and pom-poms celebrating Friday night's game as I had seen Eli do, hoping the clanging noise would summon him.

The Art Department storage room was locked. I peered through a rectangular window searching for signs of Eli. No one was in the room. Wire figures in lab coats were positioned on a stage. I made a mental note to ask Cyril if he knew about the exhibit as he often substituted in art. I shut the door on my way out.

A fear that something had happened to Eli mounted as I turned the corner. Boys bullied him. Girls objected to his smell. Even though male teachers reminded him to bathe, Eli's body odor lingered when he left a room. I continued down the corridor. Mrs. Briggs' dark empty room was locked. I texted Cyril only to find out Eli had not returned. I hurried upstairs, planning to call the dean. In the Shield Room, Cyril was brainstorming ideas with Will regarding *One Flew Over the Cuckoo's Nest*. Jenna still texted, algebra untouched.

The break-out room was dark when I left. Now a torch lamp was lit. As I entered, a sharp tang of urine crawled up my nostrils. Harsh breaths sounded from under a study table. I turned on overhead lights and found Eli hunched under a table. He must have had an accident in class and snuck into the breakout room while Cyril was occupied.

I lowered my body in a squat to talk at eye level. Exasperation turned to compassion when I confronted Eli's crouched figure. More wounded animal than child, fear and panic stripped him of his usual swagger.

Clean gym shorts were stocked in the file cabinet bottom drawer. I motioned Cyril to join us. "Mr. Banks," I said, "can you escort Eli to the locker room? Help him get cleaned up." Eli crawled from his hiding place. He followed Cyril like a puppy.

A student in need of grammar help worked on NoRedInk at a table adjacent to my desk until the bell rang. Students scattered to their next classes. A girl with wispy wheat-colored hair dressed in ballet skirt and tights entered, tears streaming down her face. I walked her to a breakout room.

A minute later she appeared in front of me holding her nose. I gestured toward an open desk. An image on her phone brought a smile. A generalized exhaustion descended over the classroom. My eyes closed a blessed second. Cyril startled me awake, rattling a folder filled with tests. "What are you doing after school?" he asked.

Too tired to devise an excuse, I said, "Nothing."

"I want to show you something," he said. We waited for the main glut of students to leave the building. Following Cyril, I descended stairs and retraced my steps past Autos and Metal Shop. Cyril opened the storage closet next to Mrs. Briggs' study hall. When he flipped the light switch, music played. Fascinated, I moved toward a concert stage constructed from discarded pipes.

"You created this?" I asked.

Cyril smiled. "The shop teacher was my best friend in first grade. He lent me this room to work. My apartment is too small. Subbing doesn't pay enough for me to rent a studio." He pointed at musicians wearing white lab coats fashioned from spirals of wire. "I call it 'splenditude.'"

"That's not a word," I said.

"Came to me in a dream. Do you keep a dream journal?" The tarot card reader had made a similar suggestion. "You should. Everything you need to know is in your dreams."

Haunting music drew me closer. I had heard the tune sounding from Cyril's phone earlier. Violin carried a jazz melody over a pulse of ancient brass. The installation was fashioned from junk I had seen in the back of his car. "Love your music," I said.

He nodded. "A tribute to Phil Cohran, the trumpeter from Sun Ra. My ex took me to see him at the Chicago Cultural Center. Cohran played Space Harp, an instrument he had fashioned himself, while projecting slides from the Hubble Space Telescope. Blew my mind. A guy sitting behind me lifted my chair with his long basketball legs as pictures expanded brighter and bigger on a ceiling mounted screen. Cohran sent the Claudia Cassidy Theater into outer space that afternoon."

Music crescendoed into a stab of ecstasy ending in a dissonant clang. He paced, pausing to drape a cloth over the plaster head he had been sculpting. Lost in his work, Cyril had transformed from a schlub sleeping in his car to a purposeful person.

"Why haven't you recorded it?"

He stopped in front of where I sat. "My band went bust." Realizing I sounded like a parrot, but unable to stop, I asked why. He swept his hand left and right as if he were trying to catch floating musical notes. "Bands break up. Artistic differences. I don't have time to tell you that story. You don't have time to listen."

"That's where you're wrong. I have time." I stayed silent so long, Cyril resumed pacing. He rearranged the position of a flutist constructed from spirals of wire.

When we'd first met, I'd guessed Cyril was sixty. Here he looked closer to forty. He had traded paint-stained jeans for a merino wool sweater over neatly pressed pants. Blonde graying hair cut around his face revealed a clear, healthy complexion. I wondered what had caused the change.

"A woman named Penelope Long upended my world. I walked into the Chicago Cultural Center during my lunch hour and heard jazz. Followed the sound toward the Randolph Street side of the building. An audience was seated in front of a small stage, listening to a woman play violin. The air around her vibrated. Her pale fingers controlled the bow as her tapping foot kept time. Head back, hair flying like a prayer flag."

"Wow," I said. "You talk like jazz piano sounds."

He draped a towel over the clay bust he had been working on. "Thought she was the love of my life. Turned out to be more limerence than love."

"Another word you made up?"

Cyril smiled. "Look it up. Horace Gregory called it love coming up in elevators. What's ailing you, I'd guess."

My attempt to hide my mental state by throwing myself into my work wasn't successful. "What's the cure?"

"Time. Spring will return to your heart and you will rid yourself of the hair shirt you wear over the scarlet A of abandonment."

"Where's Penelope now?"

"Long gone. She's never coming back." He looked so sad, I put my hand on his shoulder. Cyril hit the lights. "I gotta go." The music stopped. The room had turned cold as the boiler shut down.

"Tell me," I said. "Why the lab coats?"

"Music is a laboratory for feeling what isn't safe anywhere else," he said.

By the time I could collect my briefcase, Cyril had disappeared down the corridor.

A nauseating smell greeted me when I walked into my house. Sewage water had flooded the downstairs bathroom floor. The powder room's antique plumbing was on my list to be refurbished. I called Clem Varner, a handyman who had turned Aunt Katherine's potting shed into my writing studio. He was in the neighborhood and arrived as I finished cleaning the floor.

He explained the plumbing was so old, pipes were corroded. He used terms I had never heard, such as *drainfield trench* and *soakaway beds*. A ringing cash register of anxiety prevented me from understanding what Clem was saying. He hitched his fingers in his back pockets. "Probably have to excavate the yard."

Visions of my small savings account emptying made me dizzy. I steadied myself on the kitchen counter. Property taxes were due.

"Can't complete this job alone," Clem said. "I sure can't." His mood changed from serious to cheery as he considered the problem. "We'll need a crew. My brother-in-law and nephew can help."

As Clem sauntered to his truck, I pictured a backhoe tearing up my woodland paradise.

I had been working steadily to make Aunt Katherine's summer house habitable year-round. My salary did not cover these new repairs. I needed money. Max had sworn selling a screenplay would put more money in my pocket than selling a novel. Writing a screenplay was a risk as it was unknown territory. The reward was keeping the house I adored.

Time to read Max's notes. Get to work. I settled in an overstuffed chair covered in floral chintz. Max wrote with a blue pen, words printed in square shapes. No flowery cursive for him. Reading the edits made me feel as if he was sitting by my shoulder. As an editor, he was merciless. Clichés or predictable scenes were struck.

The time I spent with Eleanor Graham had thickened my skin for a thorough critique. My stomach jumped with gladness when I found exclamation marks next to passages Max enjoyed.

A handwritten note stuck between the pages of a story I hadn't seen when I opened the envelope fluttered out. I retrieved it and read:

> Send your script to my friend, Ryan Sturbridge. I will let him know to expect it. Remember when you found Rumi poetry in my apartment? You thought I was impressing a girl. Rumi was mine. Too bad you never knew my literary side. If I were you, I'd work on Seesaw. Finish it. Tell the story of a lifetime struggle. Tell the truth. To quote Rumi: 'Don't go back to sleep. Don't you dare go back to sleep.' Think of your insomnia as God shaking you awake. Instead of tossing and turning and losing heart, write when you can't sleep. Your energy is a gift. Harness the furious engine of your mind. Turn music into words. Write an ode to brain chemicals that exhilarate you when you see a certain slant of sunlight.
>
> Love, Max
>
> P.S. Sorry I didn't come clean about "Downtime". Shared an excerpt from Seesaw with my publisher. I proposed that you write the forward to my novella's next edition. Sorry I crossed lines I shouldn't have. Hope you still love me. I love you. M.

Clutching the note, I sank into bed. It was after midnight. As angry as Max had made me, our understanding was mysterious—shy and elusive like an animal gliding through tall grass. Our age difference had made a relationship improbable. We had little in common. He had belonged to a glittering world of smart talk and style while I hid away in the woods. Yet between us there had been a recognition of like to like, comfortable as kin.

For the first time since I'd learned of Max's death, I cried. Even if I made it my mission to meet new people, befriend other writers, I was quite sure I would never find another Max.

SIXTEEN

A CALM SPELL IN THE SHIELD ROOM WAS AN UNEXPECT-
ed gift. Students worked quietly. No one had a meltdown. I cleaned my
desk, organized paperwork, ordered supplies.

Shortly after the last bell, I found Cyril Banks near the art wing
stairs. "Can we hold a salon?" I asked. "I desperately need to get work."

Cyril sprinted downstairs, flipping on lights as soon as he entered
the storage room. A new musician complete with drum set had joined
the installation. Eager for Cyril's torrent of talk to keep my loneliness at
bay, I arranged my manuscript on a student desk. He chose a classical
station, then unveiled a plaster head.

"You write," he said. "I sculpt. No talking. Go."

Screenplay edits were stuffed in my briefcase. My disappointment at
Cyril's silence faded as I wrote a new scene on the backs of typed pages.
Experts claimed writing by hand connected body to mind. My characters
escaped the Albuquerque psych hospital, discussing life and death and
everything that scared them as they drove through the mountains. They
climbed Battleship Rock to Jemez Falls. The ache in my arm and crick
in my neck disappeared as I entered the scene, imagining a fresh woodsy
pinyon pine scent permeating dry air. I ceased to hear the clock ticking
an hour away, then two. Water ran in the sink as Cyril washed his hands,
bringing me back. My concentration had been so total, I hadn't heard
Beethoven's sonata end. Cyril's clay bust dried on a table.

"The word 'splenditude' is bothering me," I said. "Not really a word."

Cyril paced, as he often did when he was thinking. "Splenditude
is what you get when you mix solitude, attitude, aptitude, splendor, and

candor." He opened window shades. We had worked so long, darkness was descending. "The word appeared during a dream I had, chaperoning a junior high group to D.C. The Kids were so excited on the plane yelling back and forth, I'd regretted coming. I already had a headache from drinking wine and painting the night before.

"When we got students settled in their hotel rooms, it was late afternoon. I asked a teacher if she could cover while I stepped out. My plan was to pay a quick visit to Whistler and Sargent. Cabbed it to the Smithsonian on Pennsylvania Avenue. A first-floor exhibit stopped me in my tracks. 'The Throne of the Third Heaven of the Nations' Millennium General Assembly' created by James Hampton, a Federal building janitor. A placard said Hampton worked alone in a rented space to depict God's quarters in heaven. The installation was wild and beautiful, fashioned from repurposed furniture. Cardboard cutouts and light bulbs wrapped in foil sparkled silver and gold in a splendor never imagined by my Sunday school teachers. As I toured the exhibit, I planned my own tribute to the glory of existence, the power of art to enliven every cell."

I opened my mouth, but Cyril ignored me, lost in memory. "My vision made me high—not glass shattering high—just enough wind beneath my wings to catch a current and glide, man, glide. How you fly when kids are occupied a blessed moment. You dive and soar in those notebooks you pull from the bottom right drawer."

Alarm bells clanged at his mention of the exact location of my private papers. And he was so enthralled with his story, there was no way to stop his monologue.

"I stopped for a sandwich. A group of kilted men were gathered in the cafe courtyard streaming with sunlight. I asked a red bearded man with thighs like tree trunks where they were going. He handed me a brochure advertising a 2:00 p.m. performance of 'The Kirkin' o' the Tartan' at Washington National Cathedral. No way I could miss it. I followed the men outside. A van stopped to pick them up. They disappeared into the vehicle.

"Intrigued, I asked my cab driver to follow the van. The Cathedral was on Wisconsin Avenue in D.C.'s northwest quadrant. The cab driver listened to a discussion of a threatened government shutdown on news radio. When we arrived, I selected an aisle seat in time to see the band enter. Sounds of pipe and drum bounced and reverberated off massive walls."

My first impression of Cyril had been an ugly man, troll-like with his slight build and bulging, strangely-colored eyes. His cascade of words mesmerized me. "Mass came after the pipers played. I was already late, so I decided to walk back to the hotel. Flower boxes bloomed with bluebells and azaleas, roses of every color. Of course, I was late. Teachers were upset I didn't chaperone dinner. A food fight had erupted. When I returned, they fired me. Delinquent in my duties. The only employee to be fired from the school district in ten years, they told me."

I made a cluck of sympathy.

"Don't you see it was worth it?" he said. "That afternoon inspired my best work, delivered smoothly as a stork delivering a baby. Sometimes you must take a risk. Not the general you. You. Take a risk."

He hit the boom box. I couldn't classify the music. A fusion of jazz and ancient brass notes made me want to sway like a reed in the wind. "Beautiful. Have you recorded it?" I asked.

He shook his head. "Same reason you don't publish your stories," he said. "Fear of being seen. Fear of rejection. You don't have to stomp through this world, but if you want to be read, you'll have to expose yourself."

"You talk so strangely."

"Only to a kindred spirit. Eli cut his finger in Metals, so I hunted in your desk for band-aids. Your drawers are such a mess, it made me like you. The first aid kit was under a folder marked 'Tests.' I remembered you distribute tests to students who hadn't completed them in class. Stuck inside was a story called 'Seesaw.' Once I realized it wasn't a kid's paper, I read the whole thing."

I made a sound between a gurgle and gasp. He nodded. "Don't tell me you wouldn't have done the same. Artists are voyeurs by nature. We want to know what goes on in other peoples' brains, other peoples' bedrooms. Curiosity leads us to create. Makes life less lonely."

I collapsed in a canvas chair and covered my face with my hands. Cyril touched my shoulder. "Deirdre, you work like a carpenter trying to repair the broken bits. You might as well rearrange the sky."

"Isn't that art?"

He placed a leather portfolio containing his sketches into a canvas bag and slung it over his shoulder. "A discussion for another day. My cat is wondering where I am."

Cyril left the room. A new kind of pain announced itself, like a fist grabbing my heart. I hadn't talked to anyone so deeply since Max died.

Sitting in Aunt Katherine's red velvet chair, I read Max's version of our characters' meeting. I had captured the sadness but not the sweetness. Max had written:

"You're one to talk," the woman said. You crossed a boundary when you entered my life illegally. Sitting at the other edge of a screen. Tracking my movements, tracking my words."

The man drew back into himself and then took a step forward. "What kind of a novelist doesn't recognize paradox? The character you named Max had to follow you. Don't you see?" I've been tracking you, not for the reason you think. When we met at Summit, I loved you. My shrink called it imprinting, like babies do on the first loving face they see. You were the only person who listened when I was going through a tough time. That you were pretty helped. I decided it was my job to make sure you didn't leave this earth before your time. On my worst nights, I was comforted to see you safe in your bed. When you were depressed and turned your face to the wall. I worried. Don't you understand—I'd do anything for a world with you still in it?"

The man moved his face so close to the woman she could count the stubbles on his chin. She pulled a blanket from the couch and draped it around her for extra protection.

An account of our night together. Max must have written it shortly after I left. All I had remembered was his anger, not his passion.

The man raised his hand in exasperation. The woman wondered if he were going to strike her. "So I read your computer files. I had you followed when you were in danger."

Outside a taxi honked as bodega owners closed metal coiling doors. The man talked so excitedly he didn't register the woman sliding her phone inside her sleeve in case she had to call 911.

"Someone hurt you so bad you closed your heart," the man said. "What if you flipped your script and saw my actions as protection rather than aggression? What if every word you write invites the lover you crave to cross your boundaries to storm your ramparts but they can't get there because your invitation is protected by a code they can't translate?

"In the hospital you moved a horse's head ever so carefully across the chess board. You let yourself relax. I saw you. A little girl in love with life dancing in tall grass.

His words influenced my next draft. I wrote and rewrote until I infused authentic emotion. A last quarter moon shone outside my bedroom window. My heart filled with tender feelings for the Max who pushed me to excel. I pictured him disappearing down subway stairs wreathed by a cloud of cigarette smoke. That he had been afflicted with a depression no medication could cure made me question God, if not hate him.

I slept hard. The next day was Saturday. Recalling Cyril's description of me as a carpenter, I worked hours perfecting every description and tightening every line of dialogue. When I finished, I sent the script to Max's friend.

Pictures of Max driving the Pennsylvania Turnpike, chain smoking and blasting metal music invaded my thoughts. Silence made him uncomfortable. His TV job suited his outgoing personality. Max traded his dream of playwriting for a writers' room camaraderie, meals shared, drinks poured. Bars were his church, a place he shared his stories, laughter a communal high.

Max's story needed telling. I would learn playwriting, complete his play about childhood after I finished our screenplay and sent it to his friend. Google revealed a playwriting workshop in Chicago. If I could learn screenwriting, I could tackle a stage play, a play to introduce Max Fletcher's talents.

A text from the producer's assistant informed me she would get back to me after they read my screenplay. Buoyed by a sense of completion, I revisited *Seesaw*. Years of disciplined writing while remodeling Aunt Katherine's house taught me how to swim in a current of unpredictable moods rolling through my days. I submitted the title story to a literary journal Eleanor recommended, then bundled my completed manuscript into a plain brown envelope and delivered it to her Fox River writing cabin. Fog shrouded trees in a fine mist. I knocked. Her cabin was dark and locked against intruders. I slipped my manuscript into her mailbox.

A month passed and then another. The euphoria of releasing my work—tough as sending a child to the first day of school—turned to sadness when I heard nothing. I kept my flagging spirits from derailing my progress by putting one foot in front of the other and walking into each day determined to achieve one small victory. Sometimes that meant extending time with a difficult child whose lack of initiative and constant complaints set my teeth on edge. Sometimes it meant rising before dawn to write, making my bed before I could slip back under the covers.

I stopped asking questions that had no answers.

Black snow mounded staff parking. Teachers and students slogged through unexpected snow showers until Spring Break, the last week of March. Cyril didn't appear. I was surprised how much I missed his hypomanic rants.

Cyril didn't answer my text appeal for a salon until the Sunday before school was to resume. He invited me to meet him at the Clairmont Café. Cardinals and finches called each other signaling spring even though temperatures refused to budge over forty degrees. I drove into town. Cyril was finishing a plate of bacon and eggs when I arrived. I slid into a red plastic booth.

He seemed agitated, his fingernails bit close. "Let me tell you a story before I go back on tour."

"You said you were done touring. Where are you going?"

He waved off my questions. "You asked about my inspiration for splenditude."

I wondered if he had forgotten what he told me. He seemed so hyped, I could not interrupt him.

The café was quiet. An older couple sat at the counter two stools down from a man reading *Clairmont Times* behind a cash register. Bacon and grease smells wafted through the restaurant, which hadn't been remodeled since the 1950s. Posted menus kept company with pictures of Elvis at various ages.

Cyril continued, "I didn't mention I took a tab of LSD. The sidewalks were crowded with sun-stunned faces. Flowers erupted. The world was being born again that afternoon, and I was privileged to see it."

A woman clad in purple spandex glided behind him, a white angora cat draped over her left shoulder. She was a female version of Cyril, with the same wiry blonde hair turning gray. Slight build with an extra twenty pounds—voluptuous, not fat. Smoky gray eyes. A scar starting an inch above her left eyebrow continued down her cheek like a lightning bolt. She wore a cascade of gold and silver necklaces against her freckled chest and a ring on every finger.

Penelope Long picked up Cyril's monologue. "Purple everywhere— a riot of wisteria and lilac. Purple calms and stimulates, fosters creativity, sparks imagination, doesn't it, Cyril?"

Cyril's face faded. He was as white as he was the day he lost Eli in the school basement.

"I'm sure Cyril told you he's leaving town with me. We're going on tour with his latest music." The woman grabbed my hand. "My name is Penelope."

I returned her smile.

"Get that cat out of here," the owner said.

"Some people are allergic to cats," an old lady said, eating a bite of pancake dripping with syrup.

"Miss Mims wants to join our tour," Penelope said. She winked at me.

Cyril removed the cat from her shoulder and carried it outside to a 1964 Chevy Impala parked in front. Penelope took his place at our table. She ordered jasmine tea and a plate of chocolate croissants. We dropped into conversation as if we were old friends. As she bit into flaky pastry, she confided she had dreamed of being a dancer, but didn't have the right build.

We watched Cyril rearrange duffel bags and instrument cases in the back seat of a vintage Impala. Miss Mims draped herself across the dashboard.

During a lull in conversation, Penelope asked, "Did Cyril tell you about me?"

"In the past tense," I said.

Penelope stretched like her cat. "Time to hit the road." She swept a tangle of hair from my face with her bejeweled fingers. "Oh honey, you have the face of an innocent child. You believe what men tell you."

I drove slowly up the gravel drive so as not to disturb a crew building a stone wall around my garden. Clem Varner was showing a worker a blueprint to protect roses against deer who munched them like snacks. My phone rang. A breathless voice announced herself as Chloe Tremaine, assistant to Ryan Sturbridge, the producer Max had recommended.

"We loved your script. You were a friend of Max Fletcher's? Such talent, gone too soon." She rattled on, telling me about how she had met Max at a network party. How funny he was. How utterly charming. Her long-winded story gave me time to park. Metal hitting stone jarred my thoughts. I went inside and closed the door.

Chloe was still talking. "Ryan is pitching a new channel hosting fresh romcom mixed with significant social issues." She listed current hits my idea resembled. I watched so little TV I had no reference point. "Your characters are perfect. Just a tiny bit of tweaking needed. Ryan can't wait to meet you."

"I can't travel until second semester is over," I said, mentally packing my bags for California.

"Don't worry. We'll Zoom."

Knowing it was bad form to ask how much a job paid, I waited until Chloe Tremaine said goodbye and googled TV writer salaries. I found figures of $100 to $150K first year, $250 to $300K second year, depending on how many episodes I wrote.

A meeting invite appeared in my inbox. Zoom was a computer app.

I considered soliciting Eleanor Graham's opinion. Her first novella had been made into a film, which won prizes on festival circuits.

The next day, a student who volunteered in the tech center explained Zoom and installed it on my laptop. He spoke slowly and carefully as if I were a child. I rushed home. My hair was a fright. Jason had warned Zoom magnified stray hairs and wrinkles.

A woman with a cascade of blonde highlighted hair, closer in age to my students appeared in a box at the appointed time. "I'm Chloe Tremaine. Great to meet you. Ryan's on another call. He'll be right with us."

Zoom added ten years. An errant hair sprang from my crown. Looking at the screen, I realized I was smoothing the wrong side of my head.

A square-jawed earnest type appeared in a third box labeled Ryan Sturbridge. "Impressed with your work," he said. "Kat told you we're seeking a script that will humanize bipolar disorder." As Ryan outlined his idea for character development, I got an idea he wanted the female character to be twenty years younger, more madcap than manic. Max would be portrayed as brooding and romantic, not suicidal.

Kat interrupted. "Evan Trower is interested in playing Max."

I Googled Trower, lead singer from a popular boy band. "I didn't know he acted," I said.

"Picture a pop star's break-out theatrical role," Kat said. "Trower's fans will lose their minds."

Max's desire I tell the truth ran through my mind. I cleared my throat. "If I could expand on the characters."

Clem's crew yelled to each other as they shut down, pickups honking as they left the property.

Did I really look so old, or was it a trick of Zoom? I relaxed the rigid set of my jaw. "Bipolar people are stereotyped as misunderstood loners, or worse, serial killers," I said. "Almost always cast as villains. I was trying to show variations on the spectrum. How a person you work alongside every day may be struggling and you never know it. They call autism a spectrum. Mood swings are also a spectrum disorder."

Ryan shook his head sympathetically. "Totally get you. My great uncle was probably bipolar. Fascinating man—an air force veteran. He made a fortune in the stock market, lost everything. Suffered a nervous breakdown. After a long hospitalization, he recuperated and made a second fortune in real estate. When his second wife filed for divorce, he started flying alone. Crashed his Cessna into the side of a mountain at dusk. His family never knew if it was an accident or intentional. Looking back, he exhibited symptoms—he'd be life of the party then go for weeks without being in touch with anyone. Mental illness was stigmatized. Doctors didn't have knowledge we have now."

Kat unmuted herself. "The Max character dying as he did was a real downer," she said. "Remember, an audience wants to leave the theater uplifted."

Ryan nodded. "Send us a version where Max lives and meets the woman of his dreams. If we do this right, we can make real money."

Stomach sinking, I hit *leave meeting*. I wasn't sure Kat and Ryan understood my script. Maybe they hadn't read the whole thing. Still, real money would be nice. I had never had more than enough to meet expenses. I pictured myself with money to burn—a new car, a writer's conference in Greece, an in-ground pool instead of driving two towns over to a YMCA.

Selling my script meant letting someone else fiddle with my ideas. My discussion with Max in his apartment came flooding back. He had been flying high, fueled by whiskey and brain chemicals. "Tell the truth," he had said over and over, his words an admonition from God himself.

My body and brain needed an endorphin surge. I headed for the YMCA pool. Chlorine stung my eyes through fogged goggles. I struggled to complete ten laps. Usually, I swam twenty. Tired, I rested as my heart synced back to a normal rhythm. Swim team members burst from the locker room for practice, laughing and shouting. As I pulled myself onto the deck, my body shuddered with relief. The locker room was empty. I stood under a hot shower until my skin puckered.

SEVENTEEN

AN ENVELOPE WAS TAPED TO THE FRONT DOOR OF MY house. Inside was a note in elegant cursive from Eleanor Graham. Texting was not her style. She would have used smoke signals if she could. "Come see me," the note said. "I have good news."

Late afternoon sun poured through fluttering cottonwood trees lining the riverbank. I knocked.

"Come in," Eleanor said. Inside her cabin, a tart smell of lime and juniper berries permeated. She sat at her writing desk, sipping from a frosted glass.

Unable to contain my excitement, I described meeting the producer and asked what she thought.

She poured herself a fresh drink. "A director I idolized made 'Crawling Home' into a short film."

"How exciting," I said.

A redwing blackbird flew by, its call a drilling sound. Eleanor's mouth tightened around the lip of her glass revealing fine deep lines. "If you've read my work, you know my characters rarely feel good. *Crawling Home*, the movie, although praised on its own merits, didn't follow my short story. A positive benefit was being hired as keynote speaker at the Taos Writers Conference, among others. You should apply."

"Why would they hire me?"

"That new lit magazine I told you about selected your opening story from *Seesaw*. Their editor told me it will be featured in the first issue. I sent your complete manuscript to my agent. Hope you don't mind."

I had expected Eleanor to be excited about the prospect of my writing for TV. A deep fatigue that had been plaguing me pressed against my chest. As I followed the path, my heart felt like an unseen fist was squeezing it.

I fell asleep on the couch, afraid insomnia waited in my bed. A terrible headache awakened me after midnight. My jaw clenched tight, I could hardly open it to sip water. Pain trailed down my left arm. Worry kept me awake. A minute after his office opened, I called my internist. His nurse said there was nothing they could do in the office. "Go straight to the emergency room," she said. "Don't drive yourself."

I stuffed my bathrobe and a change of clothes into my gym bag and added laptop, journal, and a new manuscript I had been working on. Not wanting to spend money on an Uber, I drove myself to the hospital.

An emergency room nurse took my blood pressure several times. Ambulance crews arrived, obscuring her words. I couldn't understand if something was wrong with their equipment or with me. I lay helpless, awaiting a cardiologist. He appeared before my bed, his white lab coat paling in fluorescent glare. "I ordered an electrocardiogram. Then we'll discuss next steps." An orderly wheeled me into the elevator to take me for tests.

Five minutes or hours later, I couldn't tell, the cardiologist reappeared, trailed by the nurse I met originally and two CNAs who lifted me onto a gurney. "You're at risk for a heart attack. Ninetieth percentile." Addressing the nurse, he said, "Schedule an angiogram."

Something was wrong with my heart, not in a metaphorical way.

An older nurse, brisk and efficient, wheeled me to the cardiac floor. She settled me in my room and gave me a preview of the angiogram. I signed a waiver for the surgeon to implant stents if necessary. I could barely listen, amazed by how fast everything was moving. "The doctor will insert a tiny, flexible plastic tube called a catheter through an artery in your groin. I'll help you prepare."

My room was situated at the far end of the hall. Time alone allowed me to wonder how I had landed in the cardiac ward. I had been exercising and eating right since I moved into Aunt Katherine's house. My blood pressure had never been high. I had quit smoking twenty years ago.

Looking back, I realized my pains were not new. The first time my chest seized, I blamed it on rereading *Jane Eyre*. Pain trailing down my left arm was a physical manifestation of my overly romantic outlook, my yearning for impossible loves like Mr. Rochester. I didn't call my doctor when pain returned a second and third time.

I hadn't started taking care of myself until middle age. My extended youth was a series of weekends touring every bar in the city. A certain spring night danced around memory's edge. My heart was flying not fluttering as I embraced the city from the back seat of Nikki's Honda Civic. Spring had been buried under piles of cranky black snow buttressing parking lots. The minute snow melted, the word spread to every suburban teenager. *Time to go downtown.*

When I was nineteen, love was a gimlet cold in the flask, a tang of Rose's Lime Juice, a blush of Grenadine, a scorch of vodka traveling my throat as we flew down the expressway to celebrate the rites of spring.

Spring was a kiss on the back of my neck, a warm breeze traveling wide-open windows of Nikki's hatchback, as we joined pleasure-seekers exiting east on Ohio, north on Rush Street, honking horns swelling the chorus. City lights blinked to reveal a sea of partygoers crowding Rush Street: Butch McGuires, The Lodge Tavern, She-nanigans. Popular spots gave a nod to the ghost of Mister Kelly's Chicago, where our parents had met Frank Sinatra and Lenny Bruce.

Bar stools stocked with cute boys separated us from our friends to dance ourselves limp. Music was in the room, not shimmying through an ear bud. Music opened us petal by petal to the first warm night of spring. No matter where our adventures took us, even if we drove alone, the music rode shotgun, jazz blue if we were sad, or pound your head on the dashboard orange.

After 2:00 a.m., memories blurred. Closing time shots propelled us not to give in to soft beds and waiting parents. Nikki drove west. We stopped at a bar with a handwritten cardboard sign taped to the window: *Sorry We're Open.* A 4:00 a.m. license to speak in tongues to whoever would listen. A lone man leaning against the bar laughed when I said, "The meek won't inherit the earth, the Irish will." He said something I hoped was funny.

I leaned my head back and laughed. Nikki gave me a warning glance. "You will forgive anyone who makes you laugh," she said.

At closing time, the man asked me to step outside. Nikki warned if I didn't leave with her, I would never find my way. I waved goodbye. The man led me around a corner to a building with no address. We entered through an overhead garage door and lay down on a rusty mattress. A cold breeze blew over my exposed back. The man whose name I had already forgotten drew me toward my pleasure. It might have been the best night of my life, but I had no way of knowing. My spirit wandered in gasoline smelling air and escaped through a cracked skylight.

After the petit mort, we shared a cigarette, a catch in our throats suspending time. Death, I'll catch up with you later. Now I need to find my way home.

A CNA entered my room without illuminating overhead lights. In a halo of light, she entered data on my computer chart, approached me to take my vitals, her dark eyes wide with fatigue. I asked her to open blinds so I could watch an orange sunrise. A lightening sky illuminated a retention pond muddy with last night's rain.

The CNA slid a blood pressure cuff on my upper arm. Feeling the need to say something, I said, "Going to be a sunny day."

The cuff tightened as she checked my oxygen level. With a voice low and guttural, she said, "I prefer the rain."

Dispirited by my lack of control over my life, I lay in my hospital bed in a limbo of waiting. A nurse informed me an emergency was preempting my scheduled procedure. To pass time, I edited manuscript pages I had stuck in my purse while monitoring a conversation taking place across the hall.

A man I estimated to be in his eighties from the timbre of his voice, comforted his wife. I edited my manuscript, tuning into their conversation when a nurse entered their room. "You signed a DNR with selective treatment. You understand we will not perform CPR."

"I understand," the woman said. Her voice broke.

Real life, I thought, not rearranging words on a page.

A surgical tech, all banter and efficiency, wheeled me to Cardiac Catheterization. My surgeon introduced himself and then moved in front of a big screen to confer with nurses and techs. My angiogram revealed one artery was completely blocked and two others were partially blocked. A nurse reminded me I had signed a waiver to implant stents if necessary.

Sedated, my eyes closed. Three stents were implanted. The surgeon smiled as he visited me after the procedure, but I couldn't follow his rapid explanations. I was wheeled into Recovery and told I would have to lie still for four hours. A nurse monitored data on a computer screen above my head. An IV steadily pumped saline solution. A nurse provided a bedpan when I signaled. Staff conversed in streams of sentences humming over my head.

Back in my room, I wanted to use the bathroom by myself. I swung my legs over the side of the bed, tripping an alarm. Staff came running. The gray-haired nurse I loved sent the others away. "I'll show you how you can deactivate the bed alarm." A bit of agency made me feel like a human being again.

The nurse handed me a menu card. "Let me know what you want," she said. "You probably haven't eaten since yesterday."

"Thank you for taking care of me," I said.

She folded my clothes and placed my duffel bag in a cabinet. "My job has allowed me to meet so many interesting people. I was a nurse during the AIDS crisis." I waited for her to elaborate, but she had moved to the computer, typed some numbers, and disappeared down the hall.

Nothing interested me on TV, so I shut it off and slept. When I awoke, I got out of bed, parted the curtains. I thought I could make out the sound of horses neighing as they left their stalls at a farm adjoining the hospital property. My stomach was hollow from not eating for forty-eight hours. I ordered breakfast. An hour before a doctor discharged me, I was dressed.

Shifts had changed. I was unable to thank the veteran nurse who had helped me. I found my car in the parking lot and unlocked it. The seat was warm. Heat and a cocktail of new medications swirling through my system made me dizzy. My new life awaited. I drove carefully.

Cardiac rehab followed. Three months, three times a week, I exercised while wearing a heart monitor. Nurses and physical therapists monitored patients, all men, from a long desk equipped with computers. Every session, a nurse asked if I was depressed. The men joked with each other as they rode exercise bikes at a slow pace. I worked hard on elliptical and treadmill, determined to strengthen my heart.

Some days, I had more energy than others. Getting used to multiple medications was tough. Gradually I got stronger. Before stents were implanted, I could barely circle the block. Two months later, I was able to visit a stand of cottonwoods across from a golf course a mile away.

On my way for my last rehab session, I hit every stoplight. Across the street was a horse farm I had seen from my hospital room. During my last session, a physical therapist showed me how to incorporate weights into my routine.

Nurses congratulated me as I detached my heart monitor the last time. As I pulled from the parking lot, my phone dinged with a text from Ryan Sturbridge. I pulled into the horse farm to read it. Ryan wanted to know if I had completed my revision. He was eager to read it.

A roan mare nuzzled its offspring. Cornfields extended toward a horizon drenched in golden autumn light. The chaotic months leading up to my surgery were followed by an unwelcome silence, giving me time to think. Of my allotted hours, I had spent more time than was reasonable thinking about Max, a man I hardly knew. I had made him a vessel for all the love and longing I had left.

After surgery and rehab, the movie idea seemed from another lifetime, or someone else's life. *Wonderful meeting you*, I texted back. *Taking my project in a different direction.*

"Tell the truth," Max said. The truth was I had my illness to thank for an angle of vision that revealed beauty in unlikely places. To welcome the bare branches of winter, to see a particular signature of willow and oak. To walk in brisk winds and thank cold rain for making me feel alive.

The truth was a set of genes gifted at birth no amount of right thinking and clean living could normalize. Popular writers righted the world with happy endings. Love came early or late to everyone singers sang. Love was complicated by characters living inside me, who showed up elated or despondent at the breakfast table, depending on how they'd slept. Who could blame a weary suitor for preferring a predictable mate? Love was a puzzle piece, never the whole picture.

The truth was the chemicals produced an uneven swirl of good days and bad, never predictable, never meted out in perfect measure. Good days I couldn't take my foot off the accelerator. On bad days, I had to claw my way out of a slippery pit.

A red light made me stop short. Perhaps my method of telling the truth did not appeal to modern movie goers. Changes were needed, or a different approach altogether. As the light changed, I lurched forward. I had no one to blame but myself for the condition of my battered heart. That I loved Max I had no doubt, I had been powerless to resist his need. His love had found an entry through a crack in my heart.

EIGHTEEN

Clairmont, Illinois

May 2011

STUDENTS LEFT THE SHIELD ROOM AS SOON AS THE LAST bell sounded. My purse was stuffed with mementos from Teacher Appreciation Week: Starbucks cards and handwritten notes, a bouquet of lilacs picked from a student's garden. A mixture of happiness for warm months and a reluctance to leave my routine and colleagues made me linger at my desk, sorting supplies. Summer beckoned, days when time would stretch and expand, leaving errant moods space for mischief.

Instead of driving straight home, I stopped at a nursery to buy flowers. My plan was to create hanging baskets for my front porch. A young man helped me pack my trunk with flats of purple and pink impatiens.

My phone rang. Digging it out of my pocket, I started. Caller ID showed Max Fletcher. For a crazy moment, I thought he was alive.

"Hello," I said.

"Hello," a female voice said. "My name is Celeste Fletcher, Max Fletcher's mother. Do you have a moment?" An east coast accent featured long 'a' and 'o' sounds and clipped 'r's.' Her delivery was unhurried and sure, as if Celeste Fletcher were accustomed to getting what she wanted.

"Sure," I said. "How can I help?" My voice was full of Midwestern friendliness. I stood in front of my open trunk, surveying the faces of red, yellow, and orange marigolds nestled in flats surrounded by newspaper.

"I'm calling you from Max's phone. Your address was in his GPS the day of the accident. Did a little detective work on Google to determine where Max was headed. Am I speaking to Deirdre Collins of Clairmont, Illinois?"

"Yes."

"My husband and I are settling my son's affairs. Max had written you a check numbered 382. We wanted to let you know there are no funds in his account. His ex-wife cleaned him out."

"No worries," I said. An urge to protect Max even after his death persisted. "I use his check as a bookmark."

Celeste harrumphed. "How did you know Max, if you don't mind my asking?"

"We met in Albuquerque many years ago," I said.

Silence on the other end lasted so long, I thought Celeste had hung up.

"He told me about you," Celeste said. "Said you saved his life in the hospital."

"It was a difficult time," I said. "We shared stories."

"Even as a little boy, Max told imaginative stories."

"He told me he had two mothers, his biological mother and the college roommate who raised him. Which one are you?"

The nursery lot was filling with flower enthusiasts and would-be gardeners. I moved inside an outbuilding housing row after row of multicolored impatiens. Freshly watered, the flowers emanated a warm damp smell of life returning to the earth.

A bark of a laugh came from Celeste's end. "As I said, Max had a lively imagination. My husband and I insisted he differentiate between story and lie. I was his only mother. His childhood was quite ordinary—a house in the suburbs, an adoring younger brother, a good education. He told me you were writing partners."

"Yes," I said. "We were collaborating on a screenplay about mental illness."

"Telling stories was how Max explained his life to himself," Celeste said. "He was always searching for a reason for his highs and lows, why they set him apart."

"He sent me a play he was writing. I was thinking of completing it, producing it under both our names. There's a wonderful childhood scene where he buys airplanes for his friends."

Celeste laughed again, a more relaxed genuine laugh. "When he turned ten, Max spent his birthday money buying remote control planes. I was inside frosting his birthday cake. He led his friends out the back gate. When my husband and I finally tracked him to a local park, he was leading his friends up a hill. We let them go. Even though I was upset with him for spending all his birthday money, the sight of ten planes circling Mt. Hollyhock was stirring."

"Sounds like the Pied Piper," I said. A nursery employee watered plants with a long hose. I returned to my car.

"Why was he coming to see you?" Celeste asked. She hadn't mentioned the lawsuit I had filed against Max, so I decided not to bring it up.

"I had no knowledge of his visit. As I said, we were collaborating on a screenplay."

A family of four rolled a trolley filled with hanging baskets across the parking lot, steel wheels on asphalt obscuring Celeste's voice. I opened the door and sat in my warm car.

"I asked if you loved Max, if you were having an affair," Celeste said. "You are twenty years older, but Max's lack of boundaries often got him in trouble."

"I loved him," I said. "We didn't have an affair, more a writerly friendship. Reading a person's work is like exploring secret passageways in their brain."

Satisfied with my response, Celeste thanked me for my time. "Let me know if you finish Max's play. I'd love to read it."

Driving home, I reviewed my conversation with Celeste Fletcher. Her remarks about her son were tied too neatly, eliminating any untidy details. A dusky golden light drenched the trees lining the approach to Aunt Katherine's house. I transferred flower flats to the shed and went inside to forage for dinner. I made aglio e olio pasta tossed with broccoli.

A loud knock and a crying child startled me as I threw cooked noodles in a colander.

Eleanor pushed Alice into the house. "Can you take her tonight? I'm on deadline. Can't write with her in the house."

My first reaction was irritation. Eleanor assumed I was at her disposal. Alice tapped my knee and offered me a jonquil picked from my garden. A sweet smell almost cloying overspread the room. Alice's winsome expression, eyes blue and wide, won me over.

"Here's her bag," Eleanor said. "I'll be back late morning."

Alice moved near the window to watch Eleanor drive away. I heaped Alice's salad plate with pasta and gave her a spoonful of Parmesan, distracting her with questions about school. Between bites, she told me about singing circle, her favorite activity.

A sketchbook and a pack of colored pens sat on my writing table. I had planned to spend the evening noodling a new project.

"Can I look?" Alice asked. She examined everything on my writing desk: journals, books, finger paints, and brushes. She was gentle with an antique inkwell, picking it up and putting it down softly. Alice pointed toward a pile of paper, ran her fingers over blank pages. She was a beautiful child, pink-skinned as a pre-Raphaelite angel. Flaxen hair trailed down her back.

I stapled together ten sheets of paper. "Would you like to write a book, Alice?"

She nodded. I settled her at a coffee table. Alice chose sea green and laser lemon crayons and created a spring scene. The child was so quiet, I was able to read Max's screenplay critique.

Before bed, Alice read me her book. Alice's book was about a fairy princess named Gwendolyn who loved the first day of spring. She loved rain and ducks splashing in a pond dotted with lily pads.

"Beautiful," I said.

"Gwendolyn only likes spring," Alice said. "She rides her magic bike from town to town all over the world where every day is spring."

My adult brain considered if it were possible to live in eternal spring. Alice was already turning a page where snowdrops, crocus, daffodils, hyacinth, and tulips grew, flowers from her grandmother's garden. Alice's drawings were a miracle, a riot of color produced from a box of Crayons. "Can I sleep in your special bed?" Alice asked.

We climbed upstairs to Aunt Katherine's guest room with that four-poster bed I had slept in as a child. Alice put on a nightgown from her overnight bag. She slipped under a handmade quilt stitched with violets. She sank into sleep, listening to frogs chorusing from the pond.

I returned to my writing desk. At the suggestion of Clairmont High's drama teacher, I had applied to a summer playwright's workshop at Harold Washington Library Center with the idea of finishing Max's play about his mother.

Poems and prose snippets he supplied helped me piece together his suburban childhood—complete with a loving mother, a father away on business trips and late meetings, a younger brother he taught to play base-ball and his mother's friend who attended school plays. The same woman appeared when six-year-old Max visited a state park with his parents. The woman argued with his mother, then drove away, never to reappear.

I found a folder marked "State Park" and read: *We drove through stands of cedar and spruce stretching forever. Dad parked at a scenic overlook.*

The woman they called Francine, who sometimes attended my baseball games stood talking to my mom, smoked. As a child, I didn't question why this woman appeared where we parked. What seemed strange was she was wearing a business suit and high heels. A trail of cigarette butts led from the car to where she stood. In profile her jaw jutted severely as a bare mountain ledge.

'I couldn't,' I heard her say. 'My work consumes all my time.'

I was six years old. My legs trembled from sitting so long. I asked permission to run the trail. A white flower poked its head from a rock pile. I looked back at my parents. Mom held out her hands. Unsmiling, Francine shook her head. Why, I wondered. I picked a flower. Women liked flowers. I ran back and offered it to Francine. She took it from my sweaty palm, took a last drag from her cigarette. As she opened her car door, she dropped my flower next to the butt and crushed it with the heel of her spiky black shoe.

Details of this story synced with *Downtime*. Seeing through a six-year-old's eyes made the story so poignant, I wasn't convinced it wasn't true.

The next morning, Eleanor returned pale and shaky. I steadied her as she lumbered over the doorsill. Her hand trembled as she dropped her purse. She smelled of soap and shampoo. A paper fell. She picked it up and handed it to me. Once I made out *pancreatic cancer*, I didn't read the rest. She sank into an overstuffed chair.

Alice ran into the room. She sat on a hassock at her grandmother's feet. "Look what I made, Grammie," she said, offering Eleanor stapled pages she had decorated with pictures of yellow jonquils and pink tulips.

"Love your sense of color, Alice." Eleanor thumbed through her book. "You are an artist."

"Looks like Alice inherited your creativity," I said.

"Hopefully without the demons."

Eleanor Graham's unmistakable writing style possessed a lyricism and wit all her own. Her personal style changed, depending on how she did her makeup and hair. The first time I'd met her, she'd appeared uncluttered and mannish. A Google search showed other incarnations. Hair dyed auburn, wearing a white shirt with a black jacket, she looked like a middle manager. In another photo, gray strands, healthy as weeds, sprouted in her black hair. Frosted highlights a year later an attempt at a WASPy look. In profile, her strong nose and softening jaw suggested a Mediterranean strain of Italian or Greek, a peasant raising a spatula over a lazy man's head.

Shoulders slouched, Eleanor stood. Defeated and diminished, her pants were wrinkled as if she had slept in them. More alarming was her jaundiced complexion, staring eyes, and hollow cheeks. Why hadn't I recognized her illness encroaching?

Next to Max's book lay Eleanor's latest novel. The difference between the swagger of her back cover picture and the living Eleanor was shocking.

By contrast, Alice was growing into girlhood, her skin pearlescent, baby face morphing into beauty—feline green eyes framed by thick brows. Alice's smile was inviting yet warned she was keeping secrets. Eleanor regarded Alice.

Legs crossed, book cradled in the crook of her knee, unblemished except for a diagonal scrape. A bedspread doubling as a cape draped over her thin shoulders, the child's breathy words danced like freed puppets. I detected a series of micro-expressions passing over her grandmother's face: pride, wonder, curiosity, envy.

Crawling into Eleanor's lap, Alice closed her grandmother's yellowed hand over a tulip stem. "Thank you, Alice," Eleanor said. "Do you want to see Daddy? Get your bag."

Alice ran upstairs, singing.

"She's a beautiful child," I said. "Spent last evening working on her book. She read me a bedtime story. Did you finish your article?"

Uncrossing her legs, Eleanor leaned forward. "There was no article," she said. "I didn't want Alice to see me cry. Look, Deirdre, my time is short."

Tears pricked my eyelids.

Eleanor shook her head. "Have you read C. S. Lewis? His version of heaven is 'forests and green slopes and sweet orchards and flashing waterfalls.'"

"Lovely," I said. "Hope I see you there. Your books will live after you," I said.

"I need you to help me build a temple."

Images of crumbled New Mexican churches floated in my mind. I turned my face so Eleanor couldn't sense my thoughts. Writer that she was, she read my face as if I were a character she was creating on the page. "Not with bricks or boards. The point is, I don't want my granddaughter remembering me as a crabby old lady. I'd like to endow a line of children's books inspired by Alice. Can you help?"

Alice returned with her overnight bag slung over her shoulder.

"Of course," I said. I placed my hand on Eleanor's shoulder. A tremor traveled down her arm to her fingers.

"By the way," she said, "my agent likes *Seesaw*. You'll hear from her soon."

Happiness overtook me, although God's timing perplexed me. If only this news had come when Eleanor was still well.

To allay my sorrow over Eleanor Graham's diagnosis, I offered to watch Alice during chemotherapy days so Spencer and his wife could work.

Alice created five new books and left them at the elementary school playground and in Little Free Libraries around Clairmont. We walked to Eleanor's writing cabin, thinking we would leave one for her.

Eleanor was sitting in her Adirondack chair when we arrived. She motioned Alice to join her. "I'm working on short stories instead of the novel I had planned." She winked at me. Short stories in case she ran out of time. Eleanor's energy was more vibrant than last time we'd visited, although her complexion remained sallow.

My family was visiting from Colorado for Easter. Mom, Kevin, his wife, his two children. I set my writing aside while I cleaned house and planned a menu.

Clairmont Bakery made decorated sugar cookies from an old German recipe. Thinking Kevin's kids would like them, I stopped while I was in town.

Across the street was a new beauty shop. I crossed to take a look. Sitting in the window was Benjamin Babcock's mother giving a woman a manicure. Deb's hair was cut in a stylish bob. She spoke animatedly to her customer. A year ago, she had been living in a motel and working at the laundromat. Benjamin told me his family was renting a small house with a yard.

A table was set in the garden covered by Aunt Katherine's linen tablecloth appliqued with spring flowers. Lemonade and wine spritzers chilled in crystal pitchers. My brother Kevin filled a cooler with his favorite beer. His children, ten-year-old Grace and a five-year-old Gabe, played bocce ball. They spent a good ten minutes establishing rules, reminding me of how my brother and I played.

We toured the house. I showed Kevin how Clem Varner's crew had replaced antiquated plumbing and lighting. We ended outside. A workman had added a waterfall to the garden pool.

Kevin examined the workmanship. "We drove past the house where we grew up, driving from the airport," he said. "You wouldn't recognize our old block. The prairie is gone, of course. Houses have changed. Our neighbor's ranch homes have been torn down and replaced with country French-style and Victorians. Bloated structures on tiny yards. You have to move farther and farther from the city to feel land beneath your feet." He draped his arm over my shoulder. "Like you did. You've built Aunt Katherine's summer place into a real home. Mom and I worried about you floundering here on your own," Kevin said. "That we'd have to pick up the pieces."

A flash of anger blazed in my chest. Kevin expected me to fail? What did he know about my life? Except for holiday check-ins, we hadn't talked regularly since his Colorado move.

I walked inside, climbed upstairs to compose myself in the guest bathroom. I calmed my chest pains with a round of deep breaths.

When I returned, Kevin was leaving my writing shed with a can of bug repellent. He gave me a look I couldn't decipher. "What's for dessert?" he asked. I carried a chocolate cake made from Aunt Katherine's recipe to the table.

Mom approached, balancing on a multicolored cane decorated with butterflies. "Kevin's birthday is next week. Since we can't celebrate together, I brought you an early present."

"What is it?" he asked.

"The National Weather Service report filed the day you were born." Mom nibbled at her cake. "Deirdre was a winter baby. That's why she thrives in quiet and cold and snow. God tipped his watering can on its side the June day Kevin was born. Everyone's basement flooded."

"I wore my yellow slicker to school," I said.

Mom nodded. "Deirdre was so excited her baby brother had finally arrived, she danced in the backyard. Grandpa said you refused to come inside. Ruined your favorite dress. Luckily, I saved a picture."

A faded photograph fell. I picked it from the grass. A girl in white eyelet, tiny against a cloudless sky. Prairie wind ruffling grass, red hair flying. Little D, the girl who rollerskated and bicycled through my dreams.

When my family left for O'Hare, I collected plates and cups. After disposing of the remains of dinner, I took a lamp into my writing shed and taped the picture of Little D to my laptop, smiling at her thin arms, scraped knees, feet shod in lacy socks and black patent Mary Janes.

My phone rang. It was Kevin.

"Are you okay?" I asked. "The kids?"

"Flight was delayed. Look, I scanned your book when I was searching your writing shed for bug repellent." I hadn't intended for him to read what I wrote. "Dad was the smartest man I ever knew. You didn't write about his epilepsy."

"He wanted people to see him as a person, not a diagnosis."

"You had a bad dream about him throwing his pills in the flower beds. It wasn't a dream, Deirdre. Mom and I hauled him inside before he woke the neighbors. Can you understand I wanted a normal childhood, a dad who played golf?"

"Guess I never looked at it from your side."

"You were a pair. He tried to control his anger taking long walks, out half the night wandering the neighborhood. Then you started doing the same. He sat up, Johnny Carson mute on the TV, awaiting the click of your key to know you were safe. I was jealous of how close you were."

The first day of school every year Dad sang outside my bedroom door: *School days, school days, dear old golden rule days.* He left the bathroom warm and smelling of shaving cream.

Thunder rumbled. I opened the writing shed door and stood in humid, electrically charged air.

"You and I had good times baking together when Mom and Dad were out. Eating a pan of brownies together, watching a late movie."

The Denver flight was called. "Gotta go," Kevin said. "Don't write only the sad bits."

Rain came in soft droplets, widening in concentric circles, followed by a sharp downpour. I took shelter inside my writing shed. My dream journal sat square in the middle of my desk. I picked it up and read, amazed I didn't recognize my younger self. Too tired from a day in the sun to go inside, I rested my head on my arms and fell into a doze.

At sunrise, a woodpecker drilling a black maple tree awoke me. Finches trilled at the feeder. I rose from my desk to open the door. A line of sandhill cranes flew in pure blue sky crimped by cumulus clouds. It was a perfect June day.

Kevin had forgotten his weather report. I taped it next to a picture of my six-year-old self, dancing on the prairie.

NINETEEN

ALBUQUERQUE INTERNATIONAL SUNPORT WAS MELLOW and welcoming, compared to O'Hare's frenetic pace. Silversmiths sold earrings at turquoise-colored kiosks. Stepping outside to the car rental, the dry aromatic scent of pinyon trees threaded through dry blue air, its own particular shade of blue.

Eleanor Graham had been kind enough to blurb *Seesaw.* As her critiques had been merciless, I was touched when she called my novel "important work."

Publication led to an invitation to speak at the Taos Writer's Conference, booked at The Sagebrush Inn and Suites. The same hotel I'd stayed with Mom. Check-in wasn't until late afternoon. I decided to take the High Road.

In Espanola, I followed signs from Paseo De Onate to NM-76 toward Chimayo, where I visited a two-hundred-year-old church. New gift shops had been built since my last visit. The centuries- old sanctuary had not changed. I sank onto a wooden kneeler, making the sign of the cross, thanking God for His blessings. Not always ones I would have chosen.

After a lunch of posole and homemade tortillas, I drove north. The High Road to Truchas rose 8,000 feet above sea level. I arrived in a world untouched by time. A sign advertising a sculpture gallery pointed up a steep gravel drive where a rooster crowed from a yard filled with rusted farm implements.

The gallery was open. Light-filled spaces hung with mountain scenes, wooden planks displaying animal sculptures. I picked up a tiny bear. "Is that the one you like?" a voice behind me asked. I recognized the artist from a picture over the register. "Where are you headed?" he asked.

"A writer's conference in Taos." The artist was so welcoming, I continued, "Pretty nervous about the speech I'm giving. Looking at your paintings is calming."

"Do you think writing is something you can teach?" the artist asked. We faced a floor-to-ceiling window, the sky a pastel wash of blue, pink, and gold. "Who taught Shakespeare to write?" he asked. I paid for my tiny bear and put it in my purse. As I headed toward my car, the sculptor said, "Don't shorten your life with worry. Enjoy yourself."

Outside Chamisal, I took a picture of a barn collapsing into earth. My route continued through tiny towns called Picuris Pueblo and Penasco. The sculptor was right. In such a landscape, humanity's efforts to build and endure had been overshadowed by the land's indifference.

After checking into the Sagebrush Hotel, I dropped my bag in my room.

My speech notes were in my suitcase. I reviewed them before dinner. I lay on my bed and stared at a wooden beam ceiling. Upholstered furniture in an earthy color palette mimicked miles of high desert surrounding Taos.

My speech was targeted to a younger version of myself, sitting on a folding chair surrounded by hopeful writers. As I read, my words struck me as false. All I had done was recycle bits of information I'd gleaned from conferences and workshops.

The satisfaction of writing was hours spent alone learning craft. Waking early when the world was quiet to write and revise. I shredded what I had written and went downstairs.

Two young men holding drinks introduced themselves as Paul Sloan and Matt Hernandez. "You have the look of a writer," Paul said.

I laughed. "How can you tell?"

"Maybe those pages bulging from your purse," Matt said. "Have a drink with us."

We talked about books we were writing and our favorite authors until it was time for dinner. Paul was writing fantasy while Matt was drawn to horror. They listened carefully while I described *Seesaw*, and they asked follow-up questions. What we had in common was our love of reading. They suggested I join their digital co-write, a weekly Zoom meeting where we could write together. My speech needed to celebrate love affairs with writers who had reached me through stories they spun. How each generation continued a dialogue with those who had gone on.

Craft lectures were held at 10:00 a.m. A University of New Mexico professor spoke about D. H. Lawrence, who was buried at a ranch twenty miles outside Taos.

My speech was scheduled before lunch. Surveying the audience, I saw Paul and Matt. I was among friends.

I took a deep breath and began. "We're here because we love books.. I'm paying tribute to my first grade teacher. She taught me to read; the best thing that ever happened to me.

"Miss Johnson was tall and slender, wearing a floral print blouse tucked into a dark skirt. Smiling as she welcomed us to her room, she showed us a rectangular table arranged with copies of Dick, Jane, and Spot. As a first grader, I heard other kids making fun of them, but I loved the readers, my brightly colored, new-found friends. When I finished them, I was determined not to go home for a whole weekend without a new book. I was shy, taught never to interrupt. I tugged Miss Johnson's skirt and pointed at books stacked high. I told her I read every book.

"Our music teacher, Miss Finch, supervised singing circle," Matt continued. "I watched Miss Johnson walk outside and unlock her bicycle. 'Miss Johnson will check out books for you from our town library.' Miss Finch rested her hand on my shoulder. 'Take a seat.'

"To my first-grade self, joy was a teacher riding a bike, skirt tucked to keep it from getting stuck in the spikes of her wheel. The wonderful bike she rode to work. My child-self didn't know how much a car cost or that my teacher had thirty minutes for lunch. She flew past prairie lots turning grasshopper green, gutters singing with last night's rain. I never knew whether she changed her name from Miss to Mrs. or how many children she taught or if she served breakfast cereal. All I knew was she returned with three new books for me to read. I ran home with their brightly colored spines bumping my thin chest. I read while I crumbled saltine crackers in a bowl of tomato soup.

"Miss Johnson gave me a passport to a lifetime of reading: before sleep, on the train, in waiting rooms and in hospital beds. Never alone, heaven was any hour I opened a book. Portals to worlds where I could fly freeways with Raymond Chandler's fast boys, make strange pilgrimages with Haruki Murakami, or do laundry with Lucia Berlin and an Indian chief. Time travel with Carlos Ruiz Zafon in a misty Barcelona library."

After closing remarks and a faculty reading, I joined Matt and Paul on the patio for a parting drink. An agent in her early twenties from William Morris Endeavor who had talked about querying joined us. "What are you working on?" she asked.

"A story about two bipolar patients who meet while hospitalized. They forge a friendship over their shared experience and decide to collaborate writing a screenplay."

The agent put a business card in my hand. "Send me your manuscript," she said.

Hiding my impulse to celebrate, I shook her hand and thanked her.

The day was so fine driving south, I was reluctant to leave New Mexico. At Espanola, I stopped for lunch. While eating chips and salsa, my eyes drifted toward a muted television tuned to CNN. Occupy Wall Street protestors gathered around a stage in Lower Manhattan. New Mexico with its vast spaces and slow pace was a world away.

I was about to look away when a picture of Max flashed on the screen. Thinking I was going crazy, I dug my fingernails in my palms. A chyron headline announced, "Financier Francine Meadows Endows Suicide Prevention Foundation in Honor of Late Son". Max's headshot was the same one tucked in the kitchen drawer of his New York apartment.

Chicken enchiladas with green chile arrived, but I was too shocked to eat. A Google search revealed a *New York Times* article about Francine Meadows, former Citigroup executive turned philanthropist, who had connected with the son she gave up at birth shortly before his death.

Needing to settle my nerves, I postponed my flight and detoured toward the Jemez Mountains, heading west to Route 4. My heart slowed and my hands unclenched on the steering wheel as I entered the Village of Jemez Springs, overcome with a feeling of traveling back in history— the world's and mine.

At the Indian Monument I paid admission, half expecting to be greeted by the young brothers I had met during my last visit. On the path, a German-speaking couple consulted a *Frommer's* guide. They entered the Visitor's Center, leaving me alone. I leaned against a stone wall protecting church ruins. Warmth sank into my back and released muscles tight from sitting.

During my last visit to the village, I watched a video history of Jemez Monument. As I toured the Spanish mission, I imagined echoes of hammer on stone, a church being erected under orders of Franciscan fathers. The howls of those same priests as Jemez Indians drove the invaders from their land.

Today the quiet was disturbed only by a squeaky metal chain swinging from a "Do Not Enter" sign. Swallows flitted through chinked rock. Time expanded and contracted here, the rocky landscape indifferent.

Far above, a hawk circled. Just before he died, Dad promised he would come back as a bird. To sweep and soar where he pleased; flight being a living jazz. While Dad's references were musical, Mom spoke in play titles. Asked what album she wanted to hear after dinner, she replied, arms plunged in soapy dishwater, *You Know I Can't Hear You When the Water's Running*, a play they saw on Broadway.

Tears pricked my eyes. I had reached the spot where I almost succumbed to despair. A little boy running up the trail had startled me into dropping my knife. His open-hearted smile saved me.

An abundance of days followed. As I tended Aunt Katherine's garden, I recalled dinner table debates, nights on the town. Dandelion days with my brother in the backyard—all petals of memory flowering into stories: Stories of Dad and Max who had made me laugh but left too soon. An appreciation for Mom, who had the courage to stay. To honor Max, I would finish *The Writers' Room*. After inviting both of his mothers, I would join the roaring crowd on opening night.

To pay homage to the artists who abetted my survival by creating temporary heavens of story and song, I had to return to the Albuquerque hospital where Max and I had met.

Armed with a kaleidoscope of color, I would cover beige walls with individual escape routes. One for a woman lying face down on a plastic mattress, another for a man chain-smoking in the day room. Paths leading beyond the facility nestled in the heights of that arid city, where sunshine painted the landscape anew every morning and never set the same way.

For those who wish to set to sea, I would use my widest brush to create waves lapping a horizon where Van Gogh's startling sun rises inch by inch. For hikers, a ribboned path through grass ranges. For music lovers, I would paint the silence before the opening notes of a Ravel symphony, flutes and oboes summoning daybreak. For writers, I would build a library with quiet spaces to create and a grand auditorium to read new work.

A medallion of the sun that some call God met the horizon bright as a coin. On a day like this, I could walk forever. A tightness in my chest reminded me otherwise. Turning toward the visitor center, I prayed for grace on the last leg of my journey. My story to tell. For as long as I am able.

ACKNOWLEDGEMENTS

To my parents, for raising me in a house filled with books and music. My father for teaching me how to eavesdrop on strangers in public to pick up dialog, my mother for taking me to the symphony, ballet, and theater in Chicago as a child and traveling with me as an adult.

To Shanna McNair and Scott Wolven of High Frequency Press. Grateful for your unparalleled support as publishers, editors, and friends.

To Nancy Mellon and Steve Deal, for the haven of lifelong friendship. Ann Lyman, Paul Lukas, and Barb Stewart for their support.

To teachers, who exposed me to literature and kindled my desire to write.

To the Special Education staff at Cary-Grove High School. Their dedication to the students they serve inspired this book.

To students, learning to do hard things.

Eileen T. Lynch is a writer and educator who grew up in Park Ridge, IL, a twenty-minute train ride from downtown Chicago. A graduate of Maine South High School and Loyola University, she was influenced by her insurance man father who participated in the Hull House Playwright's Workshop and frequent trips with her mother to the Art Institute of Chicago, the Joffrey Ballet, and the Chicago Symphony Orchestra. Early jobs in retail and advertising gave her a lifelong love of Michigan Avenue and the Loop, where until Covid, 800,000 people commuted to work every day.

Her next stop was the Clothesline School of Writing at the University of Chicago which included weekly public readings at the Woodlawn Tap.

Visits to college friends in Albuquerque prompted her to visit and then to live and work in New Mexico. In Albuquerque, she joined the SouthWest Writers. Art fairs in Santa Fe and Taos combined with hiking trips throughout the state added an appreciation for the Southwest.

Returning to Chicago in 1999, she worked for the Institute of Real Estate managements as Ethics Administrator for thirteen years.

In 2015, she joined The Writer's Hotel where she workshopped two novels before writing *Splenditude*. Yearly conferences provided a vibrant writing community and an opportunity to read her work in New York City and in Maine.

Splenditude is her debut novel.

www.ingramcontent.com/pod-product-compliance
Lightning Source LLC
Chambersburg PA
CBHW041050310726
48978CB00011BA/494